Praise for
New York Times and USA Today Bestselling Author

Diane Capri

"Full of thrills and tension, but smart and human, too."
Lee Child, #1 New York Times Bestselling Author of Jack Reacher Thrillers

"[A] welcome surprise....[W]orks from the first page to 'The End'."
Larry King

"Swift pacing and ongoing suspense are always present...[L]ikable protagonist who uses her political connections for a good cause...Readers should eagerly anticipate the next [book]."
Top Pick, Romantic Times

"...offers tense legal drama with courtroom overtones, twisty plot, and loads of Florida atmosphere. Recommended."
Library Journal

"[A] fast-paced legal thriller...energetic prose...an appealing heroine...clever and capable supporting cast...[that will] keep readers waiting for the next [book]."
Publishers Weekly

"Expertise shines on every page."
Margaret Maron, Edgar, Anthony, Agatha and Macavity Award Winning MWA Past President

JACK
THE REAPER

by DIANE CAPRI

Published by: AugustBooks
http://www.AugustBooks.com

ISBN: 978-1-942633-00-6

Original cover design by: Cory Clubb
Digital formatting by: Author E.M.S.

Jack the Reaper is a work of fiction. Names, characters, places, and
incidents either are the product of the author's imagination or are used
fictitiously, and any resemblance to actual persons, living or dead,
business establishments, events, or locales is entirely coincidental.

Published in the United States of America.

Visit the author website:
http://www.DianeCapri.com

ALSO BY DIANE CAPRI

The Hunt for Jack Reacher Series:
Don't Know Jack
Jack in a Box (*novella*)
Jack and Kill (*novella*)
Get Back Jack
Jack in the Green (*novella*)
Jack and Joe
Deep Cover Jack
Jack the Reaper
Black Jack (*coming soon*)

The Jess Kimball Thrillers Series
Fatal Enemy (*novella*)
Fatal Distraction
Fatal Demand
Fatal Error
Fatal Fall
Fatal Edge
Fatal Game
Fatal Bond (*coming soon*)
Fatal Past (*coming soon*)
Fatal Dawn (*coming soon*)

The Hunt for Justice Series
Due Justice
Twisted Justice
Secret Justice
Wasted Justice
Raw Justice
Mistaken Justice (*novella*)
Cold Justice (*novella*)
False Justice (*novella*)
Fair Justice (*novella*)
True Justice (*novella*)

CAST OF PRIMARY CHARACTERS

Kim L. Otto
Carlos M. Gaspar

Charles Cooper
Lamont Finlay

Nitro Mack Parnell
Lauren Pauling
Greg Brewer
Nick Scavo
John Lawton

and

Jack Reacher

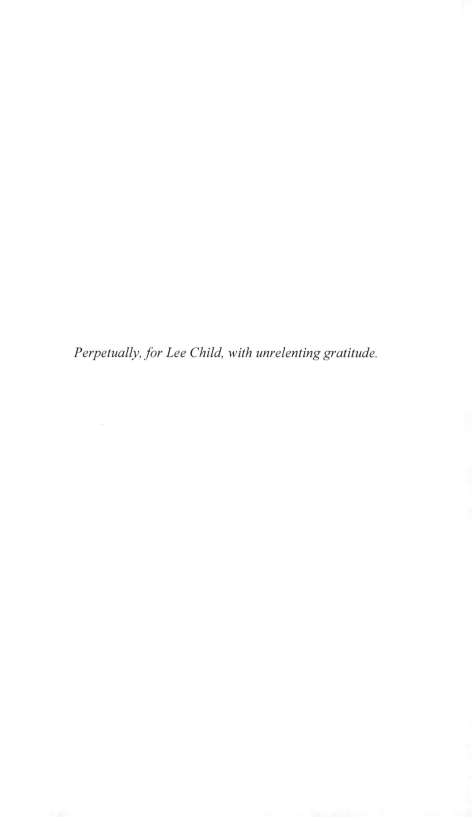

Perpetually, for Lee Child, with unrelenting gratitude.

JACK
THE REAPER

THE HARD WAY

by Lee Child

2006

"[Reacher] was calm. Just another night of business as usual in his long and spectacularly violent life. He was used to it, literally. And the remorse gene was missing from his DNA. Entirely. It just wasn't there. Where some men might have retrospectively agonized over justification, he spent his energy figuring out where best to hide the bodies."

CHAPTER ONE

September 17, 2011
Baghdad, Iraq

GENERAL MACKENZIE PARNELL WATCHED the three private military contractors enter the noisy Baghdad bar and thread through the crowd to the back-corner table. Locals and military personnel saw them enter and would see them leave under their own steam.

All a part of the plan.

Through iron will alone, Nitro Mack controlled himself.

He had earned the nickname decades ago when his quick temper and disproportionate response to everything that blocked his path had landed him in trouble.

Every day.

The years had not mellowed him. Parnell was as volatile at fifty-seven as he had been at age seven.

Both the moniker and the trait were essential elements of his DNA as well as his success.

Nobody messed with Nitro Mack and lived to brag about it.

He smiled. The three men approaching him now would learn that lesson soon enough.

He recognized them instantly.

One looked like an accountant, except his flat dead eyes resembled a shark's.

One was black.

The third was taller than the others.

The three walked well enough, but Parnell watched their arms. He'd acquired their medical records before he contacted them. All three had suffered severe breaks to their dominant upper limbs.

The first guy's shattered right humerus had been bolted together with titanium hardware and healed into an arm of limited use.

The second's crushed right wrist was now fused and stabilized, resulting in an immobile joint and limited function of the hand.

A compound fracture of the third man's left arm caused it to hang shorter than the right and bend oddly at the elbow.

Over time, Parnell had perfected the art of impulse control. Yet, this *situation*, as such things were euphemistically known in security circles, had stretched his skills to the breaking point.

He was more than angry.

He was enraged.

The slow burn had started almost a year ago and stoked hotter with every dead end he'd reached, searching for the bastard who had double-crossed him and disappeared.

Worse, his former colleague had also absconded with Parnell's retirement fund. Money he had worked hard to steal from the Army's dwindling budgets.

Whenever he thought about his missing cash, his temper

flared. Only by sheer force of will had he shoved his rage to a temporary smolder. He tapped his finger on the table rhythmically, reminding himself to keep his powder dry for another hour. Maybe not even that long.

The three contractors approached, seated themselves, ordered drinks, and settled in to receive last-minute changes to their mission from the General. It pleased him to recall that all three would be dead within the hour.

Parnell almost smiled.

He knew their names, but he thought of them as Moe, Larry, and Curly.

Not because they were clueless or funny.

Far from it. Each was a well-trained killing machine.

Tagging them with the comedic handles was one of many tricks he'd devised to manage his fury.

Moe was left-handed. Larry and Curly were right-handed.

It was surely no coincidence that their injuries were inflicted to remove them from the battlefield.

Parnell had enticed the three stooges here in the same way he had engaged their boss years ago. They were kindred spirits. Fighting men who expected violence to define their lives, which they lived without an ounce of remorse.

The type of men Parnell knew well. Nitro Mack intended to exceed their expectations today.

After the three stooges were served, Parnell said, "Did you park where I instructed? I've got a guy out there to watch your vehicle. This place is full of thieves. Fast ones."

"Yes, sir. Vehicle's twenty yards to the north, in front of the empty field, just as you ordered." Larry spoke first, marking himself as the leader of the group. "We've read the materials you sent, General. We have our gear with us. We're good to go."

Moe and Curly nodded like bobbleheads.

Parnell watched them through hooded eyes. They had never been the military's best or brightest.

Quite the opposite.

The only thing that had kept them out of Leavenworth was lack of evidence.

Charges couldn't be proved against them back when they were discharged, so they were sent on their way with little more than a hard boot to the ass.

But these three couldn't let the military go. It was an almost pathological thing with some Special Forces guys. They never moved on. They couldn't function in civilian life and had no desire to try. Naturally, they'd joined up with the only private paramilitary outfit willing to take them on.

Parnell's intel was solid.

Their leader was gone, and their team had been reduced to five. These three, and two more he hadn't located yet.

He'd wondered how the five had survived when better men had died. First order of business was to find out.

"Where's your CO? I was expecting him to be with you."

Parnell was expecting nothing of the kind.

His partner had been missing for several months, and Parnell had turned over every rock looking for him. No luck. Which was the only reason these three mouth breathers were still alive.

Moe, Larry, and Curly shared quick glances.

Larry cleared his throat and replied for them. "We believe the Colonel is, uh, dead, sir."

Parnell nodded. He believed so, too. Which meant nothing. He wanted proof. "What's your evidence?"

Larry lowered his gaze briefly before he squared his shoulders as if the information was embarrassing. "He did not return from his last mission, sir. We haven't heard from him for twelve months. We've tried to locate him with no success."

"When and where did this happen?"

Parnell had traced the Colonel and his team to London. They'd deplaned there a year ago and then vanished. As if Britain had swallowed him, his team, and even his vehicles, whole.

"A small town outside of London called Bishops Pargeter. Eleven, twelve months ago. There were eight of us, sir. Our CO and the other five embarked on the mission. We were ordered to stay behind." Briefly, Larry glanced down, and then raised his head to stare into Parnell's eyes. "None of them returned."

"I see." Parnell folded his hands in his lap and nodded slowly.

He felt his rage burning hotter, but he replied with hard and deadly calm. "And you three turned and ran. You failed to exact justice on behalf of your team. You left their bodies behind."

Moe and Curly were looking down at the table, leaving Larry to extricate them from the truth of their cowardice.

These three poor excuses for pond scum were not a team worthy of the army, and they never had been.

Parnell's decision to terminate them was justified. They should have died long ago.

He felt not even a slight twinge of remorse for his plan.

Larry cleared his throat again. "We had been disabled by the enemy and could not pursue or recover, sir."

"Disabled how? Who was the enemy?" Parnell heard the anger in his voice and clamped his jaw before he demanded too much, too soon.

These three no longer served. He held no real power to coerce them. Only greed and dysfunctional personalities glued them to their seats.

"We had a sleeper in our unit, sir. A traitor. The enemy was Major Jack Reacher. Former U.S. Army military police, retired." Larry cleared his throat. "He disabled the three of us by force and, uh, made it clear that we should let him face the others alone, sir."

Moe looked up and found his voice. "The odds were five to one against Reacher, and our guys were heavily armed. We couldn't get out there, but we expected our guys to prevail."

"It's embarrassing to admit this, General. Five to one odds. Our side lost." Curly glanced at Parnell and shrugged before lowering his gaze again. "We were all three hospitalized and when we were released and went looking for them, we found nothing. No bodies, no vehicles, no weapons. Nothing at all."

"And Reacher. You found him and took care of him." Parnell's fierce frown would have been more than adequate warning to anyone who had seen him explode.

But these three had never witnessed the fireworks. Not yet.

Curly shook his head. "Reacher just disappeared into thin air, sir."

Moe spoke up again. "We had some pretty serious injuries, and they took a while to heal. We're good to go now. We're ready for combat."

Parnell studied them briefly beneath hooded eyes. Cowards. Inept. Disloyal.

They deserved to die.

No qualms about that decision.

None at all.

CHAPTER TWO

"I SEE. THAT'S THAT, then." Parnell nodded as if he agreed with their choices. Only one important question left to be asked. "Contract payments were made to the Colonel. He held my share of revenues. Where is my money?"

Larry's eyes widened. The three glanced sideways at each other. Larry licked his lips as if his mouth had dried up. "We, uh, got paid in cash. No paper trail that way. The Colonel kept the cash locked in a room in his New York City apartment. At the Dakota."

Parnell's breath caught painfully in his chest. His nostrils flared of their own accord. "Who is living in his apartment now?"

Curly said, "We don't know. Sir."

Moe seemed to sense Nitro Mack was close to the last of his patience. He jumped in with what he probably figured would get the heat turned in the right direction. "Reacher knew the money was there. We didn't know the combination to the safe, but Reacher did. The money should be there. But if it isn't, he probably took it."

Parnell narrowed his eyes and felt his nostrils flare. He put the kind of edge in his tone that every army grunt was conditioned to fear. "This Reacher seems like a convenient scapegoat to me, gentlemen. He shows up out of nowhere, destroys your CO and your entire team, and steals my money. Then he disappears. You expect me to believe a story like that?"

Curly was the one who stepped up this time. "General, we need to work. If we'd split that nine million dollars between us, why would we be sitting here in this hellhole begging for table scraps?"

Parnell had dressed down many a soldier. He knew when he was being lied to.

Thing was, this preposterous story came across his bullshit meter and registered as true.

Unbelievable, sure.

But true.

Just one thing didn't ring solid. "Where did your CO keep the rest of the money?"

Larry arched his eyebrows. "Like we said, the money was in the apartment's safe. All nine million dollars of it."

Parnell concealed his surprise by cocking his head as if he was thinking things through. So, nine million was stashed in the apartment, but what about the rest?

These idiots had no idea.

"What about Scavo?"

Larry's eyebrows raised. "Nick Scavo? He, uh, hasn't been with our company since that revolution in Africa, sir. We figure he was killed. We lost three men there."

"Any chance he was helping Reacher in this last mission?" Parnell knew the answer to the question already.

These three had no clue where Scavo was, or whether he made it out of Africa.

Parnell tuned out Larry's feeble excuses and sipped the warm beer.

He glanced around the crowded bar. The noise level had jumped up a dozen decibels since these jokers walked in.

No one seemed to notice the four men talking quietly in the back corner.

He returned his attention to his wannabe business partners. "Okay. Here's how this is going to go. You'll do the job I hired you for here. When you're done, you'll get paid in cash. Half of what you receive is mine. Got it?"

"Yes, sir," they said in unison, nodding as if they meant it, which was not likely.

"One final thing." Parnell's frosty blue eyes pierced like lasers under the deep frown that creased his brow. "What does this Jack Reacher look like?"

The three glanced at each other. Larry cleared his throat and spoke for the crew. "Uh, well, sir, he, uh, looks a lot like you. Tall. Big. Dark blond hair. Blue eyes. Like that."

Parnell tilted his chin up and locked gazes with them one at a time. "I'm going to check your story. If I find out you've lied to me, none of us will be happy. Understand?"

"Yes, sir," they said again in unison. "No problem, sir."

Parnell nodded. "Get to work. I'll be in touch."

They scrambled to their feet and snapped a smart salute. Old habits die hard.

Parnell nodded again. The three turned away.

He watched as they wound through the crowd to the front and exited into the sun-washed desert.

After they cleared the threshold, Parnell rose and hurried toward the men's room.

At the end of the narrow hallway, he ducked out through

the back door and stepped into the blinding sunlight.

He slipped on a pair of aviator sunglasses.

Within seconds, he'd located his vehicle and sped away from the bar, raising a plume of dust behind him.

He had covered about half of a mile of the rough dirt road when the bomb exploded and shook the very ground underneath him.

He clamped both hands onto the steering wheel to avoid being thrown out of his seat, but he kept the accelerator pressed to the floor.

He glanced back to see vehicle parts and body parts still settling after the blast.

Exactly as he'd planned. The vehicle the three stooges arrived in had blasted to unidentifiable bits nicely and right on time.

He smirked with satisfaction.

Witnesses he'd paid would say the cause of the blast was a landmine beneath the vehicle.

Landmines were common enough.

Not a bad guess.

The explosion rocked everything within a two-mile radius. Too much damage for a landmine, but no one would bother to sort out the actual cause.

Life was cheap in Iraq.

The three stooges were not part of any authorized work force. No one would care why or how they'd died.

Hell, it was likely no one would even notice for a good long time.

Parnell glanced over his shoulder for a last look.

Mission partially accomplished.

He smiled again and then began to whistle an old tune from his teenaged years. *Another one bites the dust.*

Now all he had to do was find Reacher and recover his money.

Parnell figured Scavo was involved in all of this somehow. He would find Scavo, too.

All of which would need to be handled carefully. If he acted too soon, he'd attract the wrong kind of attention.

An army general's life was not his own. Privacy was impossible as long as he remained on active duty. Which was fine. Working his side deals within his current fish-bowl job was second nature to him now.

He'd be tied up here in Iraq for another few months, more or less.

Plenty of time to locate Reacher and Scavo, the last two members of the Colonel's crew.

Accumulate the resources he needed.

Plenty of time to make a solid plan.

He grinned. Hell, the first thing on the list was obvious.

Find that nine million, maybe still stashed at the Dakota. The Colonel certainly wouldn't need it.

CHAPTER THREE

Four months later
Thursday, January 13
3:00 a.m.
Detroit, Michigan

FBI SPECIAL AGENT KIM Otto's size five shoes pounded the treadmill as she ran, mouthing the words breathlessly with each footfall.

Jack Reacher was dead.

Had to be.

Everybody said so.

Time to move on.

Long past time.

Let it go.

He's dead.

It's over.

Move on.

Get a life.

That last one made her smile ruefully. A life. What was that?

She hadn't had a real life since her divorce. The Bureau was her life. And that's the way she liked it.

She'd covered ten miles already, but fatigue eluded her. She couldn't sleep until she was exhausted enough to erase the visions that plagued her dreams, and she wasn't quite there yet.

She faced the magnificent moonlit view of the Detroit River and the twinkling lights of Windsor to the South, but she noticed nothing.

Instead, she relived the explosion that killed Reacher and very nearly killed her team.

She'd visualized the events thousands of times. She knew he was dead. *Knew it* the same way she knew the basic laws of physics.

Yet, Reacher *felt* like unfinished business.

How could that be?

Only one more time, she promised herself again.

She re-experienced all of it.

Gooseflesh raised on her whole body as it had with the cold, sharp wind off the frigid Atlantic six weeks ago. The salty air stung her nostrils.

Her heart pounded hard with terror and exertion as she ran from the bomb.

She saw the magnificent old house on Maine's Rocky Pointe explode into millions of pieces.

The vision replayed in her head.

Again, and again, and again.

Her shoe tread caught on the edge of the treadmill belt, jerking her attention to the present. She stumbled and lifted her foot and worked to stay upright.

When she'd regained her balance, she cocked her head and

considered the provable facts objectively once more, arguing the evidence.

"Reacher *could have* escaped after he set that bomb and before it detonated," she had said to her partner when they argued during the post mortem.

Reacher had plenty of experience with C-4. He knew precisely how it functioned. He understood how much time he had to take cover.

Reacher was a guy who lived comfortably with violence. He accepted that he might lose his life at any moment.

But he wasn't suicidal.

Not even remotely.

He'd constructed the bomb. He would have built in enough time to run upstairs from the basement, down the back hallway, and out through the kitchen door to safety.

She believed these facts deep in her bones.

On the treadmill, she gasped with each quick inhale. Her heart pounded against her chest from exertion and exhaustion.

She struggled to stay focused. Sweat soaked her headband and glistened on her body as she argued the same hard evidence she'd covered every day since the explosion.

More likely that Reacher was inside when the C-4 detonated. That's what everyone said.

No evidence to the contrary had been located after six weeks of diligent searching by every qualified tech on the east coast and beyond.

The former owner of that house had tried to kill Reacher nine years before. Reacher won.

But this time, Reacher was nine years older. Nine years weaker. Nine years slower.

New owners of the house this time, too. Tougher ones.

Reacher had lost that last battle.

He must have.

Reacher must be dead.

He must be.

But was he?

She struggled for every ragged breath, but she didn't stop running, and her mind was mired in Reacher's horrific death like a car spinning four tires in the mud.

For twenty-six days in November, she'd chased Reacher's scent around the country and across the oceans like an old bloodhound.

But she wasn't that old, and her sense of smell wasn't that keen. Maybe that's why she'd failed. She'd never found him.

Even so, she'd noticed his scent, heard his voice, dodged bullets meant to kill him. She'd caught glimpses of him a few times, she was sure. She'd noticed his scent after he'd left the room.

No more than that.

She drew ragged breaths and wiped the sweat from her eyes with her forearm and bumped up the incline on the treadmill with her fist.

And now Reacher was dead. He must be. No alternative theories she'd conjured up over the past six weeks had panned out.

The final conclusion was the most likely answer.

The man who seemed to have survived longer than Count Dracula had finally lived his last. She didn't know much about vampires, but she recalled that even the undead could be killed with the right weapon.

What was she to do now? Return to busting drug dealers and traffickers and wannabe airplane terrorists carrying explosives in their underwear?

She felt the bile rise in her throat.

Once, her FBI job had been challenging enough. Perhaps it would be so again. Or maybe it was time to move on.

But where would she go?

Should she actually try to get a life?

CHAPTER FOUR

SHE KEPT HER HEAD high, covered another mile, heard herself panting, and still she ran.

She felt caged. At loose ends. All sixes and sevens, as the Brits put it. No longer master of her days and nights.

Face it.

She grimaced.

Okay.

Truth was, she was no longer matching wits with the most worthy adversary she'd ever hunted. The hunt for Reacher was dangerous. Deadly. But also exhilarating, in a frightening way.

Like a drug addict, she craved the adrenaline.

The real problem was, her life had returned to normal.

She'd come home to her Detroit apartment and her desk at the FBI Detroit Field Office. Her world had continued as if the Boss had never called that cold November morning at four a.m. and tasked her with the most dangerous assignment of her career. A baffling subject, no data or background on him anywhere. FBI resources off limits. An assignment she was forbidden to discuss with anyone.

Except Gaspar. She could talk to him. She'd left him a message earlier. Another one.

She kept running. What else was she to do?

Four miles later, her cell phone rang. Distracted by the phone, she stumbled on the treadmill again. She grabbed the side rails and struggled to right herself.

Her legs were as weak as the flimsy rice noodles her mother made for special family dinners. She could barely stand. *Enough.*

She pushed her weight up, placing her feet onto the stationary treads on either side of the belt. She palmed the big red off button before she stepped onto the floor, still hanging on to one side rail.

Her legs quivered with fatigue and collapsed. She landed on her ass on the floor.

She picked up the phone with a shaking hand, thumbed the talk button, and managed to squeak out a breathless, "Otto."

When he heard the greeting, FBI Special Agent Carlos Gaspar chuckled. "What're you chasing now, Suzie Wong?"

She bristled, but she had no breath to argue. They'd separated at Boston Logan Airport the day after the old house exploded. It was the last time she'd seen him.

He said, "Sorry I couldn't get back to you earlier. What's up?"

Otto glanced around the gym. It was deserted at three in the morning. Most people slept at night. She remembered those days, when she kept somewhat normal hours, the same as everyone else.

Her breath was slowly coming back. "How's the baby?"

"You called me at this hour to ask me that?" Gaspar's fifth child, his only son, had been born three days after the explosion that killed Reacher. Mother and child were fine. Whenever she'd

JACK THE REAPER | 33

asked, he said he was glad to be home and sounded like he meant
it. He'd returned to work in the Miami Field Office and never
looked back.

Otto had respected his decision. Mostly because she could
find no reason not to.

"I knew you'd be awake," she replied.

A while ago, she'd discovered that Gaspar rarely slept,
because of his injury. He didn't deny the accusation. He never
wanted to talk about his damaged body or the constant pain it
caused him, and she respected that decision, too. As long as he
did the job, the rest was none of her business. She liked
boundaries. She had her own secrets to protect, just as he did.

"The baby's fine. Everyone here is fine. Thanks for checking
in." He paused a couple of moments before he asked, "Reacher
still keeping you awake nights?"

She said nothing.

He sighed, and she heard the exasperation all the way from
Miami. "Look, Sunshine, it's over. We filled in a few blanks on
Reacher's Special Personnel Task Force Background Check.
That's all we can do. The candidate died. It happens."

"It doesn't bother you that the file remains incomplete?"

"Not really. So, Reacher's file will always be too thin. Like
many other files stowed in the U.S. Government's cavernous
inventory and forgotten. So what?"

"And the top-secret assignment Reacher was being
considered for? Such a big deal that we absolutely had to find
out every last thing about him, no matter what and nearly died
trying? You're not curious about that?"

"Whatever that job was, it'll go to a different candidate if
Uncle Sam still needs it done." He breathed deeply through his
nose a couple of times while she waited. "Look, we've been over

this. Whatever Reacher did or didn't do during all those years after he left the Army doesn't really matter now, does it?"

She hung her head and closed her eyes, worn down, in body and spirit. It was hard to argue with the cold facts. But she didn't have it in her to give up. She never had. She never would.

"Reacher's dead, Kim. It's over." Gaspar paused again, perhaps waiting for a response, but she had nothing to offer. She heard the baby crying in the background. "Quite a set of lungs on that kid, eh? I've got to get to Juan before he wakes up the whole house."

"Yeah," she said, weary.

"Otto? Seriously. You've got to move on." Gaspar's tone was kind. "You had a life before this case. Try to find that again, okay?"

Juan's crying raised another decibel.

She said, "You go. We can talk another time."

"Okay." But he hung on the open line until she disconnected.

She pushed herself off the floor, grabbed her towel, and wobbled toward the showers. She leaned against the tile, under the pounding hot water, for a full twenty minutes before she gathered her remaining energy and stepped out. She wrapped herself in an oversized terry robe, left the gym, and took the elevator down to her apartment.

Ten minutes later, she had dropped into a fitful sleep fueled by energy depletion.

She tossed and turned because Reacher once again invaded her dreams. She ran from the big old house on Rocky Pointe, full out, as fast as she could run.

But this time, when she looked back at the house for half a moment before it blasted to smithereens, she saw a shadowy figure emerge and move toward the renovated stables.

Half a breath later, the house exploded. Not in the blinding, ear-splitting, concussive blast she'd actually experienced, but a hard thump against a harder surface.

She sat bolt upright, heart still pounding, head clear and firmly in the present.

A lingering odor, something familiar, wafted from the chair in the far corner of her bedroom, but she couldn't immediately identify it.

The chair was bathed in the diffuse glow from the streetlights below through the sheer drapes across the window.

No one sitting in the chair.

No one in the room with her.

She listened hard. She caught the noise again. Not an explosion. Not a dream.

An intruder.

Thudding, fast footsteps pounded the wood floors in the hallway outside her bedroom door. Moving toward the front door.

Quietly, she pulled the bedside table drawer open, grabbed her gun, and slid her bare feet onto the cold carpet.

CHAPTER FIVE

Thursday, January 13
4:27 a.m.
Detroit

OTTO CREPT THROUGH HER open bedroom door silently on bare feet, prepared to shoot. She waited at the threshold and listened with her whole body. She heard nothing but silence.

She flattened herself against the wall and crept into her main living quarters. In the ambient light from the windows, she identified her furniture. Unoccupied. No one here.

The microwave oven clock glowed blue. 4:27 a.m.

She'd slept less than an hour.

Her eyes adjusted to the dim light. She scanned the open room. No one here. Her apartment was empty of threats. No oversized army veteran wearing work boots clomping along her highly polished floors. No ghosts, either.

She did a close sweep of the entire apartment just to be sure. Closets, bathrooms, nooks, and crannies.

The only breathing creature inside her four walls was her.

She readied her weapon and padded silently to the front door. Her breath caught. She stared at the deadbolt.

Unlocked.

Had she left the door unbolted when she returned from the gym?

She shook her head. She never left her doors unlocked. Never.

But she'd been so exhausted. Had she forgotten?

Maybe.

Not likely.

She shrugged. She had no security cameras inside her home. She lived in a building as secure as Fort Knox. Or so she'd believed.

She'd never know for sure.

She glanced at the alarm panel beside the door.

The alarm was off. Had she failed to set the alarm, too? Was that how he got inside? Or had he breached her security systems to enter and then escaped too quickly to reset them?

She considered the question briefly before she shrugged again and moved on.

Carefully, she readied her gun and, standing to the side, in one swift movement, opened the door.

She scanned the empty corridor.

Left. Right.

Nothing.

No one there. Definitely.

No audible footsteps, either.

She must be losing her mind. Reacher couldn't have been in her bedroom. Could he?

She hadn't actually heard him depart. Did she?

She shook her head. She didn't know. It was the uncertainty

that scared her the most. Reality, she could deal with. That's what her training was for. But this?

She felt herself shaking with cold. Her thin nightgown was not warm enough for January in Michigan. Even inside the heated building.

She dropped her gun to her side and glanced down. Which was when she noticed the manila envelope. It had been propped against the door and fell into her apartment when she swung the door open fast.

She kicked the envelope inside before she closed and locked the door. Securely.

She leaned back against the heavy steel, heart pounding. "This is ridiculous, Otto."

Her voice was hoarse. She cleared her throat. "Get a hold on yourself. Gaspar's right. Reacher's dead. It's over. Move on."

Her harsh words did nothing to slow her pulse rate.

She reset the alarm system before she bent to pick up the envelope and carry it along with her gun into the kitchen.

She knew what was inside the unmarked envelope and she knew who'd sent it. She wondered how it had found its way to her door, and she'd take that up with the building's security team after sunrise. For now, she placed both the envelope and her gun on the counter while she started the coffee maker.

No point in going back to bed. There would be no sleeping now, for sure.

She left the envelope in the kitchen and picked up the gun on her way to get dressed while the coffee brewed.

When she re-entered her bedroom, the faint, familiar scent reached her nose once more. She whispered as if she might be overheard. "I did *not* imagine him. He *was* here."

Even as she uttered the words, she realized how unlikely they seemed.

She flipped the lights on and examined her bedroom. Nothing was out of place. Other than the lingering aroma, growing fainter by the moment, he might have actually been a ghost. That's what her mother would have said. Her mother had tremendous respect for ghosts and spirits of all kinds.

She approached the chair and placed her palm on the upholstered seat. It was cold. No warmth from his body remained there. Which meant that she must have heard his footfalls before she'd awakened instead of after. If he'd been sitting there when her eyes first popped open, she would still feel that body warmth now. And she'd have seen him in the corridor, probably.

Maybe her mother was right. He could be a ghost.

She groaned, grabbed sweatpants and a sweatshirt, and dressed quickly. She splashed cold water on her face and slid her icy feet into slippers. She picked up her gun and her cell phone and returned to the kitchen where the coffee had finished. She poured a cup and carried it along with the envelope, her gun, and her misgivings to the table.

She plopped into a chair, ripped the envelope's seal, and dumped the burner cell phone on to the tabletop. It was the same make and model as all the others. No note. Already fired up. She didn't touch it.

The envelope had been hand-delivered to her door, which should have been impossible.

She lived on the forty-first floor of an exceptionally secure high-rise building in downtown Detroit. The entry doors were locked at seven. Every night. No exceptions. An armed doorman was on duty twenty-four-seven. The building was equipped with enough security to guard the President. All of which was designed to deter intruders.

And yet, her carefully selected security systems may have been breached twice tonight.

She shuddered. She'd always felt safe here. She'd been a fool.

Absently, she reached for her gun and pulled it closer. She figured she would not have long to wait for the Boss to call on his burner phone.

She passed the time by thinking through the explosion on Rocky Pointe again. She visualized the shadow running from the back of the house as she'd seen him in her uneasy dream. That shadow must've been Reacher. Otherwise, he couldn't have been sitting in her bedroom less than an hour ago.

But was he really here? She was exhausted. Overwrought. She might have imagined the whole thing.

She shook her head vigorously, as if to push the visions aside. "Let's not go down that road again."

She grimaced. Brutal honesty? It could go either way. Until she knew for sure, she would share tonight's events with no one. She'd seen what happened to agents deemed unreliable for much less than having paranoid delusions in the middle of the night.

She shook her head. "Nope. Not for me. Not a chance."

She might leave the Bureau, sure. But if and when she did, it would be her choice and on her own terms. She wouldn't allow herself to become an object of ridicule. She wouldn't be passed over or forced out.

"The hell with that." Who was she talking to?

She refilled her coffee at 5:02. At 5:03, the burner phone vibrated. Almost as if he could see her return to her chair before he dialed. He probably could.

She let the phone dance around on the table a few times before she cleared her throat again and picked it up.

"Otto," she said, pleased to hear the firmness in her voice. Not even an uneasy tremor.

"He could be alive." The Boss spoke quietly and cryptically, as he did whenever he could get away with it. He was paranoid about being recorded. Which was comical, really, since he had zero qualms about recording everyone else.

She wiped her tired eyes with her palm and resisted the urge to say, *No kidding.* Instead, she replied, "New evidence?"

"I'm afraid not. Or at least, not directly. Are you dressed?"

She glanced down at her sweats. "More or less."

"I'm on my way up."

The call disconnected. She gasped.

On his way up? He had never been in her apartment before. They had not met face-to-face in a very, very long time. Why was he here?

CHAPTER SIX

Thursday, January 13
5:05 a.m.
Detroit

LESS THAN A MINUTE later, the doorbell chimed loudly in
the early morning quiet. Otto pushed herself up from the chair
and made it to the door before he pushed the bell again. She
disarmed her security system and shoved the deadbolt aside.
When she turned the knob and pulled the heavy steel slab open,
she barely recognized the man standing on her welcome mat.

He was effectively disguised in outdoor gear of the high-end
variety that one might find in a sporting goods store for British
landed gentry. He wore a brimmed hat and sunglasses. His
brown tweed hunting jacket had patches on the elbows. The
collar was turned up to further shield his face. His wool flannel
slacks were tailored and fell with a perfect drape. The only
discordant notes in his ensemble were the heavy treaded work
boots on his feet.

She stepped aside, and he moved across the threshold and

toward her dining table without words. He assumed command of her home as if he owned the place, which raised the hair on her neck, but it was the sound of his boots hitting the floor that caught and stopped her breath.

The same sound she'd heard when she first awakened. She was sure of it.

Had it been the Boss in her room while she slept? Would that be any better than Reacher watching her in the middle of the night? She shivered, whether from the cold draft coming through the open door or the uncertain identity of her stalker, she couldn't say.

She stood rooted to the entrance until he reached the coffee pot, turned, removed his hat and sunglasses, and asked, "Where are your cups?"

"Left side of the sink," she said, as casually as she could. She closed and locked the door and re-engaged the alarm, even though she could be locking her intruder inside. Once, she'd trusted this man implicitly, with her career and her very life. But since he'd tasked her with hunting Reacher, their relationship had changed. She was wary of him now. With good reason.

He found the cups and poured black coffee for himself. "Freshen yours up?" he asked, which surprised her. He was rarely considerate. She nodded, and he poured.

He leaned against the counter, coffee in hand. She waited for him to speak.

"You're aware of the most recent batch of government documents released by TrueLeaks last week?"

She nodded. TrueLeaks was a website owned and operated by the nefarious Louis True. Which wasn't his birth name. He'd legally changed it from Louis Gunter when he went into the watchdog business.

True called himself an activist journalist. His mission was to disclose corruption in the U.S. Government, he claimed. There were plenty of unhappy government employees more than willing to steal sensitive and classified information for him. There were just as many enemies of the country who were thrilled to exploit the disclosures and protect True from imprisonment.

A match made in hell, she thought sourly.

"It's old stuff, though, isn't it? Two years old, at least. Some of it even older, is what I heard. No reason to be traipsing around in the middle of the night over old documents, is there?"

"We're sorting through it all now. It's going to take a while. But a few troubling things have come to light already." He paused. "Involving Reacher."

She plopped down in the same chair she'd occupied earlier and put both elbows on the table. "If Reacher's dead, how can some old references in those documents make any difference to anyone?"

He nodded. "*If* Reacher is dead, the disclosures probably won't matter much. It's hard to say. Depends on what they're about and who they implicate."

Her breath caught. "What do you mean, *if* he's dead?"

"It's been six weeks since that explosion. The crime scene has been processed down to the last grain of sand. Everything they could find has been examined several times by several of the best techs in the world. Every bit of DNA they located has been tested and run through the various databases." He paused and drank the coffee, expecting her to say something, maybe.

She held her tongue.

"And we found no evidence that Reacher died in that house. Or anywhere on the grounds, for that matter."

Her heartbeat quickened even as she nodded slowly. "I see."

"Frankly, we might all be better off if he's dead. You know more about him now than you did when you began this assignment. You know as well as anyone how unpredictable he can be." He watched her as if she was a suspect.

She wondered what he believed her guilty of, and whether he'd admit his transgressions were worse.

"Reacher's aware that you're investigating him. It's not his style to skulk around in the dark like he has been. A man with nothing to hide would have come forward by now."

What could she say to that? Reacher definitely had something to hide. But so did the Boss. And quite a few other people she'd encountered during the ten weeks since she caught the Reacher case. She said nothing.

"Look, the truth is that we don't know for sure whether he's dead or alive. And because we're dealing with Reacher, it's smarter to believe he's alive. Safer, too." He pulled a small thumb drive from his pocket and placed it on the table. "The conversations contained in the latest TrueLeaks disclosures are troubling, as situations involving Reacher tend to be."

Otto looked at the thumb drive, but she didn't touch it. The familiar tension she'd lived with since the first time she'd heard Reacher's name returned, humming through her veins like high voltage through power lines. Her stomach twisted.

"What do you want us to do?" Her voice sounded stronger than she felt because she refused to show him even the slightest weakness. She'd seen first-hand how he used the secrets he acquired. She wouldn't put herself in that position again.

"There are two witnesses. Both in New York City. One is an NYPD detective, Greg Brewer. The other is a retired FBI Special Agent, Lauren Pauling. Find them. Find out everything they know about Reacher. Fill in the gaps. If he's contacted either of them in the last six weeks, then we'll know for sure he's alive. We can make a plan from there."

She ignored the thumb drive. "And if he hasn't contacted them in the past six weeks? What does that prove?"

"Nothing. We'll still be in the same situation we're in right now. We'll talk more when you've reviewed the materials." He drained the last of his coffee and put the cup in the sink. "I've talked to Gaspar. He'll meet you at JFK. Your flight leaves from DTW in ninety minutes, unless it's delayed by weather. Which looks likely. Storms on the radar between here and JFK. My helo is on the roof. Get dressed and meet me up there. We'll drop you off."

He picked up his hat and sunglasses and walked toward the door.

The sound of his footfalls across the room triggered her sense memories.

"Were you inside my apartment earlier?"

He barely paused. "Of course not. Why do you ask?"

"Someone was here."

"Wasn't me." Without a moment's pause, he drew the deadbolt, punched the alarm's off button, unlocked the door, settled his hat on his head, and donned the sunglasses.

"We depart in twenty. Don't be late. And pack a bag. Just in case." He left, closing the door firmly behind him.

There was only one thing potentially worse than having him watch her sleeping that Otto could think of, and that was flying in his helicopter before sunrise.

She refused to think about the plane flight through bad storms coming up afterward.

Only one choice. Get dressed. Pack. Meet him on the roof.

Or quit the FBI right here and now.

She seriously considered that option for a full two minutes before she turned and headed toward the shower.

CHAPTER SEVEN

Thursday, January 13
8:50 a.m.
New York City

GENERAL MACK PARNELL, RECENTLY retired, stood at
the corner of 72nd Street and Central Park West. Gloved hands
rested in the pockets of his cashmere top coat. Scalpel-sharp air
slashed his lungs with every inhale. He'd become accustomed to
desert climates while deployed halfway around the world for the
past decade. He'd avoided biting cold for a long time, and he
didn't much like it. He planned to stay only as long as necessary.
A few days, tops.

He tilted his head up for a better look at one of the most
exclusive addresses in New York City. The Dakota Apartments
building loomed like the living legend it was. High gables, deep
roofs, and more dormers, spandrels, balustrades and the like than
any castle he'd ever seen.

While the Dakota had a long and distinguished history,
people in Parnell's generation could only think of the place as

the infamous site of resident John Lennon's murder. He wondered why Lennon's widow, Yoko Ono, had chosen to continue living here. What did she feel every day when she crossed the sidewalk where her husband was gunned down?

Parnell shook his head. Women were odd creatures. So emotional. Maybe she felt closer to her dead husband here, or some such nonsense. Parnell was a pragmatist. His career had forced him to relocate many times, and he hated the disruption. He'd have stayed because he didn't want to go. Simple as that.

He shrugged. Maybe Yoko felt the same. She had to be in her mid-eighties by now. No one wanted to move everything they owned at that age.

Which didn't explain why his former business partner, the missing Colonel, had chosen this place. He knew the history, but he'd said the Dakota offered precisely the kind of privilege and discretion he needed. His activities would never be questioned here, he said. No meddling by management or prying neighbors to worry about. Certainly, no one would dare to interfere with his business.

The money he'd spent to buy the Dakota apartment, the Colonel had said, bought privacy and freedom. Only recently had Parnell learned what the Colonel meant.

The building was a co-op, not a condo. It was owned by a corporation. The corporation was listed on the property tax rolls. The Colonel, like the other residents, held shares in the corporation. Parnell shook his head. The whole system was convoluted and a little crazy. But it meant that the corporation and the people who lived here had more control over their neighbors and their privacy.

Lennon's murder had been the sum total of Parnell's

knowledge about the Dakota sixteen months ago. He'd cared little about the Colonel's accommodations until he disappeared. Even then, Parnell was only interested in the money.

Strictly speaking, the money wasn't Parnell's. But he had a better claim to it than anyone else. If it hadn't been for him, the Colonel would have had no money to stash in this mausoleum in the first place. Damn straight.

But Parnell couldn't simply stuff nine million dollars in his pockets and walk out with it, either. Nobody had pockets that big. The cash had been delivered originally in bales of one million dollars each. One hundred-dollar bills. A hundred hundreds to a pack. A hundred packs per bale. Each bale weighed about as much as a loaded carry-on suitcase.

Parnell was in good shape for a man his age. But he couldn't carry nine loaded suitcases at once. Making nine trips, or even half that many, carrying the cash out was too awkward. Someone would notice. Which would lead to explanations. Which Parnell preferred to avoid.

He'd needed a plan. Army generals were good at plans, and he'd been planning this offensive for months.

The good news about a building like the Dakota was its historical significance. Historic buildings are not particularly private, and much was known and publicly available about this one.

Before he left the army, Parnell had pored over the city's online property records databases until he'd learned everything possible about the Colonel's fifth-floor apartment. He shook his head, still astonished at the price tag, for starters.

Ten years ago, the Colonel had paid twenty-four million dollars in cash to buy the place. Sure, that could have been a good way to launder the money. Except he didn't sell the place and get his freshly-cleaned cash out. Parnell's lip curled when he thought about it. What a fool.

Not only that, but the apartment had sucked up even more money every month like a powerful vacuum sucks air. Monthly fees were more than twenty grand a month. *A month.* Thousands in annual property taxes were included. Parking fees. Decorating expenses. The list of costs never ended.

No question about it, the Dakota co-op had made a sizeable dent in the Colonel's share of the revenue Parnell had funneled to him before he disappeared. Which was a stupid thing to do with the cash. The Colonel was a lot of things, but obviously, he was no financial genius.

Parnell could liquidate the apartment without fanfare to one of the many names on the Dakota's waiting list. Sell it fast and cheap on the private market and pocket the difference. A feasible plan.

But the problem was that the Colonel no longer owned the place. He'd screwed up. He didn't pay the monthly fees in advance before he bugged out last year. After those fees remained unpaid for a full year, ownership had transferred to the co-op's board.

Now, the board would have to sign off before Parnell could resell the place. Maybe the board would sign off, or maybe not. The process promised to be time-consuming and convoluted. Which meant, effectively, that Parnell couldn't do it.

Hard to believe the Colonel had been so stupid. In fact, Parnell hadn't believed it at first. He'd seen a small item in the *Times* about the foreclosure while he was in Iraq, searching online. A follow-up paragraph was published a couple of days later, but it had been withdrawn.

Parnell chased down the situation, which took a lot more

effort than it should have. In the end, he'd had no choice but to call in a few favors from his contacts inside the three-letter agencies to locate the withdrawn paragraph. Eventually, they found it.

He grinned. Everything that was ever stored on the internet was still sitting around out there somewhere if a man was diligent enough. Lots of men were that diligent, believe it or not. Which was only one of the reasons Parnell kept his own personal online activities to a bare minimum. The last thing he needed was to be traced like that.

The smaller item in the *Times* mentioned, oh so casually, that in a locked closet inside the apartment the co-op board had found more than nine million dollars in cash.

Only a couple of sentences. A narrow column inch. Quickly deleted and all but destroyed. A less determined man would never have found it.

The words pleased him every time he thought about them. More than nine million dollars in cash. Nine million. Dollars. Cash. He smiled broadly until the cold air touched his teeth, sending a shooting pain straight between his eyes. He clamped his mouth shut.

The good news was that the nine million was found inside the apartment a full year after the Colonel disappeared. Knowing the money was in place for that first twelve months was reassuring. Parnell felt closer to success.

Twelve months after Reacher would have returned from London, according to those three idiots. He might not have believed them if he hadn't confirmed the absence of travel records bringing Reacher back to New York.

Parnell was a student of human nature. If Reacher had wanted the money, it stood to reason that he would have returned immediately and grabbed it right away. Before anyone noticed the Colonel was gone.

Certainly, long before anyone else had a chance to find it.

Waiting an entire year made no sense at all.

Anything could happen in a full year.

Parnell nodded. He was sure. Reacher had not come back here.

In fact, everything he'd been able to turn up about Reacher suggested he had disappeared, too. Maybe the three stooges had been wrong, after all. Perhaps Reacher and the Colonel's team had killed each other.

That answer made more sense than any other he'd dreamed up so far.

Except for one slightly troubling thing.

Someone else was looking for Reacher, too. Someone big, according to Parnell's extensive search. Someone even Parnell's vast web of contacts had failed to identify.

Parnell had chased whatever leads he could find on that score, but he'd come up completely empty. Whoever was hunting Reacher had enough juice to keep himself so deep under the radar that even Parnell couldn't find out.

He shrugged. Quick or dead, Reacher was still missing. As long as Reacher and whoever hunted him stayed out of the way for a few more days, Parnell would be long gone. The good news was the Colonel's money was most likely still in that closet right now. Which was all Parnell cared about.

Well, that and his forty-two-million-dollar retirement fund.

Nine million was a nice bonus, though. It was really Parnell's money, after all. He was the one who'd risked his career and lifetime imprisonment in Leavenworth to acquire it. No one had a greater right to that money than he did.

Curiously, since they'd foreclosed on the apartment, the board had made no attempt to resell the place. He wondered why. Not that it mattered. Parnell wasn't planning to live there.

He planned to ask the co-op board president as soon as he could introduce the question casually. Thinking of the board president, he glanced at his watch. Time to meet with Simon Peck.

CHAPTER EIGHT

Thursday, January 13
8:00 a.m.
Des Moines, Iowa

LAUREN PAULING WATCHED THE young family having breakfast together from a safe distance across the dining room. A private smile brightened her face. She alone knew the whole truth about her work. But she was satisfied. She'd done good things here, for people who deserved them. No job in the world could possibly be better than this one.

Elwood lifted the spoonful of scrambled eggs to his mouth with his left hand. A few yellow crumbs fell onto his bib along the way, and he simply shook his head. Not so long ago, he would have erupted in violent frustration. His improving mental health was an important thing, to be sure. But it wasn't the only thing.

Mrs. Nicholson, the social worker, approached Pauling, carrying a clipboard and a pen and wearing a big smile. "Here's the final paperwork, Ms. Reacher. Everything paid in full through the end of the program, like you asked."

"Thank you, Joan. Where do I sign?"

Mrs. Nicholson pointed to the three lines marked with an X. The name "Jack (none) Reacher" was typed below the line. Pauling scrawled "J. Reacher" in all three places and handed the clipboard back.

Mrs. Nicholson shook her head. "You must have been teased a lot as a kid. Jack is no kind of name for a girl. What were your parents thinking?"

Pauling smiled. "I wish I knew."

She looked toward Elwood's family again.

"Don't worry, Ms. Reacher. A bit of practice and he'll be doing a lot more than eating eggs with a fork soon enough," Mrs. Nicholson said, patting Pauling on the shoulder before she hurried back to her desk.

This was the final step for returning Elwood to a functioning human being. A first-class residential rehab program, where well-qualified therapists would teach him to use his new custom-fitted right arm prostheses. His bionic arm, he joked to his young son. The arm wasn't bionic, but it was the best money could buy.

Julie Elwood and their son looked happy today, too. Pauling had moved them away from that crappy apartment and set up a decent place for them to live, which they were proud to call home. It was a starter home in a quality neighborhood and young families with whom, she hoped, they would become good friends. The contractor she'd hired refitted the house to accommodate him. After he was discharged, Elwood could navigate the new place easily.

Julie drove the new SUV to breakfast today. Afterward, she would drop their son at school and then go to work she enjoyed. The job Pauling had arranged for Elwood was waiting for him, too. Ready as soon as he was able to work.

And the money "J. Reacher" deposited in their credit union account yesterday would carry them through until they were back on their feet, with an emergency fund, just in case.

Yes, her work was done here. She'd have limited follow up with them over the next few weeks. After a couple of months, she'd check on them one last time. If they were getting along okay, she'd cross another soldier off her list.

The list of veterans she'd compiled originally had seemed overwhelmingly long, but she was making good progress now that she'd worked out the logistics. Ironically, her years at the FBI had given her everything she needed. She knew how to launder money, where to get the best counterfeit identification, and how to utilize it. She'd learned a thousand tricks of the crime trade when she was hunting criminals. Now, she was putting them to good use.

The work had settled into a comfortable pattern, of sorts. The most difficult part was finding worthy beneficiaries like Elwood. Veterans who had joined up with private military contractors after discharge from service with Uncle Sam were plentiful. But over the years, many had died in various armed conflicts, one way or another. Too many others simply fell through the cracks. Locating them was a challenge.

Elwood and his family should make it now, though. Reacher would approve. Pauling smiled again before she turned to go, pulling her leather gloves on as she walked. She glanced over her shoulder for one last look when she reached the exit. A blast of frigid air pushed against the glass door. She gave it a hard shove and left the warmth of the facility.

Time to head home for a while. She'd never been as cold in her life as she was here in Des Moines in January. She'd wait until June to come back to check on Elwood and his family. For sure.

The rental was parked around back. She shuffled through the snow, pushing the key fob to unlock the car and start the engine to warm up. She settled into the driver's seat and fastened her seat belt. The heat blasted through the vents and after a while, warmed up the interior.

She drove the rental to the airport and dropped it off in the garage. She had only one bag, which rolled easily along the concrete and into the terminal. Her flight was posted for an on-time departure.

She joined the long line of ordinary people at the security check point. She offered her boarding pass and identification for inspection, then placed her carry-on along with her purse, shoes, and coat in a plastic bin for x-ray.

She passed through the explosives trace-detection portal machine, what agents called "the puffer," without mishap. Maybe the handsome young TSA officer looked at her body's image a bit too long, but at her age, she was more flattered than offended.

She collected her belongings at the end of the process before she headed to the gate for the long flight home. Lots to do before her visitor arrived.

CHAPTER NINE

Thursday, January 13
9:15 a.m.
New York City

PARNELL CROSSED THE STREET and approached the building at the main entrance. The doorman did a double take and then stared at him like he'd seen a ghost. Before Parnell could follow up, a short, portly middle-aged man wearing round glasses rose from a wing chair in the lobby and came to greet him.

"Mr. Kern?" He lisped, extended a soft manicured hand flashing a signet pinky ring in an affected way. "We talked on the phone. I'm Simon Peck. I wanted to meet with you personally to say how sorry we are about the misunderstanding."

He looked and vamped like Truman Capote. Perhaps he was a Capote fan. Or maybe an actor, rehearsing the role. Everybody in New York was some kind of actor, weren't they? If so, he was damn good at it.

"Call me Fred." Parnell removed his right glove. His calloused paw encircled Peck's. He released the wet fish handshake quickly, barely resisting the urge to wipe the little man's sweat on his coat. "Thank you for helping me with this, Simon. My brother-in-law, the Colonel, will be glad to know you've taken such good care of things in his absence."

Peck nodded and swallowed like a kid caught with chocolate all over his face before dinner. His Adam's apple bobbed inside his fleshy neck as the words tumbled out of his mouth accompanied by a constant stream of spittle. "The board is glad you contacted us, Mr. Kern. We are mortified. Simply mortified. We are so sorry."

Parnell cocked his head, implying a question he didn't ask.

"We found out that the Colonel was on a long-term deployment only after we foreclosed on the apartment. We'd never have foreclosed if we'd known where he was. We've been sick about the whole thing." Peck didn't seem to notice that Parnell had said nothing. He babbled on, uninterrupted.

"We'll make it right as soon as he returns. Very quickly. We already have the paperwork prepared for his signature. But everything is exactly as he left it. This way, please."

"Yes, I see." Parnell nodded as if everything Peck said made sense, clasped his hands together behind his back to remind himself not to leave any fingerprints. He glanced over his shoulder to catch the doorman still staring at him, and then he followed Peck to the elevator.

"The Colonel's apartment is on the fifth floor, around the corner from the elevator." Peck pushed the button.

When the doors closed and the elevator began its ascent, Peck reached into his pocket and pulled out a single key on a ring anchored by a weighty copper replica of The Dakota. He handed the key to Parnell. "You'll have full access to everything The Dakota has to offer while you're here, of course."

"Thank you. I'm not sure how long I'll be staying." Parnell dropped the key into his pocket and offered the excuse he'd planned to cover the time required to move the money. "My meetings may last a couple of weeks, or they may wrap up in a few days."

"I understand." Peck clasped his hands below his protruding belly. "When you're ready to leave the city, just return the key to the front desk, and I'll pick it up later."

"I'll be sure to tell the Colonel how helpful you've been, Mr. Peck. Thank you. I'll call if I need anything." Parnell nodded and stepped off the elevator on five.

He walked around the corner and stopped at a heavy oak door the color of honey. He waited a few moments until he heard the elevator car depart. With luck, he wouldn't see the sweaty Simon Peck again.

Parnell reached into his pocket, fished out a pair of latex gloves, and snapped them on. He slid the key into the lock and pushed the oversized door open.

The empty apartment and his nine million dollars beckoned. Something close to pleasure flooded his belly. For the first time in sixteen months, he was glad that the Colonel had disappeared or died or whatever the hell had happened to him.

He stepped inside a small square foyer that opened onto a big square living room and closed the door firmly behind him.

He surveyed sunny yellow walls and comfortable furniture upholstered in floral prints, suggesting a woman with excellent taste had decorated the place. Which made sense. The Colonel had been married, and they'd lived here together only a few years before he fell off the face of the earth.

The next thing Parnell noticed was the stale air. He found the thermostat and flipped on the fan to get some circulation going.

The place was as quiet as a tomb. One of the articles he'd read about the Dakota said it was the most soundproofed building in the city. The builder had packed the walls and ceilings with three feet of clay excavated from Central Park. The place felt like it was carved from solid rock.

He walked through the apartment. A thin layer of dust covered every flat surface, undisturbed. No one had used the tables or chairs in quite a while.

Was the Colonel really dead? And where was his wife? No one had seen her for a couple of years, either, according to Parnell's sources. Stood to reason they were together. Somewhere.

Parnell tried briefly, but he couldn't imagine the Colonel actually living here amid the sunny yellow walls and floral prints. He was an ugly man. Crude. Sadistic. Controlling. Psychopathic, even. Useful for the kind of guerilla combat Parnell had hired him to do because he'd simply done what needed to be done, once the shackles of military ethics had been lifted from his base nature. He lacked conscience and morality of any kind.

Briefly, Parnell wondered what kind of woman would marry a man like that? Parnell was single. Married to the Army most of his life, was how he thought of it. The Colonel had had two lovely wives. Parnell shook his head, unable to grasp the mysteries of the Colonel's attraction.

Regardless, Parnell's partnership with the Colonel had worked well because he was simply a feral animal. Parnell found the deals and funneled the money. The Colonel did the dirty work. They'd made millions together.

Parnell scowled. Only problem was, Parnell never collected his share because the bastard disappeared with Parnell's money.

A situation he was about to rectify.

He walked through the entire apartment. Three bedrooms. One master. One guest. One for a kid. The framed pictures he found sitting on the dresser indicated that the kid was a girl. About seven years old at the time, give or take.

The photo showed the girl and a woman who was probably her mother. A few crayon drawings were strewn across the floor. Parnell didn't know anything about girls or drawings, but he guessed these were age appropriate for a seven-year-old.

So where was the kid? The Colonel, his wife, and the kid. All missing?

Parnell shook his head. Not likely. If the Colonel had died, as the stooges claimed, why wouldn't the wife and kid return? To collect the nine million, if for nothing else?

CHAPTER TEN

PARNELL SEARCHED THE APARTMENT with Reacher on his mind. The stooges said Reacher had killed the Colonel. But had Reacher killed the wife and kid, too? Was Reacher that kind of guy?

He shook his head again. He couldn't make that idea track. The notion didn't sit well.

He'd reviewed Reacher's entire military file, including the classified operations. Repeatedly. In detail.

Reacher's file reflected his accomplishments as an excellent killing machine, for sure. One of the best the army had ever trained. So much so that during the file review, Parnell had developed a measure of respect for his fellow warrior.

He'd have been proud to have Reacher under his command. At least, in the early years.

Later in his career, Reacher went rogue one too many times. The last time, he was invited to leave the army and told not to let the door hit him in the ass on the way out. He'd been lucky to avoid a court martial, and not for the first time.

Parnell understood the situation clearly.

Reacher was not controllable.

Which meant unacceptable for the army.

The one thing the army demanded above everything else was strict compliance with orders. Reacher, on the other hand, seemed incapable of following orders of any kind.

Parnell would have kicked him out, too. The decision was entirely justified.

But nothing Parnell had found in Reacher's history suggested he was the kind of man who would kill women and children. At least, not intentionally.

Maybe the mother and child had been collateral damage, though.

Parnell shrugged. It happens. Combat missions were notoriously unpredictable.

Whatever the reason, and Reacher might have been at the root of it, the Colonel's apartment was not occupied and hadn't been for a very long time.

Which was what he'd hoped to find.

So far, so good.

Today's visit was recon only. Get the kind of feel for things that he couldn't absorb from documents. Confirm the layouts he'd studied in the public records. Locate the cash. Figure out how he'd get it out of here.

Assuming everything checked out, he'd implement his plan to remove the nine million. Relocate it to his numbered offshore account. Dispose of the key and leave.

Simple enough. Simple plans were always easier to execute.

After the nine million was safely stashed, the next phase was to find the rest of his money and collect it, too.

The last contract he'd pointed the Colonel's way was the largest single payday for them both. It had yielded twenty-one million dollars for each of them. The nine million here might be what was left of the Colonel's share of that deal.

On top of the forty-six million Parnell had previously accumulated, the Colonel's nine would make a tidy fifty-five million nest egg.

Parnell had everything set up. He'd been planning a long time. A place where a man could live like a king on the kind of money Parnell had put together the past ten years. One thing for sure, he would never again be too cold or too hot or too anything at all.

Never.

On the architectural plans for the building and this apartment, he'd identified the room most likely to contain the Colonel's vault. He made his way back to the master bedroom.

The master had the same high ceilings as the other rooms. The walls were painted a chalky eggshell. A king-sized four-poster bed with matching bedside tables, armoire, desk, and chair.

On the desk was another copy of the same photo Parnell had seen in the kid's room. The girl and her mother were both beautiful. Too bad if they were dead.

Nothing in this room was large enough to hold a vault or nine million dollars except the two closets. Parnell crossed the room and opened the smaller door. The closet was large for New York City but small for anywhere else. It was filled with women's clothes. Expensive ones, he imagined. He swept the clothes to the side to see the back wall of the closet. No vault door there, as expected.

Parnell moved to the second closet, where the money should be. The first door opened to a shallow recess and then a smaller door with an electronic keypad next to it. He'd brought tools to disable the keypad's locking mechanism, but he saw that he wouldn't need them.

The small vault door stood wide open. He had a sinking feeling in the pit of his belly as he reached inside and pulled a chain hanging from the ceiling. The interior light came on.

He stood rooted to the floor, looking straight ahead, unwilling to believe his eyes.

The chamber was six feet by three feet. The floor was littered with thick plastic wrap. The kind of strong plastic that should be sliced with a blade because it would take a strong man's effort to tear.

The plastic on the floor, the light bulb on the ceiling, and four walls. Nothing else.

His money was gone.

Nitro Mack's nostrils flared, and his face flushed crimson. His fists clenched. He felt the familiar strength powered by rage coursing through his body.

Not yet. Not yet.

He spent another thirty minutes searching the apartment. Somewhere, the Colonel had kept the documents Parnell needed to collect his retirement funds. He knew only that they were safely hidden in offshore accounts. He hadn't wanted to know more while he remained on active duty.

That was then.

When he'd covered every possible hiding place, Parnell was forced to admit that the documents were not there.

The Colonel would not have hidden them out of arm's reach.

Which could only mean that the proof of ownership he needed to collect his nest egg had been stolen, too.

Peck. No wonder that damn sweaty little midget was

nervous. He'd rushed off quickly because he knew the money was gone. He had to know.

He was the one in charge. Not the *man* in charge. He wasn't so much a man as a toady little creature.

But Peck knew where Parnell's money was. Oh, yeah. He knew.

And Parnell would squeeze his fat throat until his eyes popped out unless he coughed up the exact location.

In fact, he might kill the little twerp either way. Why not?

Choking the life out of Simon Peck would calm Parnell like nothing else he could do right at the moment.

He smiled. He always felt calmer with a simple plan.

CHAPTER ELEVEN

Thursday, January 13
10:15 a.m.
New York City

WHEN SHE DEPLANED ON wobbly legs through the jetway at JFK, she spied Gaspar sleeping in a chair near the gate. His legs were stretched out and crossed at the ankles, hands clasped over his flat stomach, eyes closed. She'd seen the same pose dozens of times. She envied his ability to relax almost anywhere.

She felt exactly the opposite, wired. She'd swallowed too many antacids along with her coffee while the plane bounced through the expected rough weather. Combined with the lack of sleep and the creep factor whenever she allowed herself to remember the man wandering her apartment in the dark, she was as uneasy as a chicken in a fox den.

She glanced outside. Brittle sunshine failed to warm the frigid January day. The captain had said New York City expected a balmy high of twenty-two degrees this afternoon. At least she'd come from home this time, which meant she'd brought boots and a coat.

During the flight, she'd downed several cups of black coffee and gnawed on a tasteless bagel as she absorbed everything stored on the thumb drive the Boss had left in her kitchen. As always with Reacher, everything she learned generated more questions than answers.

Two significant issues were presented this time, one of which the Boss had conveniently failed to mention.

She pulled her rolling suitcase toward Gaspar and nudged the sole of his shoe. Without opening his eyes, he said, "Nice to see you again, Sunshine."

"How long have you been waiting?"

"Fifty minutes, give or take. Before you ask, yes, I reviewed all the same stuff from the Boss that you did." He opened his eyes and stood to grab his bag. "Gregory Brewer first?"

"Why?" She began walking toward the exit and Gaspar limped alongside. He'd stretch out the kinks in his leg and be fine after about twenty yards, she figured.

He kept the pace easily and didn't bother to argue. "He's an NYPD Detective. Makes him easier to find."

"You called him?"

"Yeah. He's expecting us at some greasy diner in the city, but he didn't seem happy about it."

Otto shrugged. "They never are."

"True." Gaspar grinned. "So what do you think?"

They'd reached the escalator and headed down to ground level. "What do I think about what?"

"Is Reacher alive?"

She glanced over her shoulder to look him in the eye. "What do you think?"

He grinned. "I asked you first."

And so, he had. She shrugged again.

At the bottom of the escalator, he said, "Want to stash these bags here?"

"Let's take them with us. I want to get in and get out. We might not come back, and I'd rather not make an unnecessary trip through here."

"Okay." He followed her out to the taxi line. They waited about ten minutes in the cold. When they were settled in the taxi, with the luggage and laptops in the trunk, Gaspar gave the address to the driver.

After the taxi was on the road, Gaspar picked up where he'd left off, grin firmly in place. "Well? Yes or no? I've got fifty bucks that says he's dead. Just to make it interesting,"

"You're on."

He raised one eyebrow, and the grin fell from his lips. "You really believe he's here? In the city?"

"That's another whole thing." In point of fact, she didn't believe that. Not even for a moment. She thought Reacher was still in Detroit. Probably rooting through her underwear drawer looking for whatever it was he wanted. She grimaced. "But I do believe he's alive and walking around, just like we are."

"Why?"

She took a deep breath. This was one of the things she'd decided on the plane. To tell Gaspar everything that happened last night. Because she could trust him. And she needed to trust somebody. As it was, she worried she might be losing her mind.

She opened her mouth to answer his question, but at the last moment, she changed gears. "They did a thorough job at the scene of that explosion. They found evidence from at least a dozen bodies. But no trace of him. They would have found a few identifiable specks of his DNA, at the very least."

Gaspar shrugged, his all-purpose gesture. "Maybe not. Some explosions leave more trace evidence than others. You know that."

"Which is why the Boss kept looking, even after the techs came up empty the first time. But I'm having trouble believing a guy as big as Reacher would have been reduced to dust so fine that our crime labs couldn't identify so much as a single tooth." She turned her head to gaze steadily into his eyes. "Do you really believe that?"

He shrugged again.

She smiled and nodded firmly. "Just as I thought."

The taxi stopped at the curb in front of a coffee shop on the east side of Second Avenue between 44th and 45th. It looked like a local place that survived on quick meals and coffee to go. Gaspar paid the fare and a good tip, so the driver pulled the bags out of the trunk and set them on the sidewalk.

They dodged the filthiest snow in the street and climbed over the mounds at the curb. But the sidewalks were not shoveled, either, which meant the rollers on their bags were useless. She slung the laptop case over her shoulder, hefted her travel bag, and carried it across the snowy sidewalk.

Gaspar stepped ahead and pulled the fogged glass door open. Nauseating grease fumes mingled with fried breakfast food rushed toward her from the diner as she held her breath and stepped into the steamy heat.

CHAPTER TWELVE

Thursday, January 13
11:25 a.m.
New York City

THE BREAKFAST RUSH, ASSUMING there'd been one, was over. New Yorkers were already at work. Too early for lunch, too, so there were only a handful of customers in the diner. The place had an overall brown vibe to it like it had been decorated in the 1970s. Reflected in the bronze mirrors that lined the walls, Kim saw a man sitting alone at a booth for four in the back, facing the entrance.

Brewer.

Had to be.

He looked like an NYPD detective for starters. A little heavier, maybe a little taller, although it was hard to tell while he was seated. About fifty. Gray hair a bit longer than regulations allowed. He wore a plain gold wedding band on his left hand.

Otto carried the bag in front of her along the narrow aisle

between the counter and the booths until she reached Brewer. Gaspar followed a few steps behind her.

"Detective Brewer?"

He nodded.

She extended her hand for his firm shake. "Agents Otto and Gaspar."

The seats across the aisle from his booth were open, so she plopped her bags there and sat facing him. Gaspar did the same.

"Breakfast? Coffee?" Brewer said, waving his empty mug toward a tired waitress behind the counter.

Otto was halfway through a quick shake of her head when her empty stomach reminded her of the cold bagel she hadn't eaten on the plane. This was New York City. There were great bagels to be had. She nodded, and Brewer waved the waitress over.

She brought two brown plastic mugs, which she filled from a Bunn carafe. Otto ordered a toasted bagel. Gaspar ordered a full breakfast of eggs and bacon and pancakes. When the waitress moved off with the orders, she left the carafe for refills.

Brewer spoke first, and his tone was slightly belligerent. "So you're interested in Jack Reacher. I'll tell you what I know, which isn't much. But why do you care?"

Otto was lead on the case, so she replied, "We're with the FBI Special Personnel Task Force. Reacher is being considered for a special assignment. We're updating his file. Making sure he's fit for the job."

"Sounds odd," Brewer frowned. "What's the job?"

"Truth is, we don't know. It's classified above our clearance level." Otto sipped the coffee and felt the snake in her stomach thrash, residuals of the morning's madness. The bagel should take care of that for a while.

"So you're just a couple of pencil pushers wasting my time?" Brewer stared across the table like a pugnacious bulldog ready to bite.

She shrugged. She'd told Brewer the truth. Early on, she'd wanted to know everything about the job Reacher was being fitted for. Now, she found her ignorance was useful for encounters exactly like this one.

"That's crap, and we all know it." Brewer's fuse was lit, and he wasn't about to let the question slide. "How'd you get onto me as a source?"

"The way it works is our boss identifies the sources, and we gather the intel. You don't know why your name would have come up in connection with Reacher?" The sources always knew more than Otto and Gaspar did, whether they were willing to admit it or not. No reason to pretend otherwise with a guy who was already pissed off.

The waitress returned with their breakfast, which halted the conversation for a few moments. When she left again, Gaspar dug into his food.

Otto shook her head. Nothing seemed to faze her partner. He was sleepy, he slept. Hungry, he ate. From all she'd learned about him, Reacher was the same way. Maybe it was a man thing.

"Detective Brewer, what can you tell us about Reacher?" She picked up the toasted bagel slathered with dripping butter and melting cream cheese and dropped it instantly.

Brewer smirked when she sucked the burning fat from her fingers. "Like I said, not much to tell."

"Tell us anyway," Gaspar said amiably between bites. "We're in a new era of inter-agency cooperation. All for one and one for all. Haven't you heard?"

"Yeah. And when my boss tells me to cooperate, I follow orders. But you didn't even ask him, did you?" Brewer glared across the table for a few moments.

"We can go through channels," Otto said reasonably. "I guess we had the impression you wouldn't want us to explain this situation to your boss."

Brewer's silent glare lingered until curiosity or something else got the better of him. "Okay, I met Reacher a while back. Thinking about it while I was waiting for you, seems like it was late summer. Year before last. Say fifteen, sixteen months ago. Talked to him four or five times, I guess. No more than that. He told me he was looking into an old homicide."

"See? Not so hard, right?" Otto nodded. "What did you tell Reacher?"

"Nothing." Brewer shrugged. "The case wasn't NYPD jurisdiction, so I didn't have anything useful to offer. I pointed him in the right direction, and that was pretty much it."

Gaspar was shoveling food into his mouth like a man just released from captivity. He swallowed and swilled the coffee before he asked, "If you had nothing to do with the homicide case, why did Reacher approach you?"

"He got my name from a witness. He was just getting started with his investigation. You know how that is, right? We kiss a lot of frogs in this business before we find anything useful sometimes."

Gaspar nodded and went back to sopping up the egg yolks with the pancakes. His entire plate looked disgusting. Otto wrapped her burned fingers around the cool water glass and pushed the bagel aside. Gaspar kept eating.

"You said you pointed Reacher in the right direction," Otto said. "What does that mean?"

"Nothing complicated. The witness who gave Reacher my name was a friend. She wanted me to help him out. So I pointed him to the retired FBI agent who handled the original case. Figured she could fill in the blanks for him."

Otto nodded. "And that would be Lauren Pauling?"

Brewer's eyes widened briefly as if he hadn't expected them to know. "That's right. She's a private investigator now. Office over on West Fourth Street."

"We're on our way to her next," Gaspar said.

Otto considered why the Boss had sent them to Brewer. If he'd had as little to do with Reacher as he claimed, the Boss would have known that, wouldn't he?

So there was something more here.

"How many times did you say you met with Reacher?"

"More than once. Less than ten times. Hell, probably less than five." Brewer shrugged. "I didn't count. The contact was pretty casual."

"What was the case about? The one he was interested in?"

"I told you. An old homicide."

"How old?"

"About five years at the time, I think. Maybe seven or so now. It wasn't my case."

"So you said." Otto cocked her head. "Why wasn't it your case?"

"Originally, it was a kidnapping, which is FBI jurisdiction. So we weren't involved. Which meant we didn't have a file. When the kidnapping became a homicide, they found the body on the other side of the George Washington bridge, in New Jersey, and figured she'd been killed there." He tapped his fingers on the laminated table. "Again, not NYPD jurisdiction. So we didn't have a file on the homicide case to look at or show Reacher, either. We weren't much help. Which is what I told him."

"Five meetings? To say what you just told us in five sentences?" Otto waited, but Brewer merely nodded. "You knew the witness, you said. Who was that?"

"The homicide victim's sister. That's how Reacher got on to her. Like I said, she was a friend. She's the one who sent him to me." He paused. "But again, I didn't have anything to offer him, so he moved on to Pauling."

"Why was Reacher interested in this old homicide?" Otto asked.

Brewer's gaze dropped, and he squirmed a little in his chair. He cleared his throat. "I guess you'd have to ask him."

"What was the victim's name?"

Brewer seemed to be thinking about it. "You know, I've tried to remember the name. But no luck." He shook his head.

There was more there, but she figured Brewer wouldn't say until she had some sort of incentive or a pressure point to exploit. Both of those techniques worked better with an element of surprise. If she pushed harder now, he might clam up even worse. She'd circle back. Maybe his memory would improve.

Otto nodded. "When and where was the last time you saw Reacher?"

Brewer's eyes widened as if he'd just this moment remembered. "I think it was right here. He was sitting in this very spot."

Otto held her temper, even though the guy was jerking them around and they both knew it. What she didn't know was why. "And your friend, the witness. Where is she now?"

"She moved to Washington State."

"We'll need her contact information." A demand, not a question.

He paused like he might refuse, but then he reached into his pocket for his cell phone and pulled up a contact and handed the phone to Otto. "Email it to yourself."

The woman's name was new to Otto. Patti Joseph had not been referenced in the data contained on the Boss's thumb drive. Which could mean Ms. Joseph was not relevant here. Briefly, Otto wondered why not. She handed the phone back.

"What was the homicide victim's name, again? Your friend's sister."

Brewer closed his eyes and tilted his chin as if a thorough memory search was required. "Sorry. I'm still drawing a blank. It was a short name. Kind of old fashioned. Not Madison or Ashley or one of those newer ones." His eyebrows shot up. "Ask Pauling. She'll know."

"Because it was her case. Yeah, you said that." Otto watched his eyes.

Maybe he'd been more interested in the victim's sister than he let on. Maybe that's why he conveniently didn't remember the homicide victim's name, too.

Or maybe he was lying. But why would he bother to lie for a guy he only met a few times?

"What was your sense of Reacher?" she asked, changing tack.

Brewer frowned and cocked his head. "My *sense* of him?"

"Yeah," Otto said. "I've never met the man, and you have. You're a cop. You're used to sizing people up pretty quickly. Did he seem like a reliable guy to you?"

CHAPTER THIRTEEN

BREWER NODDED AND LEANED closer across the table. He lowered his voice, which made Otto wary. First, he was all suspicious, and now he wanted to share confidences? "Honestly, I don't know. And that's one of the reasons I remember the whole situation."

"What do you mean?" Gaspar asked.

"Because I didn't know. Sometimes I'm wrong. But I always have a gut feeling, and it's usually solid. With Reacher, I didn't know. Could have gone either way." Brewer raised his eyebrows, extended his hand, flipped his palm over and back a couple of times. "On the one hand, he was one of the most controlled guys I've ever been around. Wrapped a little too tight, but not likely to react without thinking."

"And yet?" Otto prompted when he paused a bit too long.

He flipped his palm over again. "I had the feeling that the smallest little thing might push his buttons. Like with the right provocation, he might do almost anything. Like he wouldn't be the least concerned with the law or the consequences."

Brewer sat back and exhaled a long breath. "And if he was

provoked? Well, I'd be careful. My *sense* of Reacher was he seemed like the kind of guy who would always be the last man standing."

The words struck a deep chord with Otto, and she felt her nerves begin to hum with low voltage electricity like a weak Taser shot surging through her body.

Reacher's history, what little she knew of it, reflected a life of spectacular violence.

She recalled his army service records. Thirteen years. He'd seen combat, sure. Lots of medals, and a difficult career path, filled with ups and downs.

Military police. Special Investigative Unit. Ended with an honorable discharge, but a lot earlier than a guy like Reacher would typically retire. Suggesting he'd been coerced to go early, for undisclosed reasons.

In the course of his job as an army cop, the number of battered and broken men he'd left behind was surpassed only by the number of dead ones, and many of them were not enemies left on the battle field.

Brewer had nailed Reacher's army days. Spot on.

Whatever needed to be done, Reacher did it. Cop, judge, jury, and executioner. Always the last man standing. Never a drop of conscience or remorse.

Precisely.

Gaspar finished sopping up every last drop of the gooey yellow egg puddle on his plate. He eyed Otto's bagel. "Are you going to eat that?"

She pushed it toward him. The man was a bottomless pit. Where did he put all the food? None of it piled up on his bones, for sure. He could double as a scarecrow if his FBI gig didn't work out.

He made short work of the bagel and finished the coffee and pushed back from the table. Otto and Brewer both shook their heads.

Brewer laughed. "I haven't seen anybody eat like that since I coached high school football. Man, those teenagers could pack it away."

Gaspar smiled. "Were you in the army, Brewer?"

Brewer nodded. "Eat when you can. Sleep when you can."

"Exactly," Gaspar said. He pulled out a couple of bills and tossed them on the table for the waitress.

"Thanks for your help. We'll follow up with Pauling," Otto's voice quivered slightly. Probably from too much coffee and adrenaline and too little sleep or food. She stood and collected her bags. "We'll call you if we need anything else."

"You do that." Brewer's tone implied he'd be a lot less interested in taking their calls in the future.

They shook hands and just as Brewer turned to head toward the men's room, Otto said, "One more thing."

"Yes?" He turned back.

"When Reacher was here. In the city. Where was he staying?"

Brewer's face flushed and he seemed momentarily flustered. "Staying?"

"An apartment? Friends? A hotel?"

"I'm not sure. I think he had a friend with a place at the Dakota on Central Park West. Pauling will know. She spent a lot more time with him than I did." He waved them off and continued toward the men's room.

Otto watched his broad back for a moment, wondering which part of that answer was the lie, and added it to the list of things she'd ask him next time. When she had some leverage.

Because he definitely knew more than he'd admitted.

She led the way out, carrying her bags along the tight space between tables, with Gaspar trailing behind.

While Gaspar waved down a taxi, Otto waited near the building, away from the wind. She glanced around. A few pedestrians picked their way through the treacherous sidewalk, headed one way or the opposite direction. Lighter than usual New York City traffic inched along the street.

Which meant she had a partially obstructed view of a guy sitting behind the wheel of a dark sedan parked across the street. His chin rested on his chest. He was reading something in his lap. She glimpsed only his profile between passing vehicles.

Her breath caught painfully in her chest.

She shook her head to clear the fanciful thought that had popped to mind. This guy couldn't possibly be Reacher. Not if he'd been in Detroit a few hours ago. Get a grip.

Otto pulled out her phone and called Lauren Pauling Investigations. Pauling's business office was within walking distance, but with the bags and the sidewalks covered with snow and ice, a taxi was a better option.

The phone rang several times before voice mail picked up. "This is Lauren Pauling," said a low and husky voice. It sounded like she'd been recovering from laryngitis for the past thirty years. "I'm sorry I'm not available to take your call. Leave me a message, and I'll call you back."

Otto hung up. Pauling's office was a one-woman operation. She might be there, maybe with a client, or she could be out.

A taxi finally pulled up to the curb in front of the coffee shop. Gaspar came back to help with the bags. Otto felt a little twinge of déjà vu as the bags were stowed in the trunk and they settled into the back seat.

"Where to?" the driver asked. He spoke perfect English, with a slight British accent. She guessed his ethnicity was a former colony of the empire.

Otto considered the choices briefly. They were closer to Pauling's office, so she gave him the address on West Fourth Street. If Pauling wasn't there, they'd try her home.

The only other slim lead they had were the nameless friends Reacher had bunked with while he was in the city back then. Brewer said an apartment in the Dakota, which had been standing at the corner of 72nd Street and Central Park West for more than a hundred years. It would wait.

When the taxi pulled into the flow of traffic, Otto explained the unanswered phone call to Pauling and her backup plan to her partner.

"Do we know for sure that Pauling's actually in the city somewhere?" Gaspar asked.

Otto frowned. "The Boss wouldn't have sent us here otherwise."

"You still have that much faith in the guy, huh? After everything?" He smirked and wagged his head in mock consternation. "I've got another fifty bucks if you want to wager."

Otto shrugged off the fool's bet and Gaspar laughed.

CHAPTER FOURTEEN

Thursday, January 13
11:35 a.m.
New York City

PARNELL FOUND HIS CELL phone and redialed the little twerp's number. The phone rang several times and went to voice mail. The coward. He was probably standing right there, afraid to pick up. Parnell's lip curled.

He calmed his tone to coax the spineless idiot from his hiding place. "Simon, this is Fred Kern. I know you're busy and I'm sorry to bother you. But I'm afraid the key you gave me won't open the door to the apartment."

The dweeb picked up. What a fool. "Oh, Mr. Kern. I was on the other line. What? It's the wrong key?"

"I should have looked at it while you were still here. It's actually the key to the apartment above this one on the sixth floor." Parnell's right hand fisted so tight he felt his own pulse. "Could I trouble you to bring the correct key down for me? I've got a meeting I must attend, and I'm running short on time."

"Um, sure. I'll be right down." His voice squeaked, and he coughed to cover up his nerves. "But, uh, I'm on my way out with some friends, so could you meet me at the elevator again?"

Parnell could almost smell the sweat rolling off him. "Of course. Sorry to trouble you."

He ended the call before Peck could come up with any further excuses. Parnell walked to the elevator and, with gloved hands in his pockets, leaned against the wall out of sight of any passengers inside the elevator with Peck.

He didn't wait long. When the elevator arrived, and the door opened, he heard Peck and at least two other males inside. They were laughing and horsing around. Parnell stood at ease, leaning against the wall.

Peck stuck his head out and looked left first, then right. He spotted Parnell. "I have the master key here, Mr. Kern, but the one I gave you is the only key I have for that apartment."

Parnell heard Peck's friends talking. No one glanced out to get a good look at Parnell, he was fairly certain. Which meant he wouldn't need to kill them, possibly.

"Bring the master along and try it for me," Parnell tilted his head toward the honey colored door around the corner. He turned and took a few steps in that direction.

One of Peck's friends had pressed the button to hold the elevator door open, which triggered a loud bell of objection from the elevator's security system. Without turning around, Parnell raised his voice to be heard over the bell and said, "You guys go on down. He'll meet you there later."

The loud bell sounded again. Peck glanced at his friends. One said, "Go on, Simon. We'll get a head start. You can catch up."

When Peck didn't move, and the bell sounded louder,

longer, one of the men gave him a little shove toward the open door and said, "Work comes first."

Peck stumbled over the elevator's threshold. His friend must have lifted his finger from the button. The bell stopped and the doors closed.

The horrified look on Peck's sweaty face was almost comical. Almost.

Parnell slowed his stride to allow Peck to overtake him. He nodded ahead. "After you."

He followed the nervous, sweaty Peck to the honey-colored entrance. Peck extended his master key and inserted it into the lock. It turned easily, just as the one in Parnell's pocket had half an hour before. The lock was well oiled and worked perfectly, as anyone paying the maintenance fees at the Dakota had a right to expect.

Peck grasped and twisted the ornate brass knob, pushed the door open on silent hinges, and stood aside. He waved his arm, motioning Parnell to enter.

"After you, Simon," Parnell said again, in the tone he'd used to command armed soldiers for decades.

"Uh, I'm late already." Rivers of sweat ran down Peck's face and neck into the collar of his yellow golf shirt and under his sporty navy blazer with the polished brass buttons. His round Truman Capote glasses slipped to rest on the end of his nose. "I'm afraid I must go, Mr. Kern."

"Inside, Simon. I have something to show you." Parnell fisted Peck's back between his shoulder blades and shoved hard enough to propel him inside. Peck took a few stumbling steps forward while Parnell moved into the square yellow foyer and closed the door.

"You're familiar with the layout, Simon." Parnell pointed.

"Through there. I'll tell you when to stop."

They walked single file through the living room toward the interior hallway and on to the master bedroom. Peck's halting steps were annoyingly slow, so Parnell gave him a firm fist bump in the center of his back that pushed him into the bedroom. Another shove moved him through the open closet door and into the vault.

Parnell pointed. "What do you see, Simon?"

"Uh, w-what do you m-mean?" Peck's fidgeting and sweating were worse than ever now.

He resembled a kid who'd been pummeled with water balloons by a dozen playground bullies. He'd have been drier standing in a hard-pulsing shower.

What a waste of oxygen this guy was. The world would be a better place without him.

Just like that, his final plan for Peck snapped into place.

"Tell me what you see." Parnell pushed Peck's shoulder with his fist, knocking him off balance.

Peck stumbled and tripped over his own two feet. "Uh, an em-mpty closet?"

Parnell nodded. "Exactly. Where's my property?"

CHAPTER FIFTEEN

PECK'S EYES ROUNDED TO the size of dinner plates. He swiveled his head wildly as if nine million dollars could possibly be hidden in the small, empty space. His mouth worked like a fish, opening and closing. No sound came out.

"My property was in this room, Simon, when you took possession of this apartment. Now it is not here. Where is it?" Parnell reached into his pocket and pulled out the Strider SMF. He snapped the compact folding knife open in one swift move and flicked the point against Peck's fleshy neck. A narrow trickle of blood mixed with the sweat and dripped down to mingle with the stains on his collar. "Where's my property, Simon?"

"I-I-I d-don't k-know! I swear! I w-would t-tell you if I d-did!"

Parnell reached out with the sharply whetted blade and in one quick flick, sliced one of Peck's fleshy cheeks.

Peck's delayed reaction came after a split second. Blood gushed along his face down his chin. He screamed and slapped his palm on his face.

When he pulled his palm away and stared at the blood, tears fell from his eyes and snot ran from his nose and he blubbered like a two-year-old. "He took it. He took the money. Please don't hurt me again. I don't know where it is. Ask him. I don't know. I swear I don't know."

Parnell nodded. So the money had been here when the apartment was foreclosed, just as the *Times* had reported. Now it was gone. And Peck knew who stole it.

"You didn't give all that money to a total stranger, surely. You're a better board president than that, aren't you?" Parnell raised his arm as if he might slice Peck's body again and wanted Peck to see this one coming. "Who took my property, Simon? Was it Reacher?"

"Reacher? Who's Reacher? I don't know Reacher! I swear!" He shook his head furiously and crouched to make himself a smaller target. "Don't hurt me! I don't know who Reacher is!"

He was practically hyperventilating. A moment later, the overwhelming acrid odor of urine filled the six-by-three-foot space. Parnell saw the spreading stain on Peck's trousers.

What a waste of humanity.

Parnell cocked his head. The right amount of pressure must be applied. Not too much. Not too little. How hard could he push before Peck passed out or had a stroke? Always a judgment call. He'd been wrong before. But Peck was probably stronger than he pretended.

Parnell's arm darted out, and the reliable weapon sliced a deeper gash into Peck's second cheek. The blood flowed freely down to his blubbering mouth, mingling with the snot from his nose. The man was a mess.

"N-no! N-no! I swear!" Peck screamed and palmed his free hand to cover the second cut. He shook his head furiously, which was somewhat comical with both hands covering his wounds and his elbows akimbo.

Blood flew with every head shake, spattering the floor.

Parnell stepped out of the way.

Peck whimpered. "I don't know his name! A tall guy. Like you. Mean. Came here a few weeks after we foreclosed. Had a key. Said he worked for the Colonel. He's the one. He must be! He took it!"

Peck could be lying. But not likely. He didn't have the balls to lie right now.

"You should have told me that before, Simon." Parnell lowered the blade and his voice and nodded encouragingly. "What was this big guy's name?"

"Solo? Soto?" Peck's blubbering scrambled his words. "I don't know. I can't remember. I swear. He must be the one. He took it."

Parnell considered for a second. He could think of two big guys off the top of his head who knew about the money and might have had a key to the Colonel's apartment. The most recent hire, Reacher. And the former OSC Executive Vice President, Nick Scavo.

Back in that Baghdad bar, the three stooges had said Reacher left them after the bar fight in London and disappeared. They'd never seen him again, they said.

They said Scavo died in West Africa.

Parnell nodded. He knew for sure that Scavo wasn't dead because he knew precisely where Scavo was living.

Parnell cocked his head. What about Reacher? Reacher's death was unconfirmed. The three stooges had been wrong about Scavo. They could have been wrong about Reacher, too.

But Peck could have seen either Scavo or Reacher on the

premises during the months since the Colonel disappeared.

Or Peck was just trying to save his own ass.

Parnell narrowed his eyes and studied Peck's face.

He knew a liar when he saw one. The sweaty midget was lying about something. For sure.

Parnell felt his internal temperature rise. An ocular migraine distorted his vision into choppy waves like a cubist painting. He closed his eyes and watched the pulsing light cubes against his eyelids. Felt nausea in his gut.

Now. He had to control it now. Before Nitro Mack exploded.

Parnell opened his eyes and shifted his focus to the empty wall. The vision cubes melted into the solid white painted surface where they were less disorienting.

Counted his heartbeats.

Synchronized his breathing.

Clenched and released his fists, one finger at a time, until he felt his blood pressure settle and the pulsing in his ears subside.

Slowly, his vision cleared.

He regained equilibrium.

Until Peck foolishly opened his mouth and stoked the heat. So intent had he been on tamping his rage, Parnell had almost forgotten the little pile of snot shivering in the center of the room.

"I-I need a towel," Peck whined. Blood filled his hands and dripped down into the sleeves of his jacket. "P-Please."

Parnell stepped aside as Peck stumbled toward the door.

CHAPTER SIXTEEN

Thursday, January 13
12:35 p.m.
New York City

THE TAXI PULLED UP to the curb in front of Pauling's office building on West Fourth Street.

The driver stopped the taxi in the travel lane. "Are you getting out?" Gaspar asked.

"I'll go inside. You stay with the bags. If she's here, I'll call you to join me," Otto said.

The driver said, "I can't park here. We'll need to drive around the block."

"That's fine," Gaspar replied, and Otto slipped out into the cold once more. Before she'd reached the sidewalk, the taxi had rolled away.

She crossed the dirty curbside snow to the sidewalk and hiked up the steps to Pauling's office building. A small sign affixed to the corner of the glass proclaimed the street door was unlocked during business hours. A surveillance camera was mounted above the door.

The street door opened into a vestibule, which reduced heat loss from the lobby and provided an additional measure of security. Otto's bedroom closet in her Detroit apartment was larger than the small foyer, which was maybe six-by-six. The walls and ceiling were painted beige, and the floor tile was beige ceramic. The effect was similar to standing inside a dirty cloud.

Blocking the entrance to the interior lobby was the second door. Heavy steel, painted beige to blend with everything else. Sidelights, six inches wide, framed the door. She peered through to the lobby, but all she saw was a narrow staircase leading to the offices upstairs. One of those offices was Lauren Pauling Investigations.

Unlike the exterior door, the beige steel one was locked. A keypad on the wall to the left would have released the lock if she'd known the code, which she didn't.

She lifted the beige telephone receiver next to the keypad and looked up into the surveillance camera mounted on the ceiling. The fisheye lens easily captured everything in the small room.

If Reacher had come here, that camera would have recorded him. Which meant the Boss could have that footage, depending on when Reacher was here. She made a mental note to ask.

She heard nothing through the receiver for a few moments, and then a woman's voice asked, "May I help you?"

"I'm here to see Lauren Pauling."

"One moment, please."

More silence from the receiver. The vestibule was warm enough and protected from the wind, which was better than waiting outside on the stoop, but Otto felt a little claustrophobic.

Finally, the woman's voice said, "I'm sorry. Ms. Pauling's line doesn't answer. Would you like to leave a message?"

"When is she expected to return?"

"I'm sorry," she said again, perfunctorily, as if these were the first two words she'd been trained to say whenever she couldn't deliver what had been requested. "This is the answering service. I don't have that information for you. I can take a message, though."

Otto hung up. Her irritation kicked up a notch. She'd already left a message. She pushed through the outer door. She scanned the street for Gaspar's taxi.

Again, not as many people milling around as she'd expect in the summertime. But what caught her eye was the sedan idling at the curb at the opposite end of the block.

The vehicle was too far away. She narrowed her eyes. She couldn't make out the driver's features. But it was the same sedan she'd seen parked across from the coffee shop, she was sure of it. Which probably meant it was the same driver, too.

Gaspar's taxi rounded the corner and pulled up out front. She hustled down the concrete steps and ducked inside.

"Where to?" the driver asked after she'd settled in.

"One second. I'll look it up." Otto replied. She looked back. The sedan was still there. Waiting for her taxi to move, she figured.

She leaned closer to Gaspar and lowered her voice. "Looks like we've attracted some interest. That sedan back there, last one on the block, single white male driver. It was parked in front of the coffee shop, too. Same guy behind the wheel."

Gaspar turned to look while she scrolled through to find Pauling's contact information from the Boss's thumb drive on her phone.

She pushed the zoom lens on her camera and snapped a few quick photos of the car and driver. The photos wouldn't be sharp

102 | Diane Capri

enough from this distance, but they'd be better than nothing. She hoped.

Gaspar continued to watch the sedan while Otto gave Pauling's address to the taxi driver. When the taxi pulled away from the curb, the sedan didn't move. Which could mean she was wrong. Or it could mean the driver was good at following.

"As we expected. She wasn't in her office." Gaspar said, loud enough to be overheard by their driver.

He raised one eyebrow, and Otto shrugged.

They didn't see the sedan along the short drive, which signified nothing.

The taxi pulled up to a small co-op on Barrow Street near West Fourth. The brick building had once been a factory and had walls two feet thick. Inside, it probably had vaulted ceilings and exposed ductwork, too. Those were considered design elements these days.

"Do you think she's here?" Gaspar asked.

Otto shook her head. "Not likely, is it?"

"Why not?"

"Because it's the middle of the day. If she were in the city, she'd probably be at work. If she's not in her office, then she's out on a job of some kind."

"So what are we doing here?"

"Good question." Otto stared out of the taxi window. The sedan never rounded the corner behind them.

The driver was double parked, and it seemed to be making him nervous. "Are you getting out, ma'am?"

"Yeah. But I don't feel like lugging those bags." She opened the door and turned to Gaspar. "Ride around the block a few times, will you? I'll go inside. Maybe one of the neighbors knows something useful."

Gaspar snorted. "This is New York City, Sunshine. How likely do you think it is that someone's going to know anything? And even if they do, that they'll tell you?"

"You got a better idea, Chico?"

He scowled.

"That's what I thought." She stepped out of the taxi and leaned in. "Give me ten minutes. Pick me up here."

She closed the door and stepped between two parked cars and over the slush at the curb as the taxi pulled away. The sharply cold wind whipped around buildings and through the streets as if she was walking along an open river. She hunched into her coat and tramped up the snowy steps to the front door, which was locked.

She stood facing the door, but watching the street from the corner of her eye, giving the sedan long enough to catch up. When the car didn't materialize, she returned to her task.

The side panel listed unit numbers, but not names. There were four units on each floor. According to the FBI employee database, Pauling's apartment was on the second floor in the back of the building where it might have been a bit quieter. Barrow street was noisy. Taxi drivers laying on their horns. Sirens a few blocks over as ambulances screamed toward St. Vincent's.

Maybe the sedan got caught in traffic.

Otto pressed the call button for Pauling's apartment. Then she pressed the button for the other three apartments on Pauling's floor. From apartment 2A, a man said, "Yes?"

She put a smile in her voice. "Hi. I'm looking for Lauren Pauling."

"You pushed the wrong button. She's in 2C."

"I know, but—"

He'd already cut her off.

She tried pushing the four buttons on the floor below Pauling's. People Pauling might have encountered in the common areas or who might have at least spoken to her at some point. No one responded.

She then tried the four buttons for the units on the floor above and got lucky.

"Yes?" A younger man this time. His voice was a little squeaky as if he hadn't used it much today.

"I'm looking for Lauren Pauling." She turned her face up to the security camera and smiled, hoping this guy might be watching. "I'm a friend of hers. From work at the FBI." She held up her badge long enough for him to see the gold shield and her photo with FBI plainly showing.

"Hang on? I'll be right down?" Everything he said sounded like a question because his tone lifted up at the end of his sentences.

"Sure." Otto turned her collar up and stuffed her hands into her pockets. She stamped her feet to get some body warmth going and watched the street for the sedan.

It seemed to take forever, but eventually, the door swung open and she hurried inside. He closed the door behind her.

CHAPTER SEVENTEEN

"SORRY? I HAD TROUBLE finding my shoes?" He was about thirty. Skinny. Limp brown hair and a scraggly four-day growth on his face. He looked impossibly young, but he probably wasn't much younger than Otto.

"No problem. I'll just head upstairs." Otto tried to move past him, but he blocked her path.

"Well, that's the thing? See, Lauren's not here?" His eyes darted around, never resting on one spot for more than half a moment.

"How do you know that?" Great. Now he had her doing the lilting sentence thing.

He shuffled his bare feet on the cold floor. "Because when she's out of town, I look after her place? She's out of town a lot?"

"Where did she go?"

"I'm not sure? She didn't say? Maybe her condo in Palm Beach? She goes there a lot in the winter." He looked at Otto briefly, as if it had finally occurred to him that he should be a little more skeptical of strangers. "You said you work together, right?"

106 | DIANE CAPRI

"That's right."

"You could, uh, try her cell phone? She has it with her all the time?"

Otto gritted her teeth and nodded. The lilting sentences were driving her batty. If he talked like this all the time, a full interview would be excruciating. "Do you have any idea when she'll be back?"

He shook his head.

"What's your name?"

His eyes widened. "Marcus Blane?"

She pursed her lips to avoid snapping when he couldn't even state his own name with finality. She wasn't really annoyed with him, anyway. He just happened to be the guy standing in front of her at the moment. It was the situation itself that frustrated her.

Otto reached into her pocket and pulled out her phone and renewed her friendly-factor. "Marcus, give me your cell number so I can call you next time instead of bothering you by coming over."

He nodded and rattled off the number. She handed him a business card. He looked down at the raised gold seal and rubbed the pad of his thumb over it as if the solid feel provided some kind of secure vibe.

"If Lauren comes back, would you ask her to give me a call?" He nodded, and she widened her eyes with mock surprise. "Oh, shoot. I don't have her cell number with me. Give it to me quickly."

"I thought you worked together?" He seemed alarmed now, which he should have been right from the start.

"We both work for the FBI. That's right," Otto reassured him. "You have my card right there in your hand, and you already saw my badge."

He nodded slowly, still a little nervous. But he pulled his phone out of his pocket, found the number, and gave it to her.

"Thanks for the help, Marcus. I'll let you get back. Please let Lauren know I stopped by." She put her hand on the heavy brass door handle, thumbed the release button, and pulled the door open. The sharp wind gusted inside, swirling her coat around her legs.

Gaspar's taxi slowed at the curb out front.

"You've been really helpful, Marcus." She turned to face him briefly before she ducked out. "I'll be sure to tell Lauren when I catch up with her."

He smiled in that silly way that boys do when they're smitten. "Lauren's really great, you know?"

"She is. She absolutely is. Thanks again." Otto ducked through the door and glanced up and down the block for the black sedan before she hurried down the steps to the sidewalk.

When she was reseated, shivering, in the back seat of the taxi, Gaspar said, "Well?"

"We need a better plan."

"So she wasn't very helpful?" He mocked and raised both eyebrows instead of the usual one.

She shot a fierce scowl his way. "If you laugh, I swear I'll shoot you."

He pressed his lips together, but his laughter erupted anyway.

The taxi driver said, "Where to?"

Gaspar was still laughing.

Otto said the first logical place that came to mind. "The Dakota."

"You got it." The cab made a turn at the next block.

She glared at Gaspar. "Call Brewer. Get him to meet us up there. They're more likely to cooperate with a local."

"Yes, Lady Boss." He grinned, but he pulled his phone from his pocket and placed the call. While he waited for Brewer to pick up, he said quietly for her ears only, "You were right. Our watcher is waiting around the corner up ahead."

Being right wasn't what she'd wanted. Her heart broke into a full out gallop.

She pulled her phone from her pocket, flipped it to video mode, and steadied the camera to shoot through the side window.

As the taxi turned the corner and joined the slow inching crawl of mid-day traffic, she started the video. She saw the back of the sedan, idling in front of a fireplug on the left.

The car and the driver were close enough to reach out and touch when the taxi passed at a snail's pace. The driver glanced to his right at exactly the right time. She got a good look at both man and car.

Which meant her heart rate slowed to a still-painful canter. She pushed the stop record button on the video and slumped back into the passenger seat behind the driver. She had stopped breathing. When she noticed the pain, she exhaled.

She couldn't quite wrap her mind around it yet. She frowned.

This was the third time she'd seen the sedan this morning.

She shook her head. Definitely not a coincidence.

Gaspar stared at her. When she met his eyes, he nodded.

So Gaspar agreed.

The vehicle was owned by Uncle Sam.

And the driver was definitely not Reacher. He was big, but not that big. His hair was short but dark. His eyes were brown, not icy blue.

So who was he? And why was he following them?

The taxi was stopped again, one car length from the sedan.

Otto threw a hard glance toward Gaspar. "Stay in the taxi. Don't go too far. I'll catch up."

She opened the door and stuck her left leg out first.

"What the hell—" He reached for her arm, but his grasp wasn't firm enough.

She jerked her arm away and left the cab for the street. She closed the door and walked back to the sedan. On the way, she unbuttoned her coat and readied her holster, just in case.

Ten seconds later, she stood on the sidewalk beside the sedan's front door. She rapped on the window. The driver had been looking down at his phone. When he looked up, his shocked expression was almost comical.

People on the sidewalk were hustling past in the cold. One or two looked at Otto briefly, but no one stopped or asked any questions.

"You're not going anywhere," she said, gesturing toward the gridlock on the street. "Get out of the car."

He frowned, but he didn't move.

"Open the door, or I'll break the glass and pull you out." Her voice was calm. Controlled. He probably thought she couldn't or wouldn't make good on the threat. He was wrong on both counts.

After a few moments, maybe realizing he was stuck right here with her until the traffic cleared, he shrugged and opened the door. She moved to one side. He stepped out on the sidewalk.

He wasn't as tall as Reacher. Six foot two, she guessed. He wasn't as big as Reacher, either. He filled out his clothes well enough. An indicator that he worked out and took the fitness requirements seriously.

"Relax." He flashed a megawatt dazzler. "I know you're not going to shoot me, so I'll return the favor."

His voice was somewhere in the mid-range. He had a smooth, soft, Southern drawl. Not Atlanta. Nashville, maybe. "Don't bet the farm," she replied. "You're driving a government vehicle. Show me your ID."

He reached into his pocket and pulled out a badge wallet similar to hers. She recognized the badge immediately.

"You're a Treasury agent?"

"Close enough." He nodded. "Technically, IRS Criminal Investigation Division, Special Agent John Lawton, at your service. Johnny to my friends."

She shook her head to clear the confusion. "Why the hell are you following us?"

"We're not. We're watching Brewer. I saw you this morning. No one knew who you were. So," he shrugged again.

"Why are you watching Brewer?"

"Nothing to do with you. It's a Treasury matter." He was not wearing an overcoat, and the wind had picked up. She noticed he was shivering, but he seemed unconcerned about frostbite. He gave her a slightly dimmer version of the smile. "You can torture me if you want. But that's all you're getting."

She figured he meant what he said. She could stand here all day and get nothing but frozen. She glanced at the street traffic. Her taxi was a few car lengths closer to the light at the corner now.

"Let's do this," she suggested, dipping her hand into her pocket. "Here's my card. Give me one of yours."

He complied.

She looked at it. "This your personal cell number, Agent Lawton?"

"That's right. You want to invite me to dinner?" He flashed a genuine grin this time. One that caused his whole face to light up. Which made him a lot better looking in addition to infuriating. The guy was hot. And he knew it.

"Yeah. That's exactly what I had in mind." Her sarcasm was as thick as lava. "When I call you, pick up the phone. I don't like to be kept waiting."

"Yes, ma'am," he said, mocking her.

"And stop following me," she demanded.

He failed to reply, but she wouldn't have heard him anyway. She was already halfway down the block.

CHAPTER EIGHTEEN

Thursday, January 13
2:05 p.m.
Palm Beach, Florida

LAUREN PAULING WAITED OUTSIDE at Palm Beach
International Airport for her limo. She grinned and stretched in
the warm sun like a lazy cat. She felt lighter, too, without the
weight of Elwood's welfare and a winter coat on her shoulders.

She found her private cell phone and checked for calls she'd
missed during the flight. Several voice messages were waiting.
Most were not important, but two were unusual.

One caller was "unknown," which usually meant blocked
caller ID. That message was short. Probably some sort of
solicitation. She shrugged. They'd call again.

The second voice message was from Greg Brewer. She
smiled. He was her favorite NYPD detective. It had been quite a
while since she'd talked to him. She pressed the play button.

"It's Brewer. Listen, just a heads up. A couple of FBI agents
were here asking questions about Reacher. I didn't say much.

Figured I'd leave it up to you. They're on the way to you next. Thought you'd want to know."

A frown crossed her face. Jack Reacher. Several quick questions raced through her mind. Why were FBI agents interested in Reacher? And how had they identified her? Or Brewer? What did they want?

A smile crossed her lips. She had thought about Reacher a lot in the past few months. She divided her life now in two parts. Before Reacher. After Reacher.

She hadn't expected the passing fling to influence her life so profoundly. Had she known, would she have welcomed him to her bed?

She shrugged. If nothing else, Reacher had pushed her to live in the moment. Take everything exactly as it comes. Deal with what happens as it happens.

He'd shown her, in the most realistic way possible, that every moment could be her last. A lesson she should have learned at a much younger age, given the number of times her life had been on the line. She often wondered how she'd denied her own mortality before Reacher.

Before, she'd been mired in the worst of things that human beings did to one another, powerless to repair the damage or prevent the behavior from happening again.

Simply put, Reacher had changed her life.

When she saw him again, she planned to thank him properly. The thought alone sent waves of warmth through her body.

The one regret she had about her time with Reacher was that she'd never figured out how the clock in his head worked more accurately than any watch. She'd tried to duplicate his precision but never succeeded.

The limo pulled up, and the driver jumped out to open the

passenger door. She settled into the roomy back seat while he stowed her luggage. A few minutes later, he rolled into the flow of traffic, north and east toward Palm Beach Island.

The current president owned a home on the island and often visited from D.C. When he was in residence, navigating the narrow streets of the small community was a disaster area. His entourage overwhelmed everything when they were in town. Every restaurant, every street, even the boats and parties and events that were normally such a pleasure, became a nightmare of crowds, security, and inconvenience.

Luckily, he was away on an overseas diplomatic trip now. Her ride home was uneventful, and she expected to enjoy a bit of socializing without the constant pressure of his presence before he returned tomorrow night.

The drive across Flagler Memorial Bridge from West Palm Beach onto Palm Beach Island spanned what she thought of as the great divide. Those residents who were comfortably well-off on one side and those who embraced the more expensive best of everything the country had to offer on the other. Not exactly the haves and the have-nots, of course. Everything was a matter of degree.

She gazed at the sparkling Intracoastal Waterway. At Royal Palm Way, the last of her tension slipped off as they rolled into The Town of Palm Beach. America's Best Place to Live. The welcome sign and every expert said so. Pauling agreed.

Nostalgia washed over her. She and Hugh had been so happy here. He'd bought the small condo on Ocean Boulevard years before, when real estate was at least somewhat affordable and paid little attention to the place. She'd thrown herself into renovations until the bare dwelling became a comfortable home they'd both loved.

Her heart no longer ached for those days. Hugh had been the love of her life, but she'd finally let him go. She'd had no choice.

When Hugh died, she'd closed up their retreat to avoid the heart-piercing memories, and thrown herself into her work at the FBI.

Until she failed. Spectacularly. She'd resigned a half step before the stink of failure consumed her previously stellar career. She'd opened her private investigating business, and five years after that, she'd met Reacher. Because of that old failure.

The case she'd botched led to two life-altering experiences.

She shook her head. Sounded like some kind of cheap romance novel, didn't it?

She'd known Reacher only a few days, and what they shared was—what? Not a whirlwind romance. Not even remotely.

But he'd had a profound impact on her life in more ways than one.

Reacher was a big man who filled every space he entered. After he moved on, she finally noticed how empty her life was. She'd needed a change. A drastic one. Reacher gave her that.

Sixteen months later, here she was. Palm Beach in January. She'd lived in New York City her entire life, and she loved it. But the small condo on Ocean Boulevard felt more like home now.

The limo driver pulled up out front. He parked and brought her luggage inside. After he left, she was blissfully alone.

She walked through the place quickly. Everything was as expected. The housekeeping service had done an excellent job. Everything clean, fridge stocked, and the temperature inside as well as outside was perfect. She kicked off her shoes and grabbed a bottle of cold seltzer.

She hit the call back button on Brewer's message. After

several rings, the call flipped to voice mail. "Thanks for the heads up. When you have a chance, let me know what's going on."

He'd call when he could.

She slid the patio door open and walked outside. A salty breeze blew gently from the Atlantic Ocean, stinging her cheeks. She lifted her seltzer and toasted the magnificence surrounding her.

She felt glorious. "My God, Hugh was so right. This is truly paradise."

She guessed the time before she glanced at her watch. Wrong again. But she had space for a quick swim before her guest arrived.

On the way to her bedroom to change, she stopped at the small room that had once served as Hugh's office before she repurposed it. She slid the heavy oak panel away to reveal the vault's gleaming door.

Constructed of eight-inch thick Hercvlite to reduce the weight, this door was a work of art in highly polished silver, black, and gold metals. She paused to admire the craftsmanship every time.

Quickly, she entered the primary combination into the first lock and a different combination into the second one. Two locks were enough to thwart a team of three intruders with modern tools, she'd been assured. A third lock could have been added when she'd ordered the lightweight vault panel system, but that had seemed excessive.

The second lock released and she pulled the big round door open. Although the door was heavy, it swung smoothly on its hinges, simultaneously engaging the interior light. A slight whiff of orange blossom wafted to her nose from the air freshener that eliminated musty mold and mildew indigenous to Palm Beach. She stepped over the flat sill threshold. She'd test the door's inside emergency release again when she had a chance. For now, she glanced at the contents of the vault, critically measuring the stacks against her mental inventory. She nodded. Everything appeared in order. A more thorough count would have to wait.

She stepped out, closed and locked the vault, and slid the oak panel into place. Then, she hurried to change into her swimsuit. She kept her phone with her.

An hour later, after her swim, she was sunning by the pool when Brewer called.

"This is Lauren Pauling," she said, as she always did when she answered the phone. But she put a smile in her voice.

"It's Brewer. I've only got a minute. I'm right in the middle of something here."

"Okay. What's up?"

"You got my message?"

"Yes. What's going on?"

"FBI Agents Otto and Gaspar. They're asking questions about Reacher. Some bullshit about him being considered for a special project."

Pauling frowned. "What kind of project?"

"They said it was classified. Claimed they didn't know. Said they were just updating his file. But here's the thing. They knew my name and where to find me. They knew yours, too. We don't have any paper trail connecting us to Reacher or to each other. So how did they know?"

Pauling stood and paced around the pool deck. She always thought more clearly when she was in motion. "I have no idea. They didn't say, I gather?"

"No. Just thought you'd want to know. Maybe you'd want to

ask around. Let me know if there's anything I should worry about."

"What would you have to worry about, Greg?"

He blew out a long stream of air. "Beats me. Sorry. I'm being called back in. Keep me posted."

"I will," she said, but he'd already hung up.

She felt chilled all of a sudden. She picked up her towel and went inside. What could have raised the FBI's radar about Reacher? And why now? After all this time?

She knew about the TrueLeaks documents. She'd checked the media reports when the leaks were first reported. There were millions of documents and they covered a wide swath. The government loved paperwork. No doubt, many of the documents were duplicates. It could take years to sort through all that stuff.

She'd run Reacher's name through the databases she could readily locate and nothing had popped up. She'd checked her name, too. Same result.

The Colonel and his company were listed as secondary military contractors, along with hundreds of other private contractors. She hadn't found anything ominous there, either.

Nothing about the apartment at the Dakota. Or the nine million dollars he'd left there. After she'd interceded with the co-op board, all mention of the money had been removed from the foreclosure records and anywhere else it might have appeared.

She tapped a forefinger against her lips. The weak link in her situation was Simon Peck. Peck was a silly little man, with his Truman Capote obsession and his affected ways. But he took his duty to protect the Dakota and its residents very seriously. Besides, Peck adored her, and he liked Brewer. He wouldn't have volunteered anything sketchy to anyone. Certainly not to the FBI.

She considered giving Peck a call. Just to be sure. But was that the wise thing to do?

She had friends at the FBI still. She could find out who these agents were and why they were looking for her. She made a mental note to do just that. Forewarned was forearmed.

CHAPTER NINETEEN

Thursday, January 13
2:35 p.m.
New York City

TRAFFIC GREW HEAVIER. THE trip from Pauling's
apartment was thirty-five minutes of go, stop, and wait. The taxi
traveled north on Sixth Avenue to 57th Street and then two
blocks west. He turned north on Eighth, through Columbus
Circle, to Central Park West, and onto 72nd Street.

Eventually, he stopped outside the Dakota with the meter
still running.

Gaspar's phone rang. He nodded toward Otto and picked up
the call. "Yes, Brewer, thanks for calling me back. We're at the
Dakota. We want to interview the friend Reacher was visiting
here. Otto thinks they'll be more likely to cooperate with a
friendly NYPD detective than with us. When can you get up
here?"

Brewer talked for a couple of seconds before Gaspar shook
his head and his eyebrows dipped into a frown. "I understand.

Absolutely. A fresh homicide comes before a witness interview. Sure. Okay. Call me when you're done, and we'll figure something out."

When he disconnected, Otto said, "Let's see how far we can get without him."

The driver asked, "Are you getting out here? I'll need to move."

Otto glanced around for the black sedan but didn't see it. Yet. She didn't want to unload the bags and bring them along. Leaving everything in the taxi wasn't a great plan, either.

She heard her mother's voice as clearly as if she were sitting in the taxi, too. *When there's only one choice, it's the right choice.* "We'll only be a few minutes. Can you wait?"

He turned his head, looked at her, and shrugged. "You're on the meter."

Gaspar held up his phone and snapped a photo of the driver and the taxi's license. He turned on his video recording mode and held up his badge. "We're FBI agents. We're going inside for fifteen to twenty minutes, at the most. Anything happens to our property while we're inside and you've committed a federal crime. Do you understand?"

"Buddy, I've been carting you two around on the meter most of the day. You owe me a lot of money." The driver seemed uneasy, after Gaspar threatened him. And then he shrugged again. "I guess you're not going to pay me now, so I'll wait."

Otto was skeptical by nature, which made her a good lawyer and a great cop. But that same skepticism complicated her life every day. Should she trust this guy? Probably not. "Pop the trunk. I need my laptop."

The laptops were encrypted and stored classified data. They

could not be left unattended. Not if Otto and Gaspar wanted to stay out of prison.

He pushed the trunk release, and they climbed out of the taxi. She scooped up her laptop case and slung the strap over her shoulder. Gaspar grabbed his before he slammed the trunk closed and slapped the lid twice with his palm as a signal to the driver.

As they walked toward the Dakota's grand entrance, Gaspar grinned. "Ten bucks says he's there when we come back."

"You're on. Did you see his face when you flashed your badge? That guy's halfway to New Jersey by now." She slung the black leather strap over her shoulder, hunched into her coat, and hurried through the biting wind.

Gaspar said, "Nah. He wants to get paid and avoid prison. He'll wait."

Otto placed a hand on his arm and paused. "So that guy is a Treasury agent. He says they're looking at Brewer. He saw us, didn't know who we were, tried to find out. Why is Treasury interested in Brewer?"

"I have no idea. But it can't be a good thing." Gaspar's teeth were chattering already.

"You didn't recognize the guy, did you?"

"No. But can we talk about this later?" His lightweight suit and overcoat weren't doing the job. "How can it be so cold in the middle of the day with the sun shining?"

"Global warming," she said.

He laughed, and they continued toward the entrance.

The doorman waited inside the warm lobby until the last possible moment, when he opened the door and stepped outside. They hustled past, and he pulled the door closed behind them. "January weather in New York is the worst, isn't it?"

"Tell me about it," Gaspar replied, shivering and blowing warm air on his cold hands. "That's why I live in Miami."

"Lucky dog. Why aren't you soaking up the Florida sunshine today?" The doorman smiled. "I'd be there if I had that option."

"I'm FBI Special Agent Otto. This is FBI Special Agent Gaspar." Otto pulled out her badge and flashed it. Gaspar did the same. The doorman peered briefly at both badges and nodded. "What's your name?"

"Will Bishop." He pointed to the gold bar pinned to his jacket. *W. Bishop*, it said.

"Mr. Bishop, how long have you been the doorman here?"

"About eight years, I think, give or take." He closed his eyes to concentrate. "I started off on the night shift, but I've been on the day shift five days a week, oh, I guess maybe five years or so."

"So that means you see everybody that comes in and out the front door?" Gaspar asked.

"Pretty much. I mean, I have a couple of breaks during the day. But mostly, I'm right here." Bishop nodded. "We have the kind of residents who don't want to open their own doors, you know? Which is a good thing for me. Otherwise, I'd be out of a job." He smiled revealing teeth so perfect they had to be fake.

Otto nodded. "We're looking for a man who might have been visiting with one of your residents a while back."

She flipped through a few screens on her phone and found the photo of Reacher from his Army days. She had edited the photo to a tight headshot to remove all indicia of his military service, to avoid influencing the witnesses.

"This is the man we're interested in." She showed Bishop the photo.

He studied the picture for a couple of moments.

"Do you know this guy?"

Bishop shook his head. "Not really."

Gaspar frowned. "Sounds like you mean you have seen him around."

"But I didn't know the guy," Bishop nodded. "He wasn't here long. He must have been an employee or something. He came and went a few times. Sometimes on his own and sometimes with others."

"When was this?" Gaspar asked.

"It wasn't wintertime." Bishop looked up at the ceiling as if he was searching for a clue about the dates. "It was a while ago. Several months, at least. Maybe longer."

"You're certain it was him?" Otto asked.

Bishop held out his hand. "Let me look a little closer, but I think so, yeah." Otto passed him the phone, and he studied the photo a bit before handing it back. "Yeah, that's him. Like I said, he wasn't here very long. But that's the guy."

"Who was he working for?" Otto asked.

"He might not have been working. I don't know. He never talked to me." Bishop shrugged. "Sometimes he came and went solo. Other times, he hung out with some of the guys, so I just figured."

"What guys?" Otto asked.

Bishop shook his head. "I don't know. Guys I'd seen around before that one came."

Gaspar ran a hand through his hair. "Well he wasn't visiting Yoko, was he?"

Bishop grinned and shook his head. "Not likely. He wasn't her type."

"What type does she go for?"

"You know. Famous people." Bishop shrugged. "And she's way more relaxed than that guy. Way too old for him, too."

Otto was as exasperated as Gaspar was by now. "Who was Reacher visiting? We want to talk to him. Or her."

"Oh, they're gone. Left the same time that guy did." He nodded toward Otto's phone. "Never came back. The place is empty a long time now. The condo board had to foreclose on the place because they didn't pay their maintenance fees for a whole year."

Otto said, "And the owner of the apartment was?"

"Didn't I say? Well, really, I'm not sure. I just assumed, you know, because of the timing and all. Retired military. I think he was a colonel. And his family. Nice family." He paused while a slight grimace crossed his face. "Well, the wife was nice, and the little girl was adorable. *He* was all business. Lived here for years and never said a word to me. Not once. But they were good residents. No trouble. Quiet. Traveled a lot."

Otto held on to her patience, but barely. "So no one has been inside their apartment in sixteen months?"

"Well, come to think of it, there was a guy here this morning. Heard him say he was the Colonel's brother-in-law. He had an appointment with our co-op board president."

"And what was his name?" Otto asked.

Bishop cocked his head and thought it over. "Fred Kern, I think he said. You could ask Mr. Peck. Simon Peck. He's the board president. He would know."

"Is Mr. Kern still here?" Gaspar asked.

"I don't think so." Bishop wagged his head. "I'd call Mr. Peck down for you, but I know he's not around. I tried to reach him a little while ago, and the call went to voicemail. You can come back when Mr. Peck is here. I'm sure he could answer your questions."

"You have a card for Mr. Peck?" Gaspar said, annoyance plain in his tone now.

"Yeah, sure. Hang on a second. I've got one in the desk drawer over here." Bishop found the card and offered it to Gaspar, who glanced at it and stuffed it in his pocket.

"What did Mr. Kern look like?" Gaspar asked.

"Well, it's weird. Because at first, I thought he was that guy." Bishop's face flushed. "But turned out it wasn't him, I guess."

Gaspar practically growled. "You thought he was *what* guy?"

"The one in that photo you're asking me about." He nodded toward Otto's pocket where she'd slipped the phone when he'd handed it back. "Same build. Same look to him. The way he carried himself. Same military haircut. First glance, I thought it was him."

"How do you know it wasn't the same guy, then?" Gaspar leaned toward Bishop as if he might cuff him or something.

Bishop cocked his head and looked at Gaspar blankly.

Otto intervened. "You said you hadn't seen the guy in a while and you never talked to him. How can you be sure Kern wasn't him?"

"I guess you're right." Bishop shrugged. "I guess it could have been the same guy..." His voice trailed off, unsure now.

"Okay. Let's be clear," Otto said, making every effort not to lose her cool. "Since the family left a couple of years ago, you're saying no one has been in that apartment except Mr. Peck and Mr. Kern who went in this morning?"

"Well, I'm not here twenty-four-seven, so I couldn't swear to it. And now that you mention it, doesn't seem very likely that *nobody* has been in that place for sixteen months, does it?" Bishop said. "But the only other person I know about is that NYPD detective. Brewer, his name is. Comes around from time to time to keep an eye on the place."

Gaspar said, in the most official tone Otto had heard him use so far, "We'd like to see the apartment."

Bishop's eyes widened, and he wagged his head again. "You'll need to talk to Mr. Peck about that. I don't have a key to the place, anyway. Even if I had a key, I couldn't let you into a residence. I'd lose my job."

Otto took a breath. "When will Mr. Peck be back here?"

Bishop shrugged again. "He lives here. But I don't know where he went, so how can I know when he'll come home?"

"Right," Gaspar said. "What did you say the apartment owner's name was?"

Bishop's eyes widened again. "I didn't say, did I? I could get fired for that. Doormen at the Dakota are required to be discreet."

Otto put a hand on Gaspar's arm. He glared at her. She grinned. Gaspar rarely let anything get under his skin. Usually, he was the one pulling her off the ceiling.

She said, "Okay, Mr. Bishop. Thank you for your help. We'll call Mr. Peck, as you suggested."

Gaspar followed her outside. "Damn Brewer. He knew all along that Reacher was here. He knows a lot more about this whole thing than he let on, too. What the hell was he thinking?"

"Sorry. My crystal ball is cloudy on that one. When we see him, we'll ask." Otto stuck her hands in her pockets and walked toward the spot where the taxi should have been waiting.

As she rounded the corner, she stopped in her tracks.

When he looked at the empty spot where the taxi driver had promised to wait, Gaspar swore.

Otto laughed and held out her palm. "That'll be ten bucks, Chico."

"Yeah, yeah. Put it on my bill." He practically snarled at her. "I'll try to flag another cab."

She looked for the black sedan. She didn't see it hanging around. But then, if Lawton was really a pro, she never should have seen him in the first place.

Her fingers and toes had lost all feeling before Gaspar finally persuaded a taxi to stop.

They climbed into the back seat, and Otto said, "Grand Central Station."

Gaspar shot her a questioning glance, but she ignored him.

CHAPTER TWENTY

Thursday, January 13
4:25 p.m.
New York City

EVENTUALLY, THE TAXI REACHED 42nd Street and Park Avenue. He pulled over to let them out at Grand Central Station. Gaspar paid the bill and added a hefty tip, judging from the wide grin on the driver's face before he drove away.

The area around the station was crowded, teeming with pedestrians and various forms of transportation fighting for every inch of pavement, coming and going. The bustle of activity was normal at this time of day, which was why she'd chosen to come here.

Everything said, done, and barely considered around a transportation center like Grand Central was heavily monitored these days. A determined watcher like the Boss couldn't be avoided. Which was the bad news.

The good news was that they could hide amid the chaos for a short while. Which would be long enough.

Otto strode through the terminal, knowing that Gaspar would catch up. He always did. She was tired and hungry. No sleep last night, a stalker in her bedroom this morning, the Boss invading her privacy, two harrowing flights, and an entirely wasted day. Who wouldn't be annoyed?

Nothing she could do about most of it at the moment. One thing at a time.

First order of business was food. She'd had enough of diners and grease for one day. Because Gaspar never objected to food of any kind, she didn't bother to ask his preferences.

She led them to one of the better restaurants where it was still too early for the New York evening rush. A hostess seemed momentarily shocked when Otto said they'd come for dinner. She recovered quickly and seated them at a quiet booth in the back. They ordered black coffee.

Otto put her elbows on the white linen tablecloth and dropped her head into her hands, waiting until the fragrant, dark coffee arrived. She inhaled the aroma, sipped and swallowed.

Like so many other things she'd discovered in their brief partnership, the way Gaspar liked his coffee was the polar opposite of how she drank hers. The first time she'd watched him stir about half a cup of sugar and pour a huge dollop of cream into an eight-ounce cup, it literally made her teeth ache.

He'd said she'd get over it. Eventually. At the time, neither expected their partnership to last that long.

After she'd downed half a cup of liquid sanity, she wanted answers. She and Gaspar needed to be on the same page. "What have you heard about this recent batch of TrueLeaks?"

"Same things you've heard, probably." He took a swallow of the sweet, creamy liquid, grimaced, and added more sugar.

She shuddered.

"Our Miami field office personnel have been assisting with some of the less sensitive documents. I'm guessing your Detroit field office people have, too."

Otto nodded. "I haven't been involved either, but I've heard this document dump is military related. Angry private contractors dissatisfied with cutbacks. Illegal monitoring of military personnel, including private activities. Allegations of kickbacks and bribery and conduct unbecoming and the like. Of course, the anonymous leaker claims his motives are pure. Public good. Corruption at the highest levels. Yadda yadda yadda."

"I suppose you think that's somehow admirable?" Gaspar scowled and swiped a palm across his face.

"Not me, Chico." She shook her head. "You know the official position as well as I do. And there's good reason for it. Classified information is classified to save lives. You take the job, you agree to respect that. And you go to jail if you don't. Not a big mystery."

Gaspar's eyes widened and his brows arched. He feigned shock. "You don't think whistleblowers provide a worthy service? Shouldn't corruption be exposed?"

"You're mocking me. Corruption should definitely be exposed. There are legal ways to do that. I'm in favor of using them. I'm a lawyer. What else would I say?" She finished her coffee and picked up the menu. Gaspar glanced at his, too. The server came back with more coffee and took their orders.

"Here's what worries me." She leaned across the table after the server left, lowering her voice. "These leakers expose private data that can cause real harm to people. Hard to stuff the genie back in the bottle."

"This particular genie is already out there now. And besides that, we aren't handling the TrueLeaks case. We've got our own problems." Gaspar stretched his bad leg into the narrow aisle between tables. "The Boss found references to Reacher in those leaked files. We have our orders."

"That's what I want to talk about." She glanced around. The restaurant was filling up, but none of the tables nearby were occupied yet. "The transcript of that recorded telephone conversation between Brewer and Pauling. Brewer wanted Pauling to meet with Reacher. The chat was short and to the point. Brewer and Pauling were both circumspect. Brewer didn't tell Pauling much at all. She didn't ask many questions."

"They're a couple of cops. Nothing unusual about cops getting to the point and getting off the horn." Gaspar folded his hands and nodded. "And Brewer confirmed all of it today when we interviewed him. I don't see the problem here. What's your point?"

"The Boss said the files we received were part of the recent TrueLeaks dump. Maybe they were." She paused for another sip of coffee, wondering if he'd noticed on his own. If he had, he didn't act like it.

"But *why* was the Brewer/Pauling conversation recorded in the first place?"

Gaspar shrugged.

"Come on, think about it. You *know* that's odd." Otto also knew Gaspar wasn't the least bit stupid. So maybe she was reading too much into the anomaly. "One call. Only one. Took place sixteen months ago. Neither Brewer nor Pauling were involved in any military related activities at the time."

"As far as we know," Gaspar said. "Somebody at Treasury is looking at him, apparently."

"Right. Hold that thought." She raised a palm. "As far as we know, Brewer was honorably discharged from the army a couple of decades ago and has been at the NYPD all that time." Otto took a breath. "Pauling never served in the military or worked for a military contractor. She was FBI until she retired. And she retired five years before this jackpot conversation took place."

Gaspar frowned. "So what? The Boss found the needle in a haystack. The one call that mattered to him. That's explained if he set triggers for Reacher's name everywhere. Which would be the smart thing to do if he's trying to find Reacher, don't you think?"

"I do think that's what happened. I agree." She nodded.

"Then what? What are you getting at?"

She took another deep breath. If Gaspar didn't see it, maybe she was off base here. She didn't want her bias to be confirmed. She wanted the *facts* confirmed. "So why was the Brewer/Pauling conversation swept up at all?"

"How the hell should I know? We don't even know where the TrueLeaks stuff came from. Which means we don't know who was listening. We can't know why if we don't know who." Gaspar scowled. "You know how this job works as well as I do, Otto. The Boss tells us what he wants us to know, no more and no less. We go from there. Simple as that."

"And that's just fine with you?"

"You know it's not. You also know there's not a damn thing I can do about it." He inhaled about a gallon of air. "Look, I've got five kids and a wife and twenty years to go before I can relax. The only thing I can do is hang on. Show up. Follow orders."

Otto cocked her head and tried leading him in the right direction. "TrueLeaks released millions of documents less than a week ago. Most of them have not been reviewed yet." Otto paused, but Gaspar seemed to remain clueless and unwilling to speculate. "Yet, the Boss has already located *this single* phone conversation and tasked us with following up? Does that seem likely to you?"

"He has his fingers in a lot of pies. Reacher's name comes up somewhere, no matter how tangential it is, and one of the many minions at his disposal lets him know."

"Likely." Otto nodded. "And then what?"

Gaspar shrugged again. "I'm number two, remember? Thinking through all this stuff is your job."

"Okay. Here's one scenario." Otto nodded. "He gets the recorded chat between them. He does a quick background check on both Brewer and Pauling. Something he found caused him to send us here."

"Makes sense. Sure. Why not?"

"So what was it? What did he find?" She cocked her head. "Why are we here?"

Gaspar grinned. "I take it you don't mean that in the existential sense."

Otto smiled back. "You have me confused with my mother. She's the spiritual one."

The server returned with their food. Steak and potatoes and a bread basket for Gaspar. Broiled fish and grilled veggies for Otto.

"Bon appétit!" he said before he dished ahead.

Otto shook her head. She'd never cease to be amazed at how much Gaspar could pack away. And she came from farmers. Four brothers, and an extended family with more than its share of oversized people. Nobody she knew could eat as much as the rail-thin Gaspar. Honestly, the guy must have a tapeworm or something.

Gaspar stuffed half of a redskin potato in his mouth and chewed thoughtfully. Otto smiled again. Usually, he consumed his food fast, as if he'd never get another meal. He'd paused for almost three full seconds. He must have been seriously considering her point.

"So let's assume that the stuff leaked from a low-level employee. Not active military. A military contractor, because the most recent TrueLeaks document dumps have come from outside the government employee base." He put down his fork.

First time she'd ever seen that happen while food remained on his plate. Could be a good sign.

"Agreed." She nodded and continued to chew the salmon.

"Here's where it gets murky." He leaned in. "Let's also assume that this one phone conversation between Brewer and Pauling resulted from illegal surveillance. Someone or something that is somehow related to military corruption *inside* the government employee base."

Made sense that the tap was illegal. Otto considered the suggestion, swallowed, and nodded. "Go on."

"The Brewer/Pauling call was most likely swept up by mistake. Probably happened close in time to one they intended to monitor." He paused, and she nodded. "So one of them, either Brewer or Pauling, must have been talking with a targeted caller before Brewer placed the Reacher call to Pauling."

She thought about it. "Capturing the Reacher conversation was a lucky fluke?"

He shrugged. "It happens. You know it does."

"Maybe. Say you're right." She spoke slowly. "Who was actually being watched? Because I don't see either Brewer or Pauling as the target of any legitimate military corruption investigation. Do you?"

"Beats the hell outta me." Gaspar paused to think it through before he shook his head again. "But if neither Brewer nor

Pauling was the target, then that means one of them was consorting with high-level military personnel and got unintentionally snared."

Otto nodded. "That's how I'm reading the situation."

"But was it Brewer? Or Pauling?"

"This TrueLeaks thing is very, very broad." Otto swallowed another bite. Her queasy stomach was feeling better since she'd added food to the coffee and antacids. "Could go either way."

"How's that?" Gaspar must have solved his issues because he began shoveling his food into his mouth again at an amazing rate of speed.

She'd come up with a couple of guesses. "Brewer is NYPD."

Gaspar nodded.

"Those detectives don't make a lot of money and living in New York is expensive. He could be doing some moonlighting," she said. "Working security for out-of-town VIPs or something like that."

Gaspar raised one eyebrow and kept eating.

"Maybe VIPs connected to the UN or attached to one of the embassies. If his contact was being monitored, he could've been swept up, along with the pizza delivery service and the guy's kids, and who knows who."

Gaspar closed his eyes to think about it, but he didn't stop chewing. Half his food was gone already. Otto had barely touched hers. "I can buy that. Brewer seemed pretty straight with us. Confirmed what we knew. Raised nothing questionable. Volunteered info on Pauling."

"And that would explain, maybe, why Treasury is looking at Brewer. Maybe his name came up in the TrueLeaks stuff in some other way besides this conversation with Pauling." But she didn't agree with his assessment completely. Brewer hadn't told them everything he knew about Reacher. Not even close. No reason to argue about that just yet.

"I don't think Brewer would be knowingly involved in illegal activities, though. He's too close to a full pension, for one thing." Gaspar popped the last bite of steak into his mouth and chewed thoughtfully. "He didn't seem like a dirty cop to me, anyway."

"Which is too bad." She nodded. "Because that would be the easy answer. And it would explain Treasury's interest."

He noticed the fish and veggies chilling on her plate. "Want me to finish that for you?"

"No." She raised her fork and stabbed something without looking.

He grinned. He'd told her many times that she didn't eat enough to keep a bird alive. He disapproved of women who didn't eat. No father of four daughters would feel differently. "What's your theory on Pauling?"

"I don't know." Otto's words came slowly. "Her background looks good. She was with the Bureau for quite a while, and she did well inside. She retired with a solid resume. The New York field office was sorry to see her go. I checked."

"All of which means she was a great agent." He nodded slowly, watching her eat like a drill sergeant keeping her on track. "But that was a long time ago. She could've gone south since then."

"She could have. We can't rule it out." Otto took another couple of bites of her food and pushed the plate across to him. "Not until we have a chance to evaluate her."

He set into her food as if he hadn't eaten in ten years instead of ten minutes. "So you're saying you think there's more to Pauling than meets the eye."

Otto nodded slowly. "Possibly."

He sopped up her plate with the last piece of bread, and both plates now looked as if they'd been through the dishwasher already. "Let's assume you're right. You figure the Boss knows more than he's telling."

"Like you said, that's the usual situation, isn't it?" She scowled. "Every single time he sends us somewhere, there's trouble around the corner. It's like he knows that specific trouble is on the way. Why should this be any different?"

"What trouble is on the way this time, you figure?"

"What else? Reacher trouble. Something Reacher did before leads to something going down now. In this case, something that involved Brewer and Pauling happened sixteen months ago, give or take. And it's safe to guess that the Boss didn't know about any of this until this TrueLeaks dump put a spotlight on the situation." She stopped for a breath. "Because if he'd known about whatever it was before, he'd have sent us here sooner."

"Maybe." Gaspar nodded. "Problem is Pauling's location. Do we go after her or not?"

"I think Bishop was right. The guy he saw at the Dakota this morning with Peck was not Reacher." Otto took another, deeper breath before she said, slowly. "I don't believe Reacher is in New York City."

Gaspar cocked his head. "You think he's somewhere with Pauling?"

She shrugged. She didn't think Reacher was with Pauling. Unfortunately.

"Come on, Sunshine. Spit it out. What's bugging you?" When she didn't answer immediately, he frowned. "Look, either you trust me, or you don't. Which is it?"

"You already know I believe Reacher's alive." She stalled,

but not because she didn't trust him. Their relationship had grown way beyond trust. He'd saved her life, and she'd saved his. More than once. She trusted him absolutely. That wasn't the problem.

The problem was, if she said she'd *smelled Reacher* in her bedroom at four in the morning, he'd think she was insane.

He might be right.

Once she told him, she couldn't put that genie back in the bottle, either.

She wasn't ready to say the words aloud.

Not yet.

She told him half the truth instead. "I think Reacher was in Detroit last night. He might still be there."

Gaspar nodded. "Got any evidence?"

"Just a hunch so far."

Gaspar had a healthy respect for hunches. "Based on what?"

"The Boss called you on one of his cell phones. You downloaded your files from the secure satellite. He arranged your flight, and you did the rest on your own. As usual. Right?"

Gaspar nodded again, coaxing her to continue, waiting until she could spit it out.

"He didn't do that with me." She took a calming breath. "He showed up at my apartment this morning before daylight."

"That's not exactly a smoking gun."

"He was wearing…strange clothes. Some kind of weird disguise."

Gaspar's eyebrows popped up. "What kind of disguise?"

"A wide-brimmed hat. Collar turned up. Hunting clothes." She paused for another breath. "And sunglasses. Inside the building. While it was still full dark outside."

"Okay, that's strange. I agree." Gaspar cocked his head. "But there could be a thousand reasons why he came in person instead of calling. Maybe he was already in Detroit. On a hunting trip. Or maybe even working on the TrueLeaks thing."

She arched her eyebrows, mocking his favorite incredulous expression. "Has he *ever* delivered an assignment to your home? Personally? Because this was a first for me. And I've never heard of him doing that to anyone before. Have you?"

Gaspar shrugged, which she took to mean he didn't want to admit she was right. She understood. She didn't want to believe her conclusion, either. But she'd been over it in her head a thousand times, and there was only one likely explanation.

The Boss had come to her home in the wee hours, dressed to avoid recognition, for one reason only.

Because he thought Reacher was there. Nothing else would have motivated him to behave in such an odd and out of character way.

And even worse, she believed Reacher had been there, too.

A few minutes of silent thinking passed while they finished the last of the coffee and Gaspar paid the bill. Otto noticed the buzz of indistinct conversations surrounding them. The restaurant was full. People were waiting for tables.

Gaspar returned his credit card to his wallet. "You're number one. It's your call. What do you want to do?"

What she *should* do was make a full report to the Boss on the Brewer interview, say Pauling was unavailable, and wrap things up. Gaspar should go back to his family. She should return to Detroit and get a new apartment with better security. Maybe a new job, too.

She squared her shoulders and looked steadily at her partner. "Let's find Pauling. She's the key to this thing. Like you said, she could be with Reacher right now. If she is, we can find him and get some answers."

"It's not our assignment to find him. We're just filling out the paperwork, remember?" Gaspar quirked one eyebrow this time. "Besides, I thought you didn't want to find him."

"I've changed my mind." She glanced at the door where the line of waiting diners snaked around the corner. She tossed her napkin on the table and grabbed her laptop case. "Let's stash these laptops here. I'm tired of dealing with them."

"As you wish, Dragon Lady Boss," Gaspar wisecracked. But he grabbed his laptop and followed along. They stopped at a row of lockers, shoved the bags inside, and pocketed the keys.

They hustled toward the 42nd Street exit and joined the taxi line. It was full dark now, but the city's lights were almost as bright as weak January sunlight. She stuffed her hands in her pockets and stomped her feet to avoid their freezing to the pavement while they waited.

Gaspar placed a few calls, first to Brewer, who didn't answer. Then, attempting to find the first taxi driver and their stolen travel bags. She tuned him out while she ran through their options.

At this point, she could only think of two. She could call the Boss, which she rejected immediately. He already knew everything she might report, and he hadn't called her. Which meant he either couldn't or wouldn't have anything helpful to add. Contacting him would be futile as well as infuriating.

The second choice was the only choice, really. Whether she wanted to admit it or not.

Gaspar disconnected his call. "Maybe they'll find the guy. But don't hold your breath."

Otto smiled, but her heart wasn't in it. They were finally at the front of the line. A taxi pulled up. She opened the door and scooted across the bench seat. Gaspar followed her inside and closed the door.

"Where to?" the driver asked.

Gaspar turned to her. "Where are we going?"

"You don't want to know." Which was true. And he wouldn't be thrilled about the destination whether she told him or not. Why suffer his outrage twice?

CHAPTER TWENTY-ONE

Thursday, January 13
6:05 p.m.
Stanwix Village, New York

PARNELL PARKED THE RENTAL in front of a row of rectangular homes clad in white vinyl siding resting on concrete slab foundations. Probably manufactured somewhere and trailered here, he figured. Each building was thirty-feet by eighty-feet, give or take. A horizontal wall divided the buildings in half, creating two homes under one roof. Each duplex unit was thirty-by-forty, about twelve-hundred square feet of utilitarian living space.

The buildings were spaced twenty feet apart, adjacent to a sidewalk that followed the winding curves of the streets. A young tree, bare of leaves, perched on each lawn. Perhaps there were small lawns and flower gardens under the snow. Hard to tell.

No garages. Old vehicles of various kinds were parked in front of about half of the homes. Parnell figured the duplexes without vehicles were either unoccupied or the residents owned no personal transportation. Could be either. Given the population of disabled veterans who lived here, it was unlikely the residents had hopped into their trucks and headed off to work.

He had scouted the planned community only briefly after the tedious drive to Upstate New York from the city. He'd wasted too much time at the Dakota, which meant he'd arrived in Stanwix Village not long before dark. During the quick drive-through, he'd seen lights burning, and a blue television screen flickered inside the unit that interested him. Nick Scavo was home. Which was all he needed to know. He'd been searching for Scavo for a long time.

Parnell began looking for Scavo right after the business with the three stooges in Baghdad, at the same time he started his hunt for Reacher. Both men were completely off the grid. Both could have been dead. For quite a while, Parnell could find no evidence to the contrary in either case.

After months of fruitless searching, he caught a lucky break. Scavo's passport pinged at London's Heathrow airport. Scavo had used it to board a nonstop flight to JFK. Parnell had tracked him easily from that point.

When Scavo's flight arrived in New York City, he'd stayed in the city for four days. About half of those hours were spent at a hospital. The remaining hours had been unaccounted for, until Parnell's visit to the Dakota.

Thanks to the blubbery Simon Peck, Parnell now knew Scavo had spent those hours stealing his nine million dollars. While he was there, Scavo must have also taken the documents revealing the location of the rest of Parnell's funds.

When he left the city, Scavo had traveled by train to Upstate New York. He spent a few days in a VA hospital. After that, he moved into a low-rent boarding house on the edge of town, where he remained until last month. When he moved here.

Parnell had assumed the Stanwix Veterans Village duplex was subsidized by the government. Scavo had no income he had claimed on a tax return. Which meant he couldn't qualify for a mortgage or even a decent rental, but he could qualify for subsidies.

Until the Dakota, Parnell figured Scavo's living conditions were unremarkable. Scavo, like every member of the Colonel's crew, was ex-military. He'd been discharged nine years ago. He wasn't the best the army had to offer, but he wasn't the worst, either.

He'd received a general discharge in the normal course of events. Which meant he'd never been good enough to qualify for medals, but he'd never been charged with any bad acts they could actually prove.

Bottom line, because of his service and lack of income, Scavo must have been entitled to certain veteran's benefits which, in his case, apparently included subsidized housing.

Parnell turned off the engine and stepped out of the car. Cold wind blew across the powdery snow, whipping his legs and stinging his eyes. The short sidewalk leading from the curb to Scavo's duplex was shoveled recently, but blowing snow had drifted across the concrete here and there, making it treacherously slick.

He covered the distance carefully, struggling to maintain his footing. The last thing he needed was to land on his ass.

He plodded up three icy steps to the four-by-seven concrete stoop running in front of two adjacent doors, one on each side of the dividing wall leading to each unit. An aluminum awning covered the stoop and protected both doors from rain, but not from wind.

Scavo's unit was 17A, on the left. Parnell raised a gloved hand and pushed the doorbell. The first six notes of "The Star Spangled Banner" chimed in appealing tones from inside. He shook his head. *Schmaltzy.*

A minute later, the interior door swung open. Parnell stood on one side of the storm door and made every effort not to stare.

A shell of the man who had been Nick Scavo stood on the other. Warm moist air fogged the glass that separated them. Neither man moved.

Parnell was the first to blink. Scavo was barely recognizable. The big man described in his army files and depicted in his passport photo had vanished. This wreck had been aged by long, hard years rather than the mere passage of time.

But even those hardships didn't explain Scavo's skeletal appearance. His body had wasted to near nothingness.

He had lost at least sixty pounds, much of it muscle. His chest was concave, and his back bowed, like a human question mark. His left hand was wrapped around the brass handle of the heavy cane he leaned on.

Scavo's gaunt face was as emaciated as his body. A furry brow ridge protruded beyond sunken brown eyes accented by coal dark smudges, like a football player's eye black grease. The black hair in the photo was still thick, but all white now, which accentuated his colorless albino skin.

Somehow, Scavo had been separated and left behind by the Colonel's crew during that West African revolution. He hadn't died, as the three stooges assumed.

But something horrific had happened to him. Scavo probably felt the Colonel owed him. Maybe that's why he stole Parnell's money. Not that Parnell cared about his motives.

Briefly, he considered forcing his way inside. He was armed.

He was bigger, more fit, and highly motivated. Should Scavo resist, the fight would be short, and the outcome assured. At the moment, though, resistance seemed unlikely.

He'd try the easy way first. He could move on to the hard way, should the situation prove unmanageable.

Parnell raised his voice to be heard over the whistling wind and through the glass. "Nick Scavo?"

"That's right, General Parnell." Scavo nodded, surprising words spoken in a strong voice. "I've been expecting you."

Parnell paused. But Parnell was a man who took life exactly as it came, moment by moment, supremely confident that he could handle whatever came his way and conquer it. Which he always had.

"May I come in? It's damn cold out here."

Scavo paused a moment longer before he waved Parnell forward and limped away from the cold draft.

Parnell opened the storm door and stepped into Scavo's home, which was like entering the hammams, Turkish steam baths Parnell had frequented in Istanbul. The limited square footage, squeezed by the clammy heat, enveloped him with mild claustrophobia.

One glance around the place was all it took to confirm that Scavo had not spent Parnell's money on home decorating. The lightweight furnishings could have been ordered from a catalog and delivered in flat boxes for assembly. Or maybe purchased as a whole room from a discount warehouse. Everything was cheap and small and arranged in the open floor plan by someone with a sense of design beyond Scavo's expertise.

At this point, Parnell figured his nine million dollars probably wasn't stored on the premises. So where was his money?

"Are you alone?" Parnell asked. He craned his neck and peered into the hallway that probably led to one small bedroom and a smaller bath.

"Look around if it will make you more comfortable," Scavo replied while continuing his halting progress.

He moved so slowly that Parnell could have searched every square inch of the place with a magnifying glass before Scavo made it to wherever he was headed.

Parnell walked through into a short corridor, one flimsy pressboard door on either side. He opened the door on the right, which was a cheaply constructed bath. A sink, toilet, and narrow shower.

The door on the left opened into a ten-by-ten bedroom. A full-sized bed on a low frame and no headboard took up most of the floor space. No bedside tables or lamps. No pictures on the walls. No room for a small chair. One window, covered with the same plastic mini blinds that Parnell had noticed on the other windows.

The closet ran across one end of the room. Both flimsy bi-fold doors stood open. A single metal pole was the only organizing principle. Half a dozen shirts and two pairs of pants hung on plastic hangers on the pole. A cardboard box on the floor held a jumble of underwear and socks. A pair of running shoes rested next to the box.

In short, nothing here. No backup. No nine million dollars. Nothing worth stealing.

Parnell returned to the all-purpose room. Scavo's crab-like movements had eventually carried him to a straight chair at the kitchen table. Parnell waited for Scavo to get settled, which seemed to take way too long.

"Satisfied, General Parnell?" Scavo finally asked.

CHAPTER TWENTY-TWO

HE CROSSED THE ROOM in half a dozen steps and sat across the table to maintain eye contact. "Have we met before?"

The answer was inconsequential, but Parnell needed a baseline to judge Scavo's reactions later.

Scavo shook his head. "I've followed your career for a while now. I knew you'd retired. It was only a matter of time before you showed up here."

Parnell schooled his features to reveal nothing. "And why is that?"

"Because of the Colonel." Scavo shrugged. His voice was wheezy. "I was the Executive Vice President of Operational Security Consultants for a few years. I knew you were his inside contact. You funneled off-the-books military contracts to OSC."

Parnell waited while Scavo's tale was detoured by a fit of coughing. "At some point, you'd want what was yours."

Parnell neither confirmed nor denied. He noted that Scavo was smarter than the average OSC soldier. Which was probably why he was still alive.

Parnell waited through another round of hacking.

After the coughing stopped, Scavo wiped spittle from the side of his mouth with the back of his hand. "Made sense that you wouldn't want your fingerprints on any of the OSC funds until after you parted ways with Uncle Sam."

Parnell narrowed his eyes. An almost involuntary frown etched his face. Was this a setup? Some kind of sting?

He left Scavo in the kitchen and conducted a more thorough search of the premises, this time for electronic surveillance. He found no hidden cameras or listening devices anywhere.

A laptop and a cell phone rested on a table beside the sofa. The television was hooked up to cable. Parnell disconnected the cable and unplugged the television. He powered down the laptop and removed the batteries from the cell phone and shoved both under the sofa.

Satisfied that no spying devices remained in place, he returned to the kitchen and searched Scavo for tech capable of recording audio or video or both. He found none.

"Who lives next door?" Parnell asked.

"An ex-Marine. Don't worry, he's deaf as a post. Besides, he's been out of town for a couple of weeks. I figured you knew that." Scavo cocked his head. "Maybe you're not as careful as I assumed you would be."

Parnell asked, "What's wrong with you? Medically, I mean?"

Scavo shrugged. "They don't exactly know. Some kind of systemic disease, they figure. Maybe latent, from the time I spent as a POW. Most of the symptoms came on suddenly after I returned to the states."

"What's the prognosis?"

"Docs don't say. Right at the moment, it doesn't look good, does it?" He flashed a wry grin, which Parnell figured was some sort of coping thing. "The cold dry air makes it worse. Which is why it's so hot and humid in here, if you were wondering."

Parnell sat, allowing Scavo to make eye contact. "Since you've been expecting me, you know what I came for."

Scavo shrugged. "I'm guessing you want that nine million that was in the bedroom safe at the Dakota."

"For starters."

"And after that, you're looking to collect the forty-six million the Colonel socked away for you in a safe place, right?"

He smirked. "Precisely."

"I can help you with that." Scavo opened his mouth to say more, but another coughing jag possessed him for a long time. When he was able to catch his breath again, he tilted his head toward the refrigerator and croaked, "Water."

Parnell retrieved a bottle and handed it over. Scavo took a long, thirsty gulp.

"Sorry. I don't talk a lot. I'm out of practice." He rested the bottle on the table.

"Where is my money?"

"Your share of the contract payments is still where the Colonel placed it. Or at least it was the last time I checked."

"Which was when?"

"Right after I met the Colonel in London and, uh, persuaded him to tell me where to find it. I can't check from here. Too risky. You're right to be worried about surveillance in this place. Secrets do get out, one way or another." His voice was raspy and strained. He drank another few sips.

"Why did he give you that information? Were you supposed to collect the money and get it to him?"

"Not exactly. My motives were not that pure." He smiled again. "The Colonel left me for dead in West Africa. I was captured by the enemy. Let's just say it wasn't a pleasant experience. After I escaped, it took me a while to reach my evacuation kit, which I had stored in a hotel safe in London. As luck would have it, the Colonel was in London at the time, so we had a little…discussion about my…compensation."

"And what about the nine million?"

"That's a tougher question. I'm not exactly sure." He adjusted his bony ass on the chair as if the hard surface was too uncomfortable. "I'm sure you know I went to the Dakota apartment when I returned from London."

He paused, and Parnell nodded.

"I was in much better shape than I am now. I'd begun to have symptoms, but I thought it was malaria at the time. So I ignored it." He paused and leaned back in his chair. "I found the nine million cash in the safe while I was looking for the documents, but I didn't have the time to move those big bales."

"Why not?"

"I had a narrow window of opportunity to find what I needed to…collect the bigger score before the Colonel was due back. I didn't want to miss my chance."

"So you expected him back," Parnell said, nodding, as though he believed the lie.

Scavo smirked. "Your forty-six million plus his twenty, which was hidden in the same place, was more enticing."

"I can see how it would be," Parnell replied as calmly as he could manage. He hadn't expected the Colonel to hide that money in a place where Parnell could grab it. The cash situation just kept getting better and better.

"I planned to go back later for the cash. I mean, nine million isn't sixty-six, but it's not chump change, either, right?"

Parnell's mouth had dried up. He nodded.

"And I figured I'd earned it. He owed me, you know?" Scavo cocked his head and waited until Parnell nodded. "But whatever this thing is that's attacking my body accelerated. Hell, for a few weeks, I couldn't get out of bed. And then it turned out I didn't need to go back."

"Why is that?"

"Because someone, shall we say, liberated that nine million in cash first." He shook his head and wiped his lips with the back of his hand. "The likely thieves were my former OSC colleagues. At the time, I was sure they viewed it as spoils of war, rightfully theirs."

Parnell narrowed his eyes and barked, "My patience is wearing thin, Scavo."

Scavo nodded. "It took me a while to figure it out. Even now, all I have is an educated guess. I've narrowed it down to two likely suspects."

"And those two are?" Parnell's hard-edged question sliced the thick air like a blade. Scavo seemed to be cooperative. Maybe he was. Maybe he wasn't. But he needed to get to it.

"The first possibility is an NYPD detective named Brewer. Gregory Brewer. He was hanging around the first day I went to the Dakota. I didn't know who he was at the time. I found that out later." Scavo drained the water bottle and cleared his throat. He tossed the bottle toward the kitchen sink. The lightweight plastic sailed weakly in the right direction but fell short and bounced along the vinyl floor.

Parnell nodded to keep him going.

"Brewer had been inside the apartment, for sure. He'd left one of his business cards on the kitchen counter. Which means he could have gone in as many times as he needed to remove all that cash." Scavo's long bout of hacking started up again.

The Brewer story had the ring of truth to it. An NYPD detective would definitely be tempted by nine million in untraceable cash. Although a detective's salary was reasonable. Certainly, more than cops in smaller towns. Nine million dollars, sitting there for the taking, probably had been too hard for Brewer to resist.

The more Parnell thought about it, the more likely it seemed. An NYPD detective would be in a position to know everything about the security at the Dakota. He could easily have removed the money. That sweaty little fop nor the lazy doorman would have bothered to stop him, even if they'd been around.

Yes. Parnell nodded. Brewer could have been the thief. He'd also have had no trouble locating a good hiding place for that much cash in New York where no one would find it.

"And the other possibility?" Parnell asked when Scavo's painful spasm slowed.

"You know OSC had significantly reduced manpower after the West Africa debacle." Scavo raised his eyebrows, and Parnell nodded. "The Colonel had a big, old-fashioned Rolodex of candidates and he added guys to the team as necessary, depending on the job."

"Right." Parnell had seen that Rolodex once. He hoped not to spend time tracking every extra grunt listed in there. Scavo was the guy. Had to be.

"A few days before I met the Colonel in London, he hired a new gun. Army vet. Big, fair-haired guy. Bulky. About your size, or maybe bigger."

"How do you know? You weren't there."

"Same way you found out. I asked around." Scavo paused and Parnell nodded again. Scavo's body was a wreck, but his mind was still sharp enough.

"What was the new guy's name?" Parnell asked.

"Nobody at the Dakota seemed to know, and the NYPD detective wouldn't say."

"You asked Brewer?"

"Not until I had the name already. After that, I called Brewer." He smiled weakly, revealing yellowed and missing teeth. "Let's just say his reactions were enough to confirm that Brewer knows more than he's telling."

"You're saying Brewer took my cash."

"Not definitively, because obviously, I haven't seen the money in Brewer's possession with my own eyes. But I'd bet on Brewer."

"Meaning what, exactly?"

Scavo's coughing started up again. He hacked for a long, long time. His curved torso bent almost in half as he grew weaker. Parnell collected another bottle of water from the refrigerator and placed it on the table.

He had never heard of a man coughing to death, but he wondered if Scavo would be his first.

When Scavo finally managed to get himself under control, he took a few long pulls on the water bottle and tried to catch his breath.

"Sorry." His voice was raspy and subdued as if his lungs were too weak to push enough air through his vocal cords to create sound. He struggled to stand, leaning heavily on his cane. "I need rest. I'll tell you everything. Brewer has a partner."

"What do you mean?"

His next words were a mere whisper, and Parnell strained to hear. "The last hire I told you about. Bought this place. Furnished it. Paid my medical. Said the money came from the Colonel."

Parnell made no effort to conceal the malice from his tone. "What's his *name*, Scavo?"

"Reacher." Scavo hacked it out. "Jack Reacher."

The name alone heated Parnell's blood. He'd looked for Reacher on three continents and found nothing. His anger bubbled up so fast, he could barely spit out the question. "Where is Reacher?"

Scavo coughed and struggled to draw breath between long spasms. "Brewer knows. Brewer first. Then Reacher."

Parnell watched him struggle all the way to the bedroom. Simply telling his story to Parnell had all but killed the guy. He'd learn no more from Scavo tonight.

Which left Parnell free to deal with Brewer.

Parnell pulled the laptop and cell phone from beneath the sofa on his way out.

CHAPTER TWENTY-THREE

Thursday, January 13
6:20 p.m.
New York City

OTTO HAD SET UP the meeting with Finlay before she left Detroit this morning. She'd intended to finish her New York City assignment earlier in the day. She'd had two goals at the time.

She'd wanted to talk to him about Reacher. He knew a lot more than she did. During a quiet, private conversation, she thought he might be more candid.

She'd also planned to find a way to bring up her career situation. Get his take on things. He had a proven track record for advancing women on the job. She wanted to move up, which might also mean moving out of the FBI. An idea that, until recently, would never have entered her mind.

She hadn't planned to bring Gaspar with her. He didn't like Finlay because he didn't trust the man. Gaspar wasn't wrong. But he had a blind spot where Finlay was concerned. She shook her head. Couldn't be helped.

The taxi dropped them at the front entrance of the midtown hotel. Without stopping at the desk, Otto led the way to the elevator and pushed the elevator code he'd given her for the penthouse suite. The car paused briefly while security confirmed her identity and then lifted at breathtaking speed to the top floor.

His suite was directly across from the elevator. Otto stepped forward and pressed the doorbell. A man who could only have been Secret Service opened the door and waved them inside.

"Good evening, Agent Otto. Agent Gaspar. I'm Russell." His greeting sounded rather formal to Otto's ears. "He'll be with you momentarily. Please follow me."

The penthouse suite was enormous. Otto guessed the entire suite was more than 1,500 square feet. Four bedrooms, common rooms, and even outdoor space completed the pricey accommodations. Perhaps Finlay chose the suite for security reasons. Or maybe he simply enjoyed luxury.

Russell waved to a sideboard containing refreshments. "Dr. Finlay will be with you momentarily. He's finishing a call. Please make yourselves comfortable."

"I suppose the taxpayers are footing the bill for this," Gaspar said sourly.

Otto didn't bother to reply. No matter what she said, Gaspar's mind was closed to Lamont Finlay, Ph.D. Otto had stopped trying to change the situation, partly because she didn't know exactly what the source of the problem was.

Could have been his pedigree. Harvard grad, Boston born and bred. Gaspar wasn't enamored of the northeastern section of the country.

Finlay was formerly the top cop in Margrave, Georgia, where their Reacher assignment began. Not coincidentally, Margrave was the place Reacher first surfaced after he left the

JACK THE REAPER | 161

army, too. Gaspar believed Finlay was involved in the crimes that took place there. But his opinion couldn't be substantiated.

Or maybe the problem was Finlay's current position as Special Assistant to the President for Strategy. Otto had no idea what that meant, and Gaspar was openly hostile about it.

The precise nature of Finlay's job was nowhere described. He'd been selected by the highest-ranking civilian responsible for Homeland Security and Counterterrorism, and placed one heartbeat away from the U.S. Commander in Chief.

No watchdog kept tabs on him.

He reported seldom and only through verbal briefing. No paper trail so much as named the missions he'd undertaken. Process, performance, results, were also absent from the record.

Casualties, of course, were never acknowledged. She'd heard rumors. Unconfirmed.

Gaspar was opposed to all of it. Mainly what he didn't like, Otto suspected, was Finlay's undeniable power.

Like electricity, when properly harnessed Finlay might be useful. But she'd found nothing restraining him; not even his own word.

Was he friend or foe? Wiser to assume the worst, Gaspar said whenever the question came up. Even though they'd been the beneficiaries of Finlay's power more than once.

Otto viewed Finlay as a kind of defensive line in whatever game the Boss was playing here. Growing up with brothers who played football had taught her the value of giants fighting play after play from the trenches.

As if her thoughts had conjured him, Finlay entered the room.

He looked like a spokesman for financial services. Tall, straight, solid; close-cropped hair slightly gray at the temples.

Clean shaven. Well dressed. Everything polished to high gloss. Distinguished.

Experienced.

Intimidating.

A black man, but his ethnicity was not African-American. The file said his grandparents had emigrated from Trinidad to New York before settling in Boston, but that was a long time ago.

"Good to see you again, Otto, Gaspar." Finlay's big paw swallowed her hand. He shook hands with Gaspar, too, but neither looked the other in the eye or offered false smiles. "Take a seat. I don't have much time. I'm afraid I don't have a lot of information to share, either."

Gaspar raised an eyebrow in Otto's direction as if to say, *I told you so.*

"Whatever you can offer, sir, is more than we have now," Otto replied, taking the chair he'd indicated. Gaspar remained standing.

Finlay waited a moment for Gaspar to change his mind, and then shrugged and sat across from Otto. "We're all chasing our tails on this latest TrueLeaks thing. There are millions of documents, and it'll take a while to sort through it all. Most of it is military secrets, classified above your clearance level."

"Which should tell us something about where the leaks came from, shouldn't it?" Otto asked.

He leaned his forearms on his thighs and spoke more softly. "It should. Yes. And we're chasing that down now. But we don't know yet."

"These leaks are putting a lot of good people at risk." Gaspar frowned. "When you find the leaker, will he be prosecuted?"

Finlay shook his head. "That's not my call."

"What did you find out about that Reacher conversation? That's the main thing we need to know," Otto said.

"You didn't give me much time. I was only able to locate the one conversation you already have. The one between Pauling and Brewer. Which was not easy. We wouldn't have found a call that obscure for a few more weeks, at least. Not until we sorted a lot more wheat from the reams of chaff." He wagged his head and flashed his bright white smile. "Gotta give credit where credit's due. Cooper's got his finger on the pulse of all things Reacher, doesn't he?"

Otto lowered her gaze. Finlay's tone and his words conveyed reluctant admiration for the Boss, which was curious. They usually mixed as well as pouring gasoline on a raging fire. Gaspar said neither Finlay nor Cooper could be trusted. He was probably right.

"Anyway, the rest of the news, not sure if it's good or bad, is that using the one you already have, we were able to find another conversation," Finlay said. "It's the next day. Reacher made the call this time. To the woman, Pauling. Following up on the first call and scheduling a meeting. Brewer's not involved in the second call."

"Are you sure it's Reacher?" Otto asked, as her stomach started its usual churn.

"Yes. He identifies himself." Finlay nodded. "And it's been a long time since I've talked to him, but I recognized his voice."

"Can we get a copy of that call?" Gaspar asked.

Finlay shook his head. "But I can let you hear it if you keep that fact confidential for now."

He meant if they didn't tell the Boss. Otto said, "Of course."

"Reacher made both calls to Pauling from the same pay phone. The original call was scooped up because she answered on her cell phone. The same phone where she'd received the call you already have. We searched for additional conversations between Reacher and Pauling made to or from her cell number."

"Find any?" Gaspar asked.

"I'm afraid not. At least, not yet. Reacher's a bit tech phobic, I think. He doesn't talk on the phone much. Old school. Everything done in person."

Otto nodded. "Smarter that way. Why do you think we're here?"

Finlay grinned again. "Indeed."

Gaspar asked, "So does that mean Pauling is the one who was being watched? She's the common denominator in both calls."

"I can't say definitively. Not yet." Finlay narrowed his eyes. "But that wouldn't be an unreasonable hypothesis to try to prove out."

Otto cocked her head. If Pauling was the one, then why was Treasury after Brewer? Unrelated? Not likely. "Are there more conversations between Pauling and Brewer?"

Finlay nodded. "A few. Some happened around the same time as the first one. Within a day or two. Others were much later. Weeks and months later, in some cases. We're not sure how many conversations there are yet."

Gaspar said, "And you can't tell us why someone was targeting Pauling?"

"As I said, we don't know that she was a target." Finlay seemed to notice the thin platinum watch on his wrist all of a sudden, surprised at the time. He stood. "You can figure it out before we can sort through everything and find the answer. These things are usually not that complicated, you know."

Otto and Gaspar rose to their feet. They shook hands all

around again. Then Finlay looked at Otto. "Anything else you might want to discuss, I'll be here another few days. And you have my number."

Gaspar glanced at Otto, eyebrows raised.

She ignored him. "Thank you, sir."

Finlay turned to leave. But before he went, he grinned again. "Oh, and we found your luggage. Good thinking, Gaspar, to send in those photos. We've got your driver in custody. Turns out he's in the country illegally. Overstayed his visa. Claims he missed his window to renew. You scared him when you flashed your FBI badge."

"Thanks for the help," Gaspar said, but he didn't sound very grateful.

"Lighten up." Finlay smiled. "Now you don't have to sleep in your underwear. That's worth something, isn't it?"

Otto watched his retreat down the polished corridor until he reentered the room he'd emerged from ten minutes ago.

Shortly afterward, Russell, the Secret Service agent, returned with a small playback device. He handed the earphones to Otto first. When she was ready, he pushed the play button.

A woman's husky voice answered on the third ring. "Hello?"

Definitely the same voice Otto had heard on Pauling's voice mail yesterday. But she sounded sleepy as if he'd awakened her very early in the morning.

It was definitely him. Otto recognized his voice right away, although she'd only heard him speak once before, on another recording.

His voice wasn't what she'd expected that first time. The range was higher, for one thing. Tenor, not bass. His speech was clipped with a sort of nondescript Midwest American accent.

166 | Diane Capri

When she described it in her official reports, she'd said Reacher sounded less dangerous than she knew he was. Gaspar had speculated that his unruffled demeanor was how he got close to his targets. Otto disagreed.

The rest was a digitally altered scramble. Otto wondered what he'd said that was deemed classified by some tech somewhere.

They set up a meeting in Pauling's office in half an hour. So Reacher knew where Pauling's office was. And he'd met her there.

Something else, too. Even the first time they'd spoken to each other, their relationship was starting to sound a bit too, well, what? Friendly? Developed?

Reacher could flirt. Why did that come as such a surprise?

She shrugged. She glanced at Russell. "Can I hear it again?"

"Sure. Just hit the replay."

She did. The second run through was no more enlightening than the first. "What's bleeped out here?"

"The name of a civilian witness. Unrelated. The name is confidential unless someone seeks permission to unmask it. We haven't." Russell looked at her until she nodded understanding. She could get the names unmasked. Or at least, the Boss could. "Dr. Finlay said to tell you that Reacher mentions Brewer is the one who connected him to Pauling."

Otto nodded. She passed the earphones to Gaspar.

He listened twice through. "This was the morning after the first conversation? The one we pointed you to?"

"That's right," Russell said.

Gaspar and Otto exchanged glances. She pulled out one of her cards. "If you find any more conversations involving or about Reacher, please call me."

"I'll let Dr. Finlay know. Your bags are this way." Russell put her card in his pocket without looking at it and extended his arm toward the exit. Not the least bit subtle.

In the elevator, after the big gold doors closed, Gaspar grinned. "We just got what my dad would call the bum's rush."

Otto smiled, but her mind was elsewhere.

Gaspar took the hint. "Okay, why was Pauling a surveillance target and when did she become one?"

"Finlay seemed to think we could find that out easily enough. The only way I can think of to start is with Brewer. Try him again, will you?"

He found his cell phone and called Brewer's number. After several rings, voice mail picked up, and Gaspar left another message.

"Earth to Suzie Wong."

Otto glanced at him. "Sorry. Just a little preoccupied."

"We've missed our return flights already." He grinned. "Now that we have our jammies back, where will we sleep tonight?"

"Who said anything about sleeping?" She frowned. "We've got a lot of work to do."

She was still thinking about Pauling. Why was she a target of a military corruption wiretap? Nothing in her background seemed to point in that direction.

And where *was* the woman? For that matter, where was Brewer?

CHAPTER TWENTY-FOUR

Thursday, January 13
8:20 p.m.
New York City

OTTO FLOPPED DOWN ON the bed in Gaspar's hotel room
while he set up his laptop on the small desk. She was bone tired.
No need to hit the treadmill. She'd sleep like a hibernating bear
tonight. "How are Reacher, Pauling, and Brewer connected?"

Gaspar was plugging in cords and finding the secure hot spot
and connecting to the secure server. "We know that the three
were *not* connected until Reacher made that phone call to
Pauling."

"You mean the one Finlay found." Otto grinned at Gaspar's
sour face. He never wanted to give Finlay credit for anything.

"We had Pauling connected to Brewer on the call the Boss
gave us. You heard him. Without that lead, he'd never have
found the Reacher call to Pauling." Gaspar poked around to find
another electrical outlet. He'd already tried the ones on the desk,
which weren't functioning.

"So Reacher met Brewer first. Brewer connected Reacher to Pauling. Then Reacher and Pauling did what?"

Gaspar leered and wiggled his eyebrows from his spot on the floor.

"Get your mind out of the gutter." Otto threw a pillow at him, which landed wide of the mark. "This is serious."

"Okay, but you're seriously asking me that question? Did you even look at Pauling's photo? She's beautiful."

Otto frowned. "She's got to be at least ten years older than him."

"Oh, come on." Gaspar laughed. "After all the women Reacher has bedded and left in this case already? Do you need me to give you a list?"

She threw a pencil at him this time. Her aim was pretty good. The pencil eraser hit the center of his chest as if she had shot an arrow from a crossbow. He pretended to be mortally wounded, and she laughed.

"Say you're right—"

"You know I'm right." He was lying on the floor, his arm extended into a cabinet that housed the mini bar, seeking electricity.

She grimaced and ignored the interruption. "Say you're right. Pauling and Reacher talked for the first time that morning. Half an hour later, they met at her office. Which means Brewer must have told Reacher where the office was. Which means Brewer knew where her office was. Which reconfirms Brewer and Pauling knew each other a little better than a couple of colleagues across jurisdictions."

Gaspar climbed up off the floor and knocked the lint off his clothes before he booted up his electronics.

Otto asked, "Why did Reacher want to meet with Pauling?

He's not a guy who has trouble getting dates, as you pointed out. And I don't think Brewer was a matchmaking service."

"As it happens, I don't think so, either. Not in the sexual sense, anyway." Gaspar shook his head. "Brewer and Pauling were connected already. Probably that case Brewer told us about, even though he said he didn't work the case with her. Maybe more than one case, over time. Either way, Pauling retired from the FBI with a sterling record, as you noted. So the case that went south was either her last one or close to that time, and she wasn't blamed for whatever went wrong with it."

"I guess we could look at every case she had if we had an army of help and unfettered access to FBI files. Which we don't. So put your thinking cap on, Chico." Otto propped her back against the headboard. "The connection must have something to do with the Dakota. Reacher doesn't seem like the kind of guy to have friends living in the high rent district on Central Park West. Therefore, I'm going to guess that whoever he was with at the Dakota was also involved in whatever this was. Or is. And it must have some relationship to the TrueLeaks. Otherwise, none of this would have surfaced now."

Gaspar nodded. "So we get a list of residents during the relevant time frame and compare those to Pauling's cases. See if there's any overlap."

"It's a good place to start. But we still don't have the resources to do that."

"We might be able to get the list of residents from public records."

"Property tax records?"

He shook his head. "Tax rolls won't have it because the Dakota is a co-op."

Otto nodded. She was trained as a lawyer and an accountant.

She knew what a co-op meant. Essentially, a corporation owns the title to the whole building, and the board gets a single tax bill every year.

The system gave residents more privacy, which was good. But it also afforded total control when undesirables wanted to move into the building, which was even better.

"It's a little complicated, but we should be able to find records for changes of ownership for individual units. In essence, when each unit was bought and sold, it should have been recorded in the Automated City Register Information System," Gaspar said.

He was already clacking the keys, watching the screens as he flipped through from one page to another. "Some of those units will be held by corporations, and others may have otherwise concealed identities. But at least the ACRIS will be a finite list. I don't know how many apartments are in the Dakota at the moment, but originally, it only had sixty-five, and it has fewer now. A list of co-op owners will be a lot shorter than a list of Pauling's cases."

"Okay. You start there. But if you can't find it—"

"Don't worry, Sunshine." He clenched his jaw. "I'll find it."

"*When* you find the list of residents, then. Look for prior Army service. Reacher is no social butterfly. He's likely to know people he worked with before he retired. He's not likely to be besties with very many civilians."

"Agreed." Gaspar didn't look up from his laptop. "And, I'll go further and say that Reacher's host must have been an officer. Most likely at or above Reacher's rank."

"Not many Army grunts, or officers, for that matter, below the rank of major, which was Reacher's last rank, could afford to live at the Dakota." Otto nodded. "I've got ten bucks that says the list of possibles will be very short."

Gaspar grinned. "You're on. I say there will only be one name. And I'll bet you fifty."

Otto shook her head. "Too rich for me."

"Because you know I'm right. I should have the name in not more than two hours." He'd turned his full attention to the search. Absently, he said, "What are you going to do?"

Otto cocked her head. "I'll tell you, but you won't like it."

"Never mind. I'll continue trying to reach Brewer while I'm waiting."

She reached into her pocket and pulled out Lawton's card. She tossed it across the room into Gaspar's lap. "See what you can find out about that guy. And why he's nosing around Brewer."

Gaspar looked at the card. "Anything else?"

Otto found her coat and slipped her arms into it. She retrieved her gloves from the pocket. "If you get that far, call me."

"How long will you be gone?"

She shook her head on her way out the door. "Hard to say, but my guess is, not very long."

Otto left the hotel and found a taxi. She offered the address to the driver and then dialed the private number Finlay claimed he'd given to her alone. He picked up quickly.

"How may I help you?" His voice was deep and smooth as molten chocolate. He'd have made a fortune in radio. She wondered if he could sing.

"On my way. Alone. Can you spare me ten minutes?" She heard nothing but silence for several heartbeats.

"I'll do the best I can." He terminated the call, and she returned the cell phone to her pocket.

CHAPTER TWENTY-FIVE

THE TAXI DROPPED HER at the front entrance of his hotel. In the elevator, Otto used the same code for the penthouse that she had used earlier. The same Secret Service agent opened the door before she could knock.

"Good evening, Agent Otto. This way please." She heard several low voices from deeper inside the suite. Russell directed her to a small anteroom near the entrance. "Shall I send black coffee? You may need to wait a while."

She slipped out of her coat and removed her gloves. "That'll be great. Thanks."

He reached into his pocket and pulled out the same playback device she'd used earlier. "Dr. Finlay would like you to review these now. He said it would save time."

She thanked him and carried the device to a comfortable chair. He returned with the coffee almost immediately. She was already engrossed in the audio, and he left her alone with no further conversation.

She listened to the recordings straight through the first time. The second time, she paused to absorb them more thoroughly.

The contents were curious. Two brief conversations between Reacher and Pauling, that took place within a few hours of the prior call.

Four between Pauling and an unidentified man to schedule meetings in the coffee shop where Otto and Gaspar met Brewer this morning. The subject of the meetings was not discussed.

Followed by a few conversations between Pauling and Brewer. Pauling scheduled a meeting with Brewer at the same location.

Otto figured that must have been the last time Brewer saw Reacher. Assuming he'd told the truth this morning.

All the conversations took place within three days. Sixteen months ago.

Otto's exhaustion fogged her brain and slowed her reaction times. She'd had two hours of uneasy rest in the past two days. She needed sleep to make any sense of it all. In the meantime, coffee would have to suffice.

She filled the mug from the carafe and fortified herself with caffeine, sipping while she paced the room. Her thoughts jumped from one thing to another.

Pauling and Brewer had been involved in something related to the owner of the Dakota apartment. No other hypothesis made sense.

Reacher's mere presence in New York City was somewhat mystifying. She didn't believe he had trucked into the city just to visit an old army buddy. Nothing she had discovered thus far suggested that Reacher was the type to do such a thing.

He was a loner. As much as she hated to admit it, Gaspar was right. Reacher liked cops in general, and female cops in particular. Perhaps he had some sort of fetish. Maybe his mother had been particularly strong, and he craved that connection.

Otto shrugged. Psychology was not her area of expertise.

Whatever his motivations, each task she'd been assigned so far involved fallout from Reacher's previous interaction with law enforcement or military.

The guy was a trouble magnet. Wherever he went, disaster erupted.

Whether criminals were attracted to him or he went looking for them remained an open question in Otto's mind. She suspected Reacher's confrontations could arise either way. He wasn't concerned about who started what, as long as he was the guy who finished the fight.

Her brain was slow, like trudging against the incoming tide. But she felt she was moving in the right direction. The key here was Reacher's relationships with Brewer and Pauling. And more specifically, Pauling.

What was that relationship? She grimaced. Besides the likely sexual one.

She heard the door open. Finlay walked in and closed the door solidly behind him.

He glanced at the playback device. "That's all we've found so far. We're not likely to find any more."

"Why?"

"Sixteen months ago, Pauling abruptly traveled to London. We don't know why. But we do know that Reacher sat next to her on the same plane. At the same time, she stopped using this phone number," Finlay said.

"Was the phone lost or stolen?"

"If she'd simply lost it, she'd have kept the same phone number when she replaced the phone."

"So it might have been stolen."

"Possible. Either way, she got a new number."

"What happened to the old number?"

"Consistent with phone company policies, the number was retired for forty-five days and then reissued. The new owner is a grandpa in Iowa."

Otto said, "An unlikely coincidence."

"Agreed. We've been looking for Pauling's replacement number. We haven't found it. Which means she's concealing it. We still don't know where she is at the moment."

Otto nodded. She knew Pauling's current phone number. The real one. Not the ones everyone else seemed to have. The Boss had supplied it. Finlay gave her a meaningful look. He no doubt suspected she had information she wasn't sharing.

She ignored the implied question. She was here to get intel, not deliver it. "During the relevant time frame, we think Reacher was a guest of a former military officer who lived at the Dakota. We're not sure how they got connected or why Reacher was there. We don't know the officer's name. Yet."

Finlay nodded. "I might be able to help you with that."

"Gaspar thinks it will be fairly simple to figure out. If you already know, that's great. If not, I suspect he'll have it in a few minutes, and I can tell you."

Finlay nodded again. "You're thinking that the connection between Reacher, Brewer, Pauling, and this military officer was the reason Pauling was being wiretapped and got snared in the TrueLeaks case."

"It could be something else. But not likely." Otto drained her cup. "Even with everything I've learned about Reacher, I still can't tell you why he does what he does."

Finlay threw his head back and laughed heartily. "Amen to that."

She frowned, ignoring his reaction. "He's just not that

connected to people. For one thing, no one can actually find him. Even his friends. If Cooper could find him, I wouldn't be standing here. If you could find him, you wouldn't be standing here, either."

Finlay was noncommittal. "So somehow, these four got connected. They did whatever they did. And then Reacher moved on. That about it?"

"Until recently." She closed her gritty eyes briefly, seeking relief.

"So you think something else is going on now." Finlay nodded. "What changed your mind?"

Otto glanced down at the carpet for a moment and then cleared her throat. "You probably know that six weeks ago, Reacher detonated an explosion that destroyed a house in Maine. I was there. The house was reduced to rubble, along with everybody within a fifty-foot radius. We thought Reacher was dead."

"But now Cooper doesn't think so?" Finlay nodded. His lips set in a grim line.

"I wish I could tell you what he thinks. I can only tell you what he said." Otto took a deep breath. "He said no forensic evidence definitively established that Reacher died in the explosion. He said he wanted to know for sure. And he sent us here to find out."

Finlay's head nodded slowly as if he was absorbing each word. "And what does that mean to you?"

"It means Cooper has inside information that he's not sharing. He knows something that he shouldn't know." She paused. "Because he found out about it in a way that he shouldn't have. Something that leads him to believe Reacher will show up here. May already be here. Waiting."

"Cooper has always been a brilliant strategist." Finlay shook his head and chuckled appreciatively. "Did you know that he once beat the best chess player in the world during a four-day tournament? He was a teenager at the time. He was the top of his class everywhere. Never been bested. Never lost a war, a battle, or even a skirmish. I've often wondered what would happen if he and Reacher squared off."

"The outcome seems obvious." Otto shrugged. "Reacher's younger by at least a decade. He's bigger and stronger. And he's a dirty fighter."

"And he's not stupid, either." Finlay's tone was serious, now. "You should keep all of that in mind, Agent Otto. You're a pawn in a very serious tournament. Pawns are meant to be sacrificed. Never forget that."

She wasn't in the mood for a lecture. His warnings and superior attitude got her back up. "And where do you fit into this Clash of the Titans, Dr. Finlay?"

"No secret there." Finlay shook his head slowly. "Same as you. I'm looking to avoid the fallout."

Otto considered what she was about to do for another two seconds. She would have changed her mind if she had unlimited time or any other options. She had neither. She took a deep breath.

"I'm certain of two things." She held up two fingers, one at a time. "One, Cooper knows something. The other, he suspects something."

Finlay nodded and waited.

"Can I trust you, Dr. Finlay? Gaspar says no. He doesn't like you. He thinks you were a dirty cop."

"I'm aware."

"Is he right?"

"About which part?" Finlay cocked his head.

Otto nodded. "So we understand each other, I am trustworthy. My word is my bond. I am not a dirty cop. I believe that's two of the reasons I was chosen for this job."

"Maybe. But those were not the only reasons. You're deluding yourself if you think otherwise." Finlay paused briefly as if to argue with himself. He had a decision to make now. And he knew it.

Otto waited. But she wouldn't wait forever.

Finlay had been standing near the door. His mind made up, he moved to sit on the loveseat and leaned back, stretching his left arm across the back cushions. He smoothed his tie over his flat belly and then rested his right hand in his lap.

His body language was open and relaxed. "Take a seat, Otto. I want to tell you a short story about a Boston cop on his way down to the gutter who made a stop in a small town in Georgia."

He paused, waiting for her to be seated.

Otto came here for answers, and the only way she'd get them was to trust him, at least a bit. Still, she hung back.

"He was a good cop once, but life had ground him down. His wife left him. His best friend was a whiskey bottle. He landed in a sleepy town. Way off the beaten path. He ran a small department with a couple of deputies and didn't have much to do."

"Until one day a stranger walked into town," Otto said rapidly.

He smiled. "Two strangers, actually. But that's another story. We don't have the time for that one right now, and I think you know most of it already."

She tapped her foot impatiently and offered a quick nod, encouraging him to get on with it. Whatever it was.

"This second stranger was a vagrant who looked like another problem at first. Until it turned out he had, shall we say, hidden talents and qualities. Some of those talents and qualities were, uh, less than admirable, but they proved helpful in the long run."

She ran out of patience. Quickly, she said, "And the good guys won, and the bad guys died, and the stranger moved on, and everybody in the town lived happily ever after."

"Pretty much." He offered a wary chuckle. "But the cop learned some things about himself and what he wanted out of life. He also learned a few things about the stranger. Which is the part you will want to hear."

"I'll bet I can guess. The stranger is a misunderstood bad ass with a heart of gold, right?"

"Something like that." Finlay displayed his wide white teeth to full advantage. "The stranger is smart. He's a trained killer, and his gold heart is still beating, but it's tarnished by a lot of hard years. He is completely unpredictable. A fearless fighter. He never loses. Never. He will die someday. But he never gives up."

"Something we have in common, then," Otto replied.

"Indeed." Finlay nodded. "When the time comes for you to choose sides, Otto, choose wisely."

Otto cocked her head and sent a level gaze across the room. "And I suppose you're saying that you are on his side and therefore I should choose you instead of Cooper?"

"I'm saying that the outcome is predetermined. And if you want to be on the *winning* side, you know what you need to do."

Otto narrowed her eyes and considered Finlay's words for a few moments. He was a cocky son of a bitch. And she was not in the mood.

Which didn't mean he was wrong.

But it did mean he was irritating as hell.

"Thanks for the advice. I know you're busy and I have a lot to do tonight, too." She gathered her coat and gloves. She held the playback device in her outstretched hand, offering it to him.

"You can keep that. Gaspar will want to hear it. And I have copies."

She nodded and slipped the device into her pocket before he could change his mind.

As she opened the door to leave, Finlay's voice filled her ears. "Don't forget what I said."

Otto left without further comment. In the taxi on the way back to the hotel, she called the Boss.

"What did Finlay tell you?"

She shook her head. "You mean you can't see and hear everything that goes on in his world? I'm shocked."

He laughed. "Only if I make the effort."

She wondered briefly if he could see her inside the dark taxi. He probably could.

"He's playing catch up on this Pauling and Brewer and Reacher thing. But he's a fast learner, and he has a lot of minions at his disposal, just like you do." She rubbed the slight headache forming between her eyebrows. "We're barely ahead of him at the moment."

"How so?"

"We have Lauren Pauling's phone number. He doesn't. Yet. He says it's concealed, somehow." The taxi was five minutes out from her hotel. "Can you ping the phone and find her exact location?"

"She's not in the city, I take it?"

"She could be. But one of her neighbors said otherwise." She closed her eyes a moment. "I believe the guy."

"Okay. I'll find her and let you know."

"And something else."

"Yes?"

"You know Pauling's old number was being traced. Which is how you got the conversation you gave us originally. You also know that Pauling talked to Reacher on that number a few times."

He didn't respond, which was confirmation enough.

"Has Pauling talked to Reacher since those original mid-September conversations? Meaning, since she got the new phone number. Can you search that?"

He answered the questions in reverse order. "It's not a quick process. But no. So far, we've found no conversations with Reacher."

The taxi stopped on the street, a block west of the hotel. "Ma'am. You'll need to get out here. I can't drive up any closer."

Otto glanced out the windshield. The hotel's front entrance was surrounded by flashing lights atop police, fire, and rescue vehicles. "What's going on?"

"I don't know, Ma'am. But they won't allow me any closer. The street is closed. See?"

She craned her neck to see around the obstacles. Indeed, a police cruiser had closed the street on each side of the hotel entrance.

To the Boss, she said, "Okay, keep looking. I've got to go."

His tone was solid steel. "I'm taking orders from you now?"

She disconnected the call.

She called Gaspar's number, handed the driver a twenty for the seven-dollar fare, and slipped into the cold night.

CHAPTER TWENTY-SIX

Thursday, January 13
11:20 p.m.
New York City

SHE CALLED GASPAR'S PHONE, but he didn't pick up. She left a quick, "Call me," voice mail, and then made her way to the pretty Latino NYPD officer blocking pedestrians from using the sidewalk to reach the hotel entrance.

"I'm staying at this hotel. Is there another entrance I can use, Officer—" She peered at the name plate, "Cruz?"

Officer Cruz had her arms at her sides, within easy reach of the equipment on her duty belt. "The other entrance is also closed at the moment, ma'am."

"What's going on here?"

"We were told the building is being evacuated. That's all the information I have." Officer Cruz sounded genuinely sympathetic, and maybe she was. She might have noticed Otto's shivering, too. "You can wait at the coffee shop in the next block until we get the all clear. It'll be warmer inside."

Otto pulled her ID from her pocket. She opened the bi-fold wallet and showed Officer Cruz her credentials.

Cruz examined the ID. She nodded once and pointed to another officer standing halfway down the block. "Agent Otto, that's the captain. He should know more."

Otto looked ahead, toward the hotel entrance. From her vantage point, she could see nothing but a lot of broad backs and emergency flashers in several colors. People were filing out of the hotel doors in quick but orderly fashion. She didn't see anyone with obvious injuries.

"Thank you, Officer Cruz." She approached the captain, but only walked about ten feet before her phone vibrated. "Gaspar. I'm out front. Can't get in. Where are you?"

"Headed your way. Five minutes out." His tone was serious and official. "Stay there. I'll find you."

Otto walked another few yards toward the Captain when she heard quick footsteps coming up behind her. She turned fast, ready to deflect until she recognized Detective Brewer. Out of shape and out of breath, he slowed and waved her toward him.

She reversed course. Brewer had backed into a wide doorway, protected from the biting wind. He grabbed her arm and pulled her into the alcove, out of sight.

She jerked her arm from his grasp. "Brewer, what the hell?"

"Where's Gaspar?" he said, furtively.

"On his way. We've been trying to reach you all day."

"I want to show you something. And then you need to go."

"Show me what? Go where?"

Brewer stuck his head beyond the alcove and ducked back. "Wait until he gets here."

"What's going on?" She frowned. "And who are you hiding from?"

"Just about every cop out there knows me. I don't want to get pulled into what's going on out there." He spoke quietly as if he might actually be overheard amid the cacophony.

Pedestrians were steadily passing the alcove moving in both directions. Reporters with cameras and microphones, guests in their pajamas, emergency personnel, sirens headed toward the hotel. The chaotic scene bordered on pandemonium as more seconds passed.

"What is going on out there?" She jerked her thumb to point over her shoulder. "I was on my way to find out when you grabbed me."

"Look, it's complicated. I only want to say this once. Not start over for Gaspar."

Otto let out a harsh breath and counted to ten. "Why'd you pull me in here? If we want Gaspar to find us, standing on the sidewalk in plain view would help, don't you think?"

"Just take my word for it, will you?"

"You've already lied to me twice." Otto's patience snapped. "Why should I take your word for anything?"

"Believe me, I wish I had told you the whole story to start with." Brewer grimaced, and his shoulders slumped. "A man I liked might still be alive if I had. I was trying to let Pauling handle things. That was a mistake."

Otto cocked her head. He'd finally succeeded in capturing her curiosity. "You wait here. I'm stepping out where Gaspar can see me."

"Gaspar isn't the only one watching you, Otto."

She shrugged, but only because she didn't want to reinforce how right he was. She moved out of the alcove and looked up and down the crowded sidewalk. Gaspar was half a block down, struggling to break a trail through the people who blocked his path, like a salmon swimming upstream against a strong current. He had the laptop cases, one over each shoulder, but no travel bags wheeling along behind him.

She caught his eye. He nodded. She held his gaze as she moved back into the alcove with Brewer.

Another few minutes later Gaspar finally reached their location, slightly breathless, Otto noticed. His eyes widened when he saw Brewer. "Where the hell have you been?"

Brewer said, "I caught a homicide case. I told you that. But it resolved about an hour ago. Which is when I picked up your messages. Let's go."

"Go where?" Gaspar asked, but Brewer was already walking away.

Otto said, "What happened at the hotel?"

"Hard to say. The fire alarm sounded. Shortly after that, security personnel knocked on the door. Said we had to evacuate immediately and wouldn't take no for an answer. I grabbed up the electronics, but I couldn't get the travel bags. It took a while to get down to ground level in the elevators. I'd have taken the stairs, but we were on the forty-third floor."

Otto glanced at the fire trucks parked in the street. None of the hoses had been removed. Fire fighters were milling around. "Doesn't look like a fire."

"Didn't smell like one, either. And no smoke anywhere that I saw." Gaspar handed over her laptop.

Otto slung the shoulder strap over her left shoulder to leave her gun hand free, just in case. "Let's deal with Brewer. We can come back after. Maybe they'll let us collect our bags, at least."

Gaspar shrugged. "I swear those things are cursed."

She left the alcove and Gaspar followed. There were too many people milling around. They couldn't walk side-by-side.

She kept an eye on Brewer, half a block ahead by now. He bobbed and weaved through the swarm. At the corner, he turned left.

Threading the crowd, Otto reached the turn twenty yards behind him. The throng continued straight in both directions. Brewer was making better time. He was ahead another half-block. She waited for Gaspar.

"Where's Brewer?" he asked when he reached her position.

"Straight on." The crowd on this street was smaller, typical for New York pedestrians in this neighborhood on a weeknight, thin enough to make walking together possible.

Gaspar switched his laptop to the other shoulder. "Where's he going?"

"Beats me." She shook her head.

At the next corner, Brewer waited. He'd hailed a taxi.

"Where are we going?" Gaspar asked when they reached him.

"The Dakota."

"Why?" Otto asked.

"Get in. I'll answer all your questions, but we've got to go."

Gaspar walked around and climbed in on the opposite side. Otto slipped across the bench seat to the middle.

Brewer stepped inside, closed the door, and gave directions to the driver.

"Well?" Otto asked.

"Pauling is not in the city."

"Do you know where she is?" Gaspar asked.

"I can make a pretty solid guess. She has a condo in Palm Beach. The weather's a hell of a lot better there."

Gaspar raised his eyebrows.

Otto replied, "Her private investigations business must pay a lot better than her FBI salary did."

"The Palm Beach place belonged to her late husband. He bought it in foreclosure a couple of decades ago. He was an investment banker, I guess. Back in the 1980s when those guys were all drowning in cash."

"Do you have an address?" Otto asked.

Brewer shook his head. "We can get it from her, though."

The taxi made relatively good time and stopped on 72nd Street sooner than Otto expected. They piled out, and Brewer paid the fare before the driver headed downtown.

"This way," Brewer said. He walked at a good clip toward the main entrance.

Otto and Gaspar exchanged glances before they followed behind. The doorman they'd met earlier, Bishop, must have finished his shift a few hours ago.

Brewer waited for a dignified old gentleman to open the door.

"Good evening, Detective Brewer." His voice resonated with the same sort of dignity the historic building emitted.

Brewer nodded without slowing his stride. "Good evening, Mr. Clark."

Otto and Gaspar followed Brewer to the elevator. He pushed the call button. While they waited, he reached into his pocket and pulled out latex gloves for each of them.

"Put these on."

"Why?"

"We can talk when we get there." The elevator arrived, and they filed in. He pushed the button for the fifth floor.

Otto had tired of asking Brewer questions he didn't answer, but Gaspar said, "Where are we going?"

"To the apartment Reacher stayed in while he was in the city sixteen months ago. When I met him. When Pauling met him."

"It's too late to bang on the door and ask for a home tour, don't you think?" Gaspar asked.

Brewer said nothing.

The elevator car came to a stop. The doors opened soundlessly, and Brewer stepped out. "The apartment has been unoccupied since Reacher left town."

Brewer led the way around the corner and stopped at a heavy oak door the color of honey. He already had the key in hand. He slipped it into the lock, which turned easily. He pushed the door open.

"Let's get inside. We'll have some privacy." They moved into a small, square foyer, and Brewer closed the big door behind them. "Go straight into the living room. We can talk there."

The abandoned living room was tastefully decorated. Sunshine yellow walls offered the illusion of good cheer, but the place had a strong negative vibe to it, as her mother would say. Dust wafted to her nose, and she sneezed.

"Bless you," Gaspar said.

"Thanks. Okay, Brewer. Out with it. Why are we here?" Otto demanded. She'd been chasing Pauling all over New York when Brewer knew she'd left town. He'd refused to tell them about this apartment. He'd wasted her time. And he'd better have a damned good reason for it.

"Let me start, to keep the conversation honest," Gaspar said. Brewer had the grace to wince. "This apartment was held by a corporation called Operational Security Consultants, the sole shareholder of which was also the occupant. Former U.S. Army Colonel Edward Lane lived here briefly with his first wife, and then with his second wife and his step-daughter. So far, so good?"

Brewer nodded.

"The apartment has been unoccupied for the past sixteen months," Gaspar continued. "In September, four months ago, the co-op board foreclosed. Failure to pay some pretty hefty fees for a full year. Shares were transferred to the co-op, but the apartment was not put on the market or resold to any of the pre-approved buyers on the Dakota's long waiting list."

Otto asked, "Why go to all the hassle of foreclosing and then not resell?"

"Brewer knows the answer to that, don't you Brewer?" Gaspar said.

Brewer nodded. "When they foreclosed on the place and entered the apartment for the inspection afterward, they found a vault containing a lot of cash."

"So they realized that the owner had the ability to pay the fees, but must have had a good reason for not doing so?" Otto asked.

Brewer nodded. "The Dakota always wants to avoid scandal and respect the privacy of the owners. That's why celebrities live here. For the special protections."

"Foreclosures are public records, though," Gaspar said. "That's how I found out about this one."

Brewer nodded. "True. They'd already stepped in a big pile of crap by proceeding down that path. When they found the money, they really started to worry."

"So they called you, the friendly neighborhood NYPD detective?" Otto asked.

"Exactly." Brewer shrugged. "And I called Pauling."

Otto frowned. "Why Pauling?"

"I regret it now. But at the time, I figured it had something to do with Reacher," Brewer said. "I knew Lane was the guy Reacher had been working for. And that's why I'd put Reacher and Pauling together in the first place. So I thought she might have better intel and would know what to do about the situation."

"And did she? Know what to do?" Otto asked.

Brewer replied, "She connected with the president of the board and paid the overdue fees. She paid the fees through the following two years, too. She persuaded the president to wait until the owner returned to do anything more with the place."

Gaspar shook his head. "Doesn't make any sense. Why did Pauling get involved in this?"

"Because of Reacher. She said he'd want her to deal with it. And remember, she was the one who handled the original situation, not me." Brewer shrugged. "I didn't think much of it at the time. I'm not in the property management business, and the situation didn't have anything to do with me or NYPD at that point. I'm a homicide detective, you know?"

Otto crossed her arms over her chest. "So that was the end of it? You passed it off to Pauling four months ago and never heard anything else?"

"Until this afternoon," Brewer spoke slowly. "Bishop, the daytime doorman, got an attack of conscience after you left. Called me and said he'd given you my name. I asked him if he'd put you in touch with Peck. He said he'd passed along Peck's number."

Otto shrugged. "None of that sounds ominous."

"Here's the ominous part." Brewer took a deep breath and paced the room. "Bishop told me about the guy who came to see Peck this morning, too. He said the guy reminded him of Reacher."

"He told us it definitely *wasn't* Reacher," Gaspar replied.

"I know. And I think he was right. But that was curious," Brewer said.

"Why?" Gaspar asked.

"Think about it from Bishop's perspective. No one has come

around here since Reacher left sixteen months ago. Including the people who lived here. And now, a guy shows up, and then on the same day, you show up. And this guy just happened to remind Bishop of Reacher." Brewer breathed deeply again. "It was strange. Got the hair up on my neck. Call it cop's intuition or whatever you like. But it didn't feel right."

"So you came here to check it out," Otto said.

Brewer nodded. "And I wish I hadn't."

"Because?" Otto asked.

"Let me show you." Brewer walked through the living room to the back hallway and into the master bedroom. Gaspar followed first, then Otto.

Gaspar's limp was pronounced, which meant he was tired. Otto stifled a yawn and glanced at her watch. It was well after 1:00 a.m. She was tired, too. Whatever Brewer had found, they'd look at it briefly now and come back later. They could follow up with Pauling tomorrow. Once they'd had some sleep.

Brewer stopped in front of a small closet. Inside the painted wood door was a recess where a heavy metal door had been installed. The second door opened electronically.

"This is where they found the money. I found out later that Reacher gave Pauling the combination." Brewer reached up with his gloved index finger and punched 3785 into the keypad mounted on the left.

The keypad beeped.

Brewer opened the inner door and reached inside to turn on the light.

Otto caught the unmistakable scent of early decomposition first. A single glance was enough to take in the grisly body mutilated by multiple knife wounds.

CHAPTER TWENTY-SEVEN

HE HADN'T BEEN DEAD very long. Twelve hours, give or take, probably. Looked like most of his blood was pooled around him on the floor. No point in checking for a pulse.

Brewer said, "This was Simon Peck. The co-op board president. Bishop said Peck met with the mystery man who arrived today. He also said Peck hadn't been answering his phone since then."

"Have you called this in to your homicide desk?" Gaspar asked.

"Not yet. I'm having trouble coming up with a plausible reason for being here," Brewer said.

Gaspar smirked. "Yeah, that seems like a problem for you."

Brewer frowned. "Thought you might help me out with a solution."

"Which is why you brought us here," Gaspar replied. "You're starting to piss me off, Brewer."

"We can argue about this later." Otto held up a gloved hand. She looked at Brewer. "This is where the money was found after the foreclosure, you said. How much money are we talking about?"

196 | DIANE CAPRI

"I never saw the money. And everyone involved tried to hush the situation up as soon as the money was found." Brewer cleared his throat. "But I heard it was something around the neighborhood of nine million dollars."

Gaspar whistled. "Nice neighborhood."

"Who'd you hear that from? Pauling?" Otto asked.

Brewer leaned his head toward the body. "Peck, here, told me."

Gaspar's eyebrows arched higher than usual. "That's a lot of bulk cash to have lying around. Most people would put it in a bank. This guy some kind of wacky survivalist or something?"

Brewer said, "Or something."

Gaspar nodded. "And it would take time to move all of that paper. What happened to it?"

Brewer shook his head. "I really don't know. But I think Pauling does."

Otto squatted down near the body, careful to avoid the congealing blood. A knife, presumably the murder weapon, lay open and partially covered by the darkening goop. "This is a Strider SMF. Marines Special Ops weapon. Created for their Detachment One unit."

"Not the kind of thing an ordinary street punk would be swinging around at more than seven hundred dollars to buy," Gaspar said.

"So it's a military guy? A Marine?" Brewer asked.

"Maybe," Gaspar replied.

"Looks like most of the blood came from the deep cut across his throat. But he's got several more superficial cuts around his face and hands," Otto said. "The killer must have been trying to get some information from the guy or something. Otherwise, he'd have killed him immediately without bothering to carve him up first."

"Hang on. The doorman gave me a cell phone number for Peck this afternoon." Gaspar pulled Peck's business card from his pocket and dialed the number.

It rang several times, and Peck's voice mail picked up. But they heard no ringing from Peck's pockets or inside the vault. Gaspar disconnected.

"The killer took Peck's phone," Brewer said. "We can ping it. Find him that way."

"Unless he destroyed the phone and disposed of it already. Which is what he probably did," Otto said. She pushed up off the floor. "I don't see any obvious prints on that knife. Killer probably wore gloves."

"I guess we'd better find Pauling before the guy who killed Peck finds her first," Otto said. "Do you have her address in Palm Beach?"

Brewer shook his head again. "Wish I did."

Gaspar said, "You're not a lot of help, Brewer."

"I realize that. But there's nothing I can do about it." He pulled his cell phone out of his pocket. "I've got to make the call to start getting this homicide processed. NYPD will get on this mystery visitor. Maybe he's still in the city."

"Chances of that are pretty slim," Gaspar said.

Brewer nodded. "You could get your FBI whiz kids to find Pauling by pinging her phone."

"Yeah. We can do that," Otto said. "We'll find her. You find the killer."

Brewer hovered his thumb over the touch screen on his phone.

Before he made the call, Otto said, "And I want to know what happened to bring out the cavalry at our hotel tonight. What do you know about that?"

"Nothing. What I heard on my radio on my way over was that some civilian had called in a potential suicide bomber. You might be able to pick up more on the news by now." He made the call and put the phone to his ear to report the homicide. "Keep in touch."

"Yeah, you, too," Gaspar replied on the way out.

Otto's phone vibrated in her pocket.

CHAPTER TWENTY-EIGHT

Friday, January 14
1:20 a.m.
New York City

GASPAR PUSHED THE BUTTON for the elevator while Otto answered the Boss's call.

"Since you've already heard everything, any chance you can find us a place to sleep?" She asked before he had a chance to speak. "Our hotel has been evacuated. Bomb threat or something. We can't get back in."

"You can sleep on the plane. You're booked from JFK to Palm Beach at five a.m."

"You found Pauling?" Otto had learned to ask. Gaspar smirked, and she punched him in the bicep hard enough to make him stop.

The elevator arrived, and they stepped inside.

"Encrypted files are on your secure server. It's a small island. She won't be hard to find."

Otto grabbed a strand of hair that had escaped the tight

chignon at the back of her neck and tucked it into place. "How did you find her?"

"Brewer narrowed it down for us."

"You're welcome," Otto said, sarcastically. The elevator stopped on the first floor. Gaspar walked out, and she followed. "And you've got eyes on her? I'm not interested in another wild goose chase."

He sighed. "We got lucky. Unlike many phones, her cell won't ping unless she's using it."

"She's not your average citizen." Otto frowned. "Who's she talking to at this hour?"

"Not Reacher, if that's what you're thinking."

Gaspar had rounded the corner to the open lobby.

Otto paused and lowered her voice. "Do you have surveillance of the guy who killed Peck?"

"Not yet. Nothing usable, anyway."

"Send us what you have."

He said nothing.

She didn't press him, only because there was no point. He'd do whatever he wanted, no matter what she said. "Why did they evacuate our hotel tonight?"

"You might ask your pal Finlay about that. Rumor is that he made the call."

She widened her eyes. "Why?"

"Who knows why he does anything?" He sounded bored. "This TrueLeaks thing has everybody on edge."

"Nobody likes to think about military corruption at the highest levels," she said.

"After you got Finlay's curiosity up, he's paying attention. My guess is he's got a flag on both of you and everything that might have to do with Reacher. When Gaspar started nosing around in the databases tonight checking into private military contractors and their real estate holdings in historic buildings, somebody probably got nervous about it. Nothing more than a civilian phone call with an unconfirmed tip would be necessary to get a Manhattan hotel evacuated."

"He doesn't have a current location on our source."

"Not yet," he snapped. "And no thanks to you."

He'd hung up on her. She was holding nothing but dead air. She shook her head and dropped the phone into her pocket.

She rounded the corner into the lobby of the Dakota. The distinguished old gentleman stood near the door talking casually with Gaspar. Otto looked around for surveillance cameras. Most buildings had security systems in place these days. The Boss could hack into any ongoing signal. If he hadn't found good images of Peck's killer, it meant that the guy was savvy enough to avoid the cameras.

Brewer would follow up. There were hundreds of cameras around New York. Maybe he'd find another way to get some good images.

If this guy was connected to Pauling in some way, a picture could be way more effective with her. Otto didn't have a good feeling about Pauling's level of cooperation. How many times had she been down this road already? Reacher's women hadn't been particularly helpful so far. Why should Pauling be different?

"What's the best way for us to get a taxi to JFK?" Gaspar asked the old gentleman as Otto approached.

"I can handle that for you, sir." He moved to a telephone on the desk and lifted the receiver. He pushed a single button three times and replaced the receiver. "I've signaled the driver. He will be here momentarily, sir. Please wait here until he pulls up. It's too cold to be outside tonight."

"Thank you," Gaspar said. "This is Mr. Clark, Agent Otto." He extended his white-gloved hand. "Alfred Clark, ma'am." Otto shook hands with him. Maybe he'd lived to a healthy old age because he shook hands with his gloves on. Fewer germs. "How long have you been working here, Mr. Clark?" He smiled and wagged his head. "Feels like half my life I've been at the Dakota. Nowhere else to go anymore."

"No family?"

He clasped his white-gloved hands together. "My wife passed years ago. We didn't have any kids. So it's just me. The Dakota's always been my home and my family, too."

"Did you know Mr. Lane and his family that lived on the fifth floor?"

"Of course, I did." He nodded. "Both Mrs. Lanes were very nice. The little girl was adorable. A shame they moved."

Otto cocked her head. "You said *both* Mrs. Lanes?"

"Terrible thing about the first Mrs. Lane. She was murdered. Sad, sad day." He shook his head and closed his eyes briefly as if he was offering up a prayer. "Seems like some of these rich folks who live here have too many tragedies, you know?"

"Is that how you met Lauren Pauling?" Gaspar asked, as if he knew for sure that Clark knew Pauling. "When the first Mrs. Lane died?"

"Yes, sir. Ms. Pauling is a really nice person. She was with the FBI then. She took it hard. Detective Brewer, too. It wasn't his case, but he was upset about it. Hell, we all were."

"Have you seen Ms. Pauling lately?" Otto asked.

He wagged his head slowly from side to side, thinking about it, maybe. "Probably been a few months since she's been around. She'll be back though. Mr. Peck's a friend of hers."

He glanced outside. "Your ride is here. You stay warm out there, now."

"Thank you, Mr. Clark," Otto said. "We will. Thanks for the help."

Gaspar shook hands with the old gentleman again before he pushed the glass door open and they hurried to the limo. Within the hour, they'd reached JFK.

CHAPTER TWENTY-NINE

INSIDE THE TERMINAL, OTTO asked, "You hungry?"

Gaspar grinned. "You've forgotten who you're talking to. But we're not going to find anything open here at this hour."

"Maybe not. But let's check around."

The shops and eateries they passed as they walked the corridors were closed for the night. Metal gates were pulled to the floor and locked. New York might be the city that never sleeps, but the airport was as dead after two o'clock in the morning as any farm town in Nebraska.

"I give up. Let's get to the gate and download those files. See what we're dealing with here," Otto said, turning around and heading to the gate.

She'd never seen JFK like this. The effect was eerily like a futuristic ghost town. Without the usual mobs of travelers, bustling to and fro and stopping in the middle of the walkways, their gate seemed like a million miles away down the empty hallways.

"Tell me what happened back at the hotel," Otto said since no civilians were around to overhear their conversation. "The

Boss says it's your fault we got evacuated. Something you were searching online triggered someone to freak out."

Gaspar frowned, "Let me guess. Finlay's doing."

"That's a reasonable guess. There are probably others." Otto shrugged.

"You already know most of it. After I found the name of the corporation that owned the Dakota apartment, I started searching for whatever I could find about OSC and the owner. I broadened the search to OSC's list of mercenaries on the payroll." Gaspar grinned and shifted his laptop bag again. He had so much stuff in there. It had to weigh twenty pounds, at least. "Mercenaries get a steady paycheck, with taxes and everything. Who knew? You'd think putting your life on the line on a daily basis in some of the most dangerous places on earth would pay better."

Otto gave him the side-eye. "You mean OSC paid them off the books. In cash. Which may explain why OSC had all that cash in the apartment safe."

"There's no way to find under the table cash payments in the records I found so far. But the payroll stuff showed salaries at about what you'd expect for a new hire at a burger joint." Gaspar shrugged. "If the OSC guys weren't being paid a lot more from somewhere else, they were the biggest idiots on earth."

"You don't believe in working for the joy of the job, Chico?" She grinned, but her heart wasn't in it.

"Joy of the job is one thing. But the whole point of being a mercenary is to make money." Gaspar's scowl deepened. "And most of the OSC guys died in one campaign or another. Why would they agree to give their lives for a pittance?"

They'd reached their posted departure gate, and Otto plopped down in one of the sling back vinyl seats. "How many OSC fighters are we talking about?"

"Again, hard to say. OSC is a smallish outfit, for a military contractor." Gaspar dropped his laptop bag into another seat in the row across from hers. "But not counting the Colonel, I only found records on one who is still alive."

Otto stared at him. "Seriously? Only one?"

"Seems like employment with OSC is a one-way ticket to hell." He pulled his laptop out and set up his secure satellite hot spot. In a couple of minutes, he'd reconnected to his private server where he'd stored the work he'd done back at the hotel.

Otto watched him nod and frown and shake his head for a couple more minutes before she said, "Okay, Chico. The suspense is killing me."

He grinned. "I'm looking at what I have on the lone survivor. His name is Nick Scavo. He was the Executive VP for OSC until he was captured in a revolution in West Africa. Presumed dead for about five or so years."

He scanned the screens, flipping through quickly. "Here it is. He's now living at a place called Stanwix Village in Upstate New York. He's being treated at a VA facility and this community is nearby."

"Treated for what?"

"Dunno. VA medical records are a little harder to hack into. It'll take a bit more time."

"Let's do that. But first," Otto nodded, "did you find anything that would have freaked Finlay out?"

Gaspar pushed a few more keys to switch to different files. "Nothing much right away. But then I went to the TrueLeaks document dump. It's online at several different media outlets. And it's a lot of stuff that's not very well indexed at all."

Otto nodded. Made sense. According to the Boss, the new TrueLeaks dump was where he'd somehow found the original

Pauling/Brewer telephone call mentioning Reacher.

"My TrueLeaks searches turned up a few hits for OSC and the Colonel. I found a longer list of OSC personnel, going back a few years. Before I could check everything out, the fire alarm sounded and I got rousted." He paused and seemed to be thinking about something. "Immediately before the alarm, I saw two or three hits that mentioned the Panama Papers."

Otto's eyes widened of their own accord. "The Panama Papers? Connected to the TrueLeaks documents?"

"That's how it looked on the screen. But you know how the media stories go. The two could be unrelated, and some reporter is only trying to hook them up to get eyeballs on his story." He paused. "But I saved my searches. I'll check them out as soon as I can get up and running again in a better environment."

She knew what he meant. An environment away from the airport. Where every word and every move wasn't being monitored and recorded by multiple agencies, governments, and civilians of all types.

In fact, sitting around here for another few hours was a monumental waste of time.

Otto stood. Gaspar glanced up from his screen. She tilted her head toward the exit.

His eyes widened briefly as his eyebrows shot up. She waved him up with her hand.

She started off slowly, giving him time to catch up. A few moments later, he had stashed his laptop and collected his case and followed.

Otto used her cell phone to reserve a rental car. She said nothing more until they reached the rental lot where she picked up the keys from the sleepy attendant.

Gaspar tossed his laptop into the back seat of the SUV and

settled in behind the wheel. Otto climbed into the passenger seat, fished her alligator clamp from her laptop case, and placed it at the retractor of her shoulder harness.

When they were on the road, traveling away from the airport and outside the intense surveillance perimeter, Gaspar grinned. "Was it something I didn't say?"

She replied, "The Panama Papers were all about shell corporations and offshore bank accounts for hiding assets. Tax evasion. Money laundering."

"Right."

"Makes sense that military corruption could have produced some dirty money. Nine million dollars or so wouldn't be out of the realm of possibility." Otto nodded. The more she considered the connection between Gaspar's computer work and the hotel's evacuation, the more likely it seemed. "That hotel is a big place. Rooms, restaurants, bars, events. Thousands of guests were there last night. Anything could have been going on. And we don't know what actually triggered the alarm."

"Not likely it was something else, though." Gaspar scowled. "Fifty bucks says one of them got nervous. Finlay or the Boss."

"Hell, I'm working for the joy of the job," Otto said sourly. "Why don't you just take my whole paycheck?"

Gaspar laughed out loud, and the sound was good to hear. "Where to, Dragon Boss Lady?"

"I'm pulling up directions to Stanwix Village now." She watched the choices as they popped up on her phone.

"I'll keep a lookout for a place to eat."

She didn't bother to argue.

CHAPTER THIRTY

Friday, January 14
2:35 a.m.
Staten Island, New York

Nitro Mack had approached Brewer's bucolic residential
neighborhood on Staten Island long after nightfall. He had
prepared his plan of attack carefully. Recon a few hours ago had
revealed the best entry point was the side door.

Unfortunately, there were no alleys behind the single-family
homes that lined the residential street. Most of the houses were
wood construction, built in the 1920s before Parnell Ford had put
a car in every driveway.

The lots were thirty feet wide and one hundred feet deep.
The homes were back-to-back, although small green spaces
filled the area behind the house. A ten-foot easement on either
side of the property line made the green space seem almost twice
as vast as it actually was.

Brewer's fifteen-hundred-square-foot house was a well-
maintained three-bedroom colonial in Port Richmond. It was

212 | D I A N E C A P R I

minutes away from the metro area with easy access to
transportation. No doubt this was convenient for Brewer's wife.
According to online DMV records, she did not own a car or have
a driver's license.

Parnell had tracked down everything he could find but did
not discover a good explanation. She might be unable to drive.
Possibly handicapped or disabled, but he'd found no records
reflecting that, either. Maybe she was afraid to drive, or maybe
she had no need to. Parnell had long ago ceased to be amazed at
the number of New Yorkers who did not have a driver's license
and knew nothing about cars.

Brewer's job provided a city-owned vehicle of some sort,
which he probably drove to and from work every day.
Otherwise, the Brewers must have used public transportation.

The street was cleared of snow, and the frigid weather
discouraged pedestrians on the sidewalks. Brewer's house had a
green awning over the front door that barely covered the small
cement stoop, four steps up from the sidewalk. Forcing his way
into the house from the front stoop would be awkward.

The side door was at ground level and not illuminated by the
streetlights. A wooden fence separated Brewer's house from the
house next door for privacy, which was exactly what Parnell
wanted. The side door was definitely a better option than the front.

Brewer worked the day shift, 9:30 a.m. to 6:00 p.m., five
days a week. His shift had ended hours ago.

Parnell tapped his thumb impatiently on the steering wheel.
Maybe Brewer had caught a new case. No matter. Parnell could
wait.

His plan was solid. Enter the house after Brewer was home
for the night, relaxed, expecting nothing. When he wouldn't have
his weapon on him.

But Brewer was too late. Parnell considered alternatives. He shook his head once. No need to improvise. Poorly planned improvisation in the field had killed more soldiers under his command than any other misguided stupidity.

He would follow the plan he'd worked out on his way from Scavo's place. He'd stopped once at a DIY hardware store and again at a Wal-Mart to pick up the supplies he needed. Two more stops and he was on his way.

He glanced at the clock on the dashboard again. 2:42 a.m. Brewer's meat and potatoes went cold hours ago. Mrs. Brewer had prepared dinner and placed it on the table promptly at seven o'clock, which seemed like her routine. Detective Brewer was not a man who missed many meals.

Two hours later, Mrs. Brewer ate alone. An hour afterward, she cleared the table and washed up the dishes. Perhaps she left a plate for her husband in the oven. She seemed like the kind of wife who might. She turned off the kitchen light and walked deeper into the house.

The blue glow from a television emitted from the master bedroom window. She settled into bed to wait for him. She had a long wait tonight.

At 2:52 a.m., Brewer finally pulled the NYPD unmarked sedan into the driveway. The garage door opened with the push of a button on his remote, and Brewer drove straight back into the detached garage. The interior light came on automatically as the garage door slid up. Brewer shut off the engine, left the car, and pushed the button on the door frame.

The garage door began its descent. Brewer ducked under the moving steel and hustled toward the house. He used the side entrance. No doubt the storm door's hinges squeaked when Brewer pulled it open, just as they had when Parnell tried the door earlier.

Brewer turned the knob and leaned his shoulder into the interior steel door. He stomped and scraped his shoes on the brown coir doormat and slipped into the warmth of home before the garage door settled onto the concrete. Parnell could have heard the storm door's squeaking hinges as it slowly closed and snugged shut if he'd been close enough.

He watched for another fifteen minutes. Satisfied that Brewer and his wife were now home for the rest of the night, Parnell drove past the house and parked two blocks away. He left the rental unlocked and tossed the keys onto the floor where he could grab them in a hurry.

But he shouldn't need to do that. His plan was solid. He'd have plenty of time.

Parnell grabbed the small duffel bag, turned up the collar on his coat and, careful to keep his face in shadow, walked normally down the sidewalk toward the house behind Brewer's. As it had been all night, the house was dark. Perhaps the family was out of town. A stroke of good luck.

He sidled along the property line behind a row of evergreen shrubs until he reached the back of Brewer's garage. From this vantage point, he could see the back of the house. A bay window curved from the kitchen, offering Parnell an unobstructed view. Brewer and his wife were seated at the kitchen table. She'd probably pulled his plate from the oven. She watched while he ate the dinner.

Parnell sneered. A real Normal Rockwell moment. She was wearing a red and white robe that stretched across her ample bosom and belly. He had a napkin tucked into his collar beneath his chin. He paid close attention to the food on his plate, shoveling it in like a stevedore while she watched, not talking.

Parnell waited a moment longer, listening. He heard only the distant traffic and abnormal silence of the cold, winter night. No dogs, drunks, or nosy neighbors interrupted. A mixed blessing. He wouldn't be noticed, but no bits of noise would cover his activities, either.

He shrugged. Field conditions were precisely what he'd expected.

He grabbed a pair of latex gloves from his pocket and pulled them on, snugging the fingers into place one at a time.

Soundlessly, he stepped away from the garage, careful to avoid the light wash from the big bay window, and approached the side entrance.

The storm door was not locked, and the house was not equipped with an alarm system or surveillance cameras. Maybe the squeaky hinges were usually enough to alert the Brewers of visitors, welcome or otherwise.

Or maybe an NYPD detective figured no man would be stupid enough to break into a cop's house.

Either way, Parnell wasn't concerned about Brewer or his defenses. Brewer had Parnell's nine million dollars, and he was here to take it back. Simple as that.

Parnell pulled the small plastic bottle from his duffel and squeezed ample drops of Eezox onto the storm door's hinges. He inhaled the familiar sweet smell. He'd used Eezox premium synthetic gun lubricant on locks, hinges, latches, and more. No residue. Effective at cold temperatures. Worked every time.

He capped the bottle and returned it to the duffel. The storm door opened silently on its lubricated hinges, and Parnell grinned. *Slides like a hot knife on butter.*

With the glass storm resting against his back, he turned his attention to the steel door, which was locked and bolted.

It was a standard residential door. The kind people installed themselves. Reasonable quality for most homes. Stronger than a wood door, but not as strong as a bank vault.

Parnell grabbed the door breaching tool from his bag. He'd selected the non-hydraulic extendable ratchet system because it was faster, quieter, and had the highest torque force in its class. The unit weighed twelve pounds. It would apply 13,000 pounds of force between the door and the doorjamb. The steel door would open in twenty-five seconds or less.

With luck, Brewer would come to check out the disturbance. Parnell would meet him head on. If he didn't show up, Parnell would find him soon enough.

Half a second after the door popped open, Parnell pivoted on his left foot and shoved the steel door inside, hard and fast, expecting resistance from Brewer.

The door swung too easily. Which meant Brewer wasn't blocking from the other side.

Parnell's momentum propelled him forward. He let the storm door close behind him. He pushed the steel door back into place and pulled his weapon.

CHAPTER THIRTY-ONE

HE FORGED THROUGH TO the kitchen where Brewer and his wife were seated at the dinner table, eyes wide, mouths hanging open.

Half-chewed food spilled onto Brewer's bib.

Brewer jumped up from his chair, ready to fight, but he had to swallow the food first.

Which was long enough for Parnell to push forward on his left foot and slam his balled fist hard into Brewer's stomach.

The blow drove Brewer back into the chair. Brewer's momentum knocked the chair back onto the floor.

With Brewer temporarily neutralized, Parnell reached up and flipped off the kitchen lights.

Which was when Mrs. Brewer finally screamed.

Parnell slipped on his night vision headset and pulled a zip tie from his pocket.

Brewer was cursing and scrambling to get away from the chair and off the floor. Before he could untangle himself, Parnell kicked him savagely in the kidney.

Brewer grunted and cried out, "I'll kill you!"

But his words were weak and breathless, the threat harmless. Parnell kicked him again, harder the second time. Brewer groaned and clamped his mouth shut, writhing on the floor.

Parnell knelt and slipped the zip tie around both ankles. Then he pushed Brewer onto his stomach. "Hands behind your back."

"Screw you!"

Parnell kicked him again and grabbed one of Brewer's arms as the detective's other arm reached to protect himself from another blow.

Parnell grabbed Brewer's second arm and secured the zip tie around both wrists quickly, expertly.

Mrs. Brewer's screams turned to wailing.

"Shut up!" Parnell ordered.

She wailed louder.

Parnell stepped around Brewer's bound legs and took two long steps to reach her. He raised his gun and slammed it into the side of her head.

He didn't want to kill her. Not yet.

The blow was only hard enough to silence her. For now.

"What the hell are you doing?" Brewer yelled.

"Shut up!" Parnell yelled back.

"Leave her alone!" Brewer screamed.

Parnell found the duct tape in the duffel, tore off a piece with his teeth, and slapped it over her mouth. He tore off a second piece and slapped it over Brewer's mouth, which was opened to yell again.

The guy was a stupid asshole if nothing else. Let him lie like that for a while and see how brave he was.

With the two of them silenced, Parnell found the smaller syringes he'd stashed in his breast pocket. A fast-acting anesthetic that would keep them both sedated while he searched the house. He injected Brewer first. Then the bitch.

He waited less than a minute for both to succumb. And then he dragged them from the kitchen, down the short hallway into a bedroom.

He checked the windows, which were locked, and closed the shades. He used two more zip ties to bind Mrs. Brewer's hands and feet. He checked their carotid pulses. Slow and steady.

They should remain sedated long enough.

He left the lights off, closed the bedroom door, and began his search.

Nine million dollars. It shouldn't be hard to find that much cash in a place this size. He'd start with the basement because that's where he would have hidden the money. Away from prying eyes of all types.

Parnell found the stairs to the basement behind a closed door off the landing where he'd entered the house. He searched briefly for a light switch but didn't find one. He turned on his flashlight, pointed it toward the wooden staircase, and trudged down into the oppressive damp.

At the bottom of the stairs was a naked bulb on the ceiling with a long pull cord. He yanked on it. Instantly, blinding light flooded his pupils. The bulb's light coned from the source to the floor like a theater spotlight. Outside the cone of light, the basement remained as black as a cave.

He shined the flashlight into the abyss toward the ceiling. Similar bulbs spaced ten feet apart dotted the floor joists overhead. Carefully, he advanced from one bulb to the next, averting his eyes when he pulled each cord.

When light was flowing from eight bulbs, the full basement was illuminated. It resembled a dungeon. A hole in the ground covered by a dwelling. The house was built in 1920, so the basement must have been dug by hand. The dirt walls and dirt floor suggested it had once been a root cellar. Or maybe illegal booze was stored here during prohibition.

Lawn furniture was piled in the South corner. Two stacks of empty terra-cotta flower pots probably held annuals on the patio during the summer.

The air was damp, cold, and musty. Nothing of value could be stored here for a long time without damage.

No doors lead to additional rooms. No large cabinets. A few plastic boxes were stacked along the north wall. Boxes too small to store nine million dollars.

No windows. No plumbing. A thick layer of dust covered everything, indicating that Mrs. Brewer rarely cleaned here. No wonder. The place was downright creepy. And it was as quiet as a tomb.

Parnell grinned. "Perfect."

He moved two of the lawn chairs into the center of the basement, one behind the other. He placed each chair directly under a separate bulb, and inside the cone of light it threw onto the floor. He trudged up the stairs and returned to the back bedroom.

When he opened the door and flipped on the lights, Detective and Mrs. Brewer were still unconscious. He grabbed her ankles and dragged her down the hallway to the basement stairs. He considered pushing her down, but he figured Brewer was more likely to cooperate if his wife was still alive.

Parnell changed his position and grabbed Mrs. Brewer's wrists to lift her head. He dragged her down the stairs, legs and feet flopping hard down each step. Damn, the bitch was heavy.

At the bottom, he dragged her across the dirt floor to one of the lawn chairs. He secured her ankles to the chair's legs and her wrists to the chair's arms. Her head flopped forward onto her chest. He left it there and headed back up the rickety stairs.

He dragged Brewer the same way and secured him to the chair in the center of the room facing away from his wife.

Once they were both settled, Parnell pulled all the cords and extinguished the lights one at a time until the dungeon was once again in total darkness. Light spilled down the stairs, and he followed it up. At the landing, he closed the door and slid the deadbolt into place.

If they woke up before he finished searching the house, they could scream their heads off behind that duct tape down there, and no one would hear them. Served them right.

Searching the house didn't take long. Nine million dollars in cash was harder to use than many people realized. It could not be deposited in the bank or used to buy money orders or other negotiable instruments. Any effort like that would trigger the bank's federal reporting requirements, which would require specific identification and lead to the obvious questions. Such as, where did the money come from? How did the depositor come to possess it? Was it drug money? And on and on.

If nine million dollars in cash was hard to spend, it was harder to smuggle out of the country. Airports, cruise ships, trains, and buses ran luggage through x-ray machines that would identify the cash immediately by the metal strips embedded in each bill. And all shipping containers were inspected.

Even driving the money across the border in a truck was problematic. Nine million dollars in cash, even assuming the entire amount consisted of $100 bills, and depending on how it was packaged, would take up a significant amount of space. The three-by-six closet at the Dakota must have been stuffed almost to the ceiling. Nine million dollars would fill nine large duffel

222 | DIANE CAPRI

bags, which would be a lot of luggage for a single passenger on any commercial flight. Border guards could be bribed, but men who accepted bribes were inherently untrustworthy, and Nitro Mack Parnell trusted no one.

Brewer was a New York City police detective. Which should have meant that none of the illegal methods of removing the money from the country would be necessary because he shouldn't have the money or the need to move it.

Parnell shrugged. He was a two-star general retired from the U.S. Army after a distinguished career. Many people would say the same about him.

Brewer's record looked fairly clean for a cop who had been on the job twenty years. But not squeaky clean enough. Brewer took the money, and he knew where it was. Before Parnell left this house, Brewer would give it up. One way or another.

CHAPTER THIRTY-TWO

PARNELL STARTED HIS SEARCH on the second floor this time. It was the next best place to hide contraband, after the basement. He trotted up the staircase, which ran from the living room to the center of a short hallway upstairs. Two bedrooms and one shared bath between them were located on this floor, according to the real estate tax records.

He saw three doors, all closed. One on either side of the hallway and one at the end. He opened the doors and turned on the lights briefly in each of the three rooms. All were tidy and furnished as they should have been. Each bedroom had a large closet. The bathroom contained a small linen closet. A total of six places his nine million dollars could have been stored. A total of six places where he didn't find it.

Would Brewer have stored that much stolen cash on the first floor of his home? Unlikely. Parnell already knew the money was not in the garage. Which only left the first floor, the one Brewer and his wife spent most of their time in, was the last place to look.

Parnell completed a thorough search in less than ten minutes.

When he finished, his patience was gone. He searched through the kitchen drawers until he found the implements he needed and made his way back to the basement.

He could smell their fear wafting up the stairs from the dungeon. The foul odor grew stronger and put a spring in his step as he descended. At the bottom of the stairs, the stench was overwhelming. He smiled. *You ain't seen nothing yet, Detective Brewer.*

He walked toward Brewer, averted his eyes, reached up, and yanked the cord above Brewer's head. The light erupted from the single bulb like a lighthouse beacon at ten feet instead of ten miles.

Brewer had not expected the assault on his retinas. He jerked back, squeezed his eyes shut, and emitted a strangled scream. Coupled with the effects of the sedative, he must have felt a knife-like pain shoot through his skull, front to back, ricocheting a few times.

The mental image pleased Parnell no end.

He waited until Brewer calmed down enough to focus. "Detective Brewer."

Brewer's eyes rounded, his eyebrows shot up, and his nostrils flared. To his credit, he made no further noises.

"You have something that belongs to me. I've searched the entire premises, and my property is not here." Parnell raised the items he had foraged from the kitchen. A chef's knife in one hand and a potato peeler in the other.

He watched as Brewer's battered brain registered the implements.

"Make no mistake. You will tell me where to find my property." Parnell tilted his head to the left, slightly behind Brewer and outside the cone of light. "Your wife is sitting there, in the dark. She can see and hear you. If you fail to answer my question, you will hear her screams, I promise you."

Sweat popped out on Brewer's forehead and dripped down his temples. A strangled cry escaped through the duct tape and his face reddened with outrage.

"There are two ways to do things, Detective Brewer. The easy way, which is where you simply tell me what I want to know. Do it immediately, and we're done here."

Parnell paused and pressed his lips together and pointed his head toward Mrs. Brewer sitting in the darkness. "Or we can do this the hard way. Surely you realize that the easy way is preferable. Would you like a brief demonstration to help you decide?"

Brewer made the wrong choice. His chest rose with a deep inhale. His face flushed darker crimson. Defiant noises erupted from his throat behind the duct tape.

"That's fine." Parnell shrugged again. "If she was my wife, I would probably have made the same decision. She's such a cow. And cows should be slaughtered. I totally agree."

Parnell stepped outside the light where Brewer could no longer see him. As he walked through the darkness toward her, he said, "Mary, you've been listening to my conversation with your husband, haven't you? You know this is not my decision. It seems he doesn't care about you as much as he cares about my money. After all the years you've been together. Sad, don't you think?"

He stopped within arm's reach of her. Quickly, his hand darted forward and slapped her. Hard. The sound rang out through the quiet dirt pit. A startled scream of shock and pain was held back by the duct tape across her mouth. Parnell grabbed a corner of the tape and yanked. She screamed again, and he slapped her a second time.

Three blows. How long would Brewer let her suffer? The entire business was distasteful, to say the least. Nitro Mack Parnell wasn't a sadist. He derived no pleasure from torture. But he knew its value, even if the politicians disagreed.

When her screams subsided, Mary Brewer began to sob. Much better. Sobbing women made their men more pliable than defiant ones in Parnell's experience.

"Mary, your husband stole nine million dollars from me." Her eyes widened even as the sobbing continued. "Yes, that's a lot of money. My colleague left my money safely stored in a vault inside his home. Your husband took it. I've searched your house, and my money is not here. I want your husband to tell me where it is."

He paused a few moments to let the problem sink into her muddled thinking.

"I'm going to give him another chance to make the right decision here, Mary. But if he doesn't, I'll be back in a moment." Parnell pulled a tissue from his pocket and wiped her nose. He dropped the tissue on the ground. "Do you have anything you want to say to your husband? Perhaps you'd like to ask him to answer my questions. Otherwise, Mary, I'm afraid this isn't going to work out very well for you. You understand I'll have no other options."

Mrs. Brewer nodded vigorously. Parnell waited while she summoned her nerve.

"Greg, honey." When she spoke, her voice was deep and sexy, and the mystery of their relationship fell immediately into place. Parnell imagined she must have been attractive enough as a young woman. Hormones raging, young Private Brewer must have been smitten from the first hello. "Greg? If you know where his money is, for the love of God, please tell him."

Parnell nodded. So she didn't know. She didn't know anything about the money or what Brewer had done with it. Which made the situation simpler. No point in pressing her for information she did not possess.

"Thank you, Mary." Parnell replaced the duct tape across her mouth and patted it gently into place. "If your husband does as you've asked, your ordeal will be over."

In the darkness, he couldn't see the gentle tears that leaked from her eyes, but he knew they were there. What a shame. Why did women make such lousy choices in men?

Parnell stood outside the cone of light while Brewer worked things through for himself.

Brewer was no stooge. He'd been regular Army long ago, and then NYPD. Which meant he was good when he entered the police academy and even better when he came out. He rose through the ranks to detective, a position he'd held for several years.

In short, Brewer was well trained and seasoned. He was not a fool. And he was desperate.

The combination was dangerous. Brewer was a worthy enemy, and Parnell never underestimated his enemies.

When he judged Brewer had had enough time to work things out, Parnell moved into the cone of light and stood where Brewer could see him. A career officer who knew what to do. A man who had ordered thousands of soldiers into battles too many had not survived. Because it had to be done.

Parnell was respectful of Brewer's skills, but not afraid of him. Not in the least. All of which General Nitro Mack Parnell conveyed with a single stare and assurance of the outcome. *Bring it on if you dare.*

Brewer raised his head and looked directly into Parnell's flat gaze, a stare Brewer recognized. He simply nodded, acknowledging defeat and a willingness to cooperate.

Parnell said, "Wise decision, Detective Brewer. I advise you not to try anything stupid. Give me my property, and this will end."

Brewer nodded again. Parnell stepped forward and yanked the tape from his mouth. Brewer worked his jaw and wet his lips with his tongue. He cleared his throat as if he couldn't quite get words past his voice box.

"Don't make me ask the question again," Parnell said. His words, or perhaps his tone, triggered Mary's whimpering and quiet sobs from behind Brewer in the dark.

Brewer's eyes narrowed when he responded. "Hear me out. I don't have your money, and I don't know where it is." He must have sensed Parnell's instant rage, because he rushed on. "But I know who knows."

Parnell's hands fisted at his sides, struggling to tamp the fire inside. "I'm listening."

"Her name is Lauren Pauling. Retired FBI. She and Reacher worked it out." Brewer took a breath. "I don't know what they agreed to. I wasn't there. But I know she took the money from the apartment. What she did with it after that, I can't say."

Parnell stared at Brewer for two full seconds and judged him to be speaking the truth as far as he knew it.

Scavo had said Brewer or Reacher.

Brewer had blamed Reacher without prompting.

Reacher. Again. Everything came back to him. Where was the bastard?

Maybe Reacher was with Pauling. Maybe not. But Brewer didn't have the nine million dollars and didn't know where it was. That much, Parnell believed.

Which was too bad, actually.

"Where is Pauling now?"

"I haven't seen her in at least a year. She has an office on Fourth Street. I'd start there."

Parnell nodded. "See? The easy way is always best."

In one fluid motion that he'd practiced a million times, he reached into his deep coat pocket and pulled out his gun, already fitted with a sound suppressor.

He lifted his arm in a slow, deliberate arc and pointed the barrel directly at the center of Brewer's forehead.

He shot two muffled rounds that hit slightly above the bridge of Brewer's nose, killing him instantly.

Mary's gasp followed the shots.

Parnell walked around to her chair, turned his head aside, and pulled the chain over her head. The light flooded down and blinded her temporarily. Half a moment later, she was dead. She never saw it coming.

Parnell patted Brewer's pockets to locate his cell phone. He rolled through the contact list until he found a number for Lauren Pauling. He dropped the phone into his pocket.

Parnell pulled both cords to return the dungeon to darkness. He turned on his flashlight and followed the beam up the wooden stairs. At the top, he closed and bolted the basement door.

He replaced his items into the duffel and let himself out. He closed the steel door as well as possible. The storm door would conceal the damage from casual observers, which should suffice for a while.

Five minutes later, Parnell was seated in the rental car, on the road to the city.

Lauren Pauling wasn't likely to be in her office at this hour. Within twenty minutes, he'd know where to find her.

CHAPTER THIRTY-THREE

Friday, January 14
4:10 a.m.
New York City

PARNELL KEPT BREWER'S PHONE because it was the easiest and fastest way to find Pauling, although carrying Brewer's cell phone dormant in his pocket was like wearing a bull's-eye on his chest.

Cell phones were routinely monitored, as even the general public was aware because of the damn TrueLeaks crap over the past few years. Many of his fellow citizens seemed shocked and appalled by the practice.

Most civilians either didn't know what to do or didn't bother. Which meant cell phones were constantly sending and receiving signals from cell towers and those signals were easily exploited.

Parnell considered the monitoring prudent and part of the national defense effort.

But it was damned inconvenient at the moment.

Cloning phones was beyond his expertise, and he didn't trust hackers to do it for him. Instead, he employed simple evasive maneuvers. He used throwaway phones. He paid cash and never bought phones from the same place twice. He never carried the same phone for more than a single day, and he kept that one turned off whenever possible.

Which meant that as soon as someone with rudimentary expertise started looking, Parnell was at risk every moment that Brewer's phone remained in his pocket.

But it couldn't be helped until he found Pauling and dealt with her. Sooner was better. Scavo could wait a bit longer.

Pauling was a private investigator, licensed by the state and the city. He could find her address online.

He needed a computer for that. Scavo's laptop was in the trunk.

He ignored the risks associated with that decision, too. It was the fastest alternative.

He needed an internet connection. Public internet was another risk he'd need to take. As he left Brewer's neighborhood, he scanned for a public place with free Wi-Fi still open at this hour.

Ten miles later, he parked in the lot of an all-night gas station that catered to truckers. The attached sandwich shop served twenty-four-seven-three-sixty-five, the sign said. Another sign said free Wi-Fi with purchase.

He ordered black coffee and requested the password.

"Here you go, Pops." The bored hipster behind the counter handed over a receipt for the coffee with the password printed at the bottom.

Parnell gritted his teeth and didn't slap the little pierced and tattooed snot.

He carried the coffee and password to a small table and set up the laptop. He connected to the state licensing database instantly. Not much internet traffic on the site at this hour. Good. He searched Lauren Pauling Investigations and found what he needed right away. He made a note of the business address and phone number.

Next, he entered her personal telephone number from Brewer's list of cell phone contacts into a search engine. The number popped up on the screen after a fraction of a second.

Pauling's area code placed the number in New York City. After that, his luck ran out. No name or fixed address attached to the number, according to the search results.

Parnell checked the number, again and again, using several browsers, with the same result.

He attacked the problem from a different angle. He tried searching for cell providers. Three websites listed Pauling's number as a personal cell phone, but no additional data. No name, no billing information, no provider identification.

All of which meant that Pauling was not one of those careless civilians who ignored the reality of cell phone tracking.

He nodded. Props to Pauling. He enjoyed a clever adversary, even as she thwarted his immediate goal. Because he would prevail. He always did.

Parnell would have continued with more sophisticated searches but he happened to glimpse the television screen mounted on the wall across from his seat. The sound was muted, which was okay. All he needed to see was the looming image of the Dakota and read the crawler across the bottom of the screen, which was not okay.

He scowled and pursed his lips to suppress the string of curses he wanted to bellow. The crawler said police had discovered a mutilated body in one of the apartments a few hours ago. The victim's identity was withheld pending notification of the family.

Parnell already knew who the dead man was. Someone would learn soon enough that the owner's fictitious brother-in-law was the likely prime suspect. It was just a matter of time and much less time than he'd expected.

Every moment he stayed in the city with Brewer's phone in his pocket increased his risk to unacceptable levels. He closed the laptop and returned to his rental. The plan was still simple.

Find Pauling. Eliminate her. Destroy Brewer's phone. Do it fast.

He paused when his hand pushed the key into the ignition.

Find Pauling.

Do it fast.

How?

Think it through.

Pauling would not be in her office at this hour.

If she rented her apartment, her name might not appear in any local databases.

However, if she owned any sort of real estate interest, the city of New York would collect taxes. Which could mean that she was listed in the real estate databases.

He returned to the sandwich shop and fired up the laptop again. This time, he pulled up real estate records for the city. He searched last name first and returned three pages of Paulings organized by a multiple digit tax ID without names. He searched that list for Lauren Pauling and came up empty. When he searched for Pauling, L., three tax ID numbers populated the screen.

Two of the properties were in Queens. The third was a

transfer to a shareholder for a co-op on Barrow Street in Manhattan. He figured most single women without children would prefer to live in the city. Parnell made note of the address and closed down the laptop and left the coffee shop again.

The digital clock on the dash of the rental car now reflected 4:40 a.m. Many New Yorkers were night owls. By law, bars could serve only until 4:00 a.m. Pauling could be a partier. Or an insomniac. Either way, she should be home by now.

He could be at her place in half an hour. Sooner was better. He started the rental and rolled into the street.

New York might be the city that never sleeps, but it definitely slowed after hours. Many New Yorkers never drove anywhere, even if they could. He ran into very little traffic, by New York standards and reached Pauling's building on Barrow Street faster than he expected.

He pulled into an empty parking spot at the curb. The building was a residential co-op now. Once upon a time, it had probably been a warehouse. He guessed there were four units on each floor, more or less.

Pauling's records suggested her co-op was on the third floor. Safe bet that her share of the building's taxes was higher than the units on the lower floors.

Parnell craned his neck to look up at Pauling's windows. No lights on. Pauling was already in bed, or not home. No lights on in any of the other windows, either.

He rechecked Brewer's recent calls log. One call to Pauling, placed yesterday, early afternoon. The call lasted fifteen seconds. Long enough to leave a voicemail, but not long enough for a conversation, Parnell figured.

After that, Brewer must have been working a homicide case not involving the Dakota, because there were at least a dozen calls placed and received inside the city to various NYPD departments.

Late in the day, another call to Pauling. This one lasted three minutes.

Parnell went back to the top and scrolled through the recent calls again. He found one he'd missed on the first pass. Or maybe it was delivered late by the cell provider. Sometimes, voice mail delivery could be days late. Maybe Brewer never actually heard the message.

From Pauling, yesterday morning. The call was short.

Parnell located the message and played it back. Her voice was rough, like a lounge singer who had belted out jazz over a full ensemble in a smoky room for a couple of decades.

She did not sound like any FBI agent he had ever met. He wondered briefly what she looked like. Wrinkled and worn out, like her voice, probably.

She was returning Brewer's call. She said she was out of town. She didn't say where she was or when she'd return. From the looks of her place, she wasn't back yet.

Parnell slammed his palm onto the steering wheel. He felt the overwhelming desire to explode.

But then he realized he was finally done in the city. There was nothing else for him to do here. His money was gone. Brewer was dead. Pauling was not here.

His business here was finished.

It felt like progress

He could move on with a slight adjustment to his plan.

Scavo first. Then Pauling.

Perfect.

He turned the rental north.

Parnell headed upstate for the last time. He stopped once for gas and to grab a bite to eat. He was tired, but he felt energized at the same time. He was close. So close.

He spent the drive time formulating plans. One to handle Scavo. One for recovering his nine million dollars from Pauling. One to deal with Reacher.

Reacher stoked anger in his belly. Anger he controlled because Scavo possessed intel Parnell wanted. If he'd been ambivalent about eliminating Scavo before, that indecision had hardened to granite resolve. These hours would be the last of Scavo's life.

CHAPTER THIRTY-FOUR

Friday, January 14
6:15 a.m.
Stanwix Village, New York

THEY'D MADE GOOD TIME from JFK and arrived upstate about an hour before sunrise. The time of day between daylight and darkness when the sky is diffused and pinkish, and the sun is still below the horizon.

Gaspar had stopped only once, at a fast food place near a twenty-four-hour pharmacy immediately off the expressway. At the pharmacy, they'd picked up a few essential toiletries. Shaving supplies for him, cheap tinted lip gloss for her. Deodorant, toothpaste, and a folding toothbrush for each.

At the burger joint, they'd briefly used the public restrooms, making an effort to look more like FBI agents and less like vagrants.

Otto had splashed water on her face and peered into a mottled mirror. Even in the bad lighting, she looked like she hadn't slept for a while. In daylight, she'd scare small children if she came across any.

Her mother's Vietnamese genes had blessed her with a good complexion, and dark eyebrows and lashes, unlike her blond German dad and brothers. She could get away without much makeup. Which was a good thing, since her makeup was stuck inside her travel bag, somewhere in a Manhattan hotel.

She tidied her hair and slapped on lip gloss. Nothing would erase the circles under her eyes except sleep. Which wouldn't happen any time soon.

"Sorry kids. This is the best it's going to get."

She shrugged and rejoined Gaspar at the front counter, noting that his results were somewhat better than hers. He was better with kids than she was, too. They grabbed burgers and fries and more coffee. The whole stop sucked up thirty minutes before they got back on the road.

The rest of the drive was a straight shot. Light traffic. No tie-ups. Even the weather cooperated. The predicted snowstorm held off.

Sitting in front of Scavo's modest duplex, the rental's motor running and the heat blasting, Gaspar said, "You know the odds that we'll get anything out of this guy are slim, right?"

She nodded. Scavo's house was dark. No lights were burning inside, as far as she could tell from this vantage point.

Gaspar said, "Chances are, he never met Reacher at all. He was still in Africa when Reacher and Pauling were involved with whatever they were doing."

Otto nodded. The other half of Scavo's duplex was dark, too. Perhaps unoccupied. Or maybe both occupants were still sleeping.

Gaspar sighed. "Tell me again what you expect us to gain here?"

"Dunno. Scavo was close by. It seemed stupid to ignore him

while we chased off to confront Pauling." She shrugged.

A white panel van marked with a red cross pulled into the space ahead of the rental. A heavyset woman opened the driver's door and climbed to the ground. She carried a tote bag in her right hand. She flipped the fur-trimmed hood of her parka over her head on her way to the sidewalk leading to Scavo's home.

When she reached the stairs leading to the front steps, she held onto the wrought iron railing and climbed the concrete stoop. At the door, she stood on her toes and ran her hand above the door first, feeling along the ledge for something. A door key, probably. She pulled the storm open and grabbed the knob. Pushing the door open, she stepped inside and flipped a light on.

Otto said, "Let's go."

She stepped into the bitterly cold morning and hustled to follow the woman, assuming Gaspar would follow. At the door, she raised her hand to knock. But on a hunch, she grabbed the doorknob and turned instead.

The door was unlocked. She pushed it open and let the storm close behind her. She stepped into a wall of overwhelmingly hot, humid air.

The woman had dropped her parka and her bag on the couch. She had moved into the kitchen to make coffee.

The storm door clicked into place, and the noise caught her attention in the silence.

She looked toward the noise and gasped. Her eyes rounded to golf-ball size. "Who are you? What do you want?"

Otto reached into her pocket for her badge. "FBI Special Agent Otto Gaspar, ma'am," she said, holding the badge out where the woman could see it.

Her alarm had calmed only slightly when Gaspar came through the storm door, and she gasped again.

Before she could totally freak out, Otto said, "He's with me. Special Agent Carlos Gaspar."

The woman seemed to come down off the ceiling slightly.

"What's your name?" Otto nodded, to keep her calm more than anything else. The coffee had begun to brew. The aroma filled the small room and hung on the humidity like a blanket.

"Beth Ayers, R.N. I'm Mr. Scavo's day nurse. I come for a home visit every morning." Her face clouded over. "He's usually awake when I get here, though. I need to check on him."

"I'll come with you," Otto said. Nurse Ayers didn't seem to know how to respond to that plan. Indecision held her rooted to the spot for a few moments before she moved to the couch, collected her bag, and walked toward the back of the duplex.

Otto glanced at Gaspar, who was searching high and low for something. Opening cabinets, lifting cushions, feeling under the tables. Otto wondered what he hoped to find there. Nine million dollars in cash would be hard to miss, and it wouldn't fit in cubbies like those, either.

Perhaps he felt her eyes on him. He looked up briefly. She tilted her head toward Nurse Ayers' retreating back. He nodded.

Ayers had entered a doorway on the left. Otto unsnapped her holster, grabbed her weapon, and followed.

Otto pushed the door open wide with her left hand and immediately returned to her shooter's grip. She scanned everything, taking in the scene with a mixture of confusion and disappointment, although she wasn't sure exactly what she'd expected.

The sparsely furnished bedroom was overwhelmed by a full-sized bed. Nurse Ayers leaned over a prone figure, blocking Otto's view of his face. She stepped into the room to make a positive ID on Scavo.

She stood behind Nurse Ayers, who was busy working on her patient. She knew Scavo had been through hell. She hadn't expected him to look like his passport photo and his last army photo. But she wasn't prepared for the skeletal head resting on Scavo's pillow. Otto had seen many cadavers that looked better.

Scavo wasn't conscious. Ayers spoke to him, and he didn't respond. The blankets over his body moved as he breathed, but barely.

Whatever was going on with Scavo, she had nothing to fear from him. Or from Ayers. She returned her weapon. A quick scan of the bedroom revealed no threats and nothing of interest. She left Ayers to her work.

Back in the main room of the duplex, Gaspar had poured coffee and was seated at the kitchen table. He raised his eyebrows in question. She shook her head. He nodded.

Ten minutes later, Nurse Ayers returned with her bag. "I gave him a sedative. He's resting comfortably."

"What's wrong with him?" Gaspar asked.

"I'm not authorized to talk about his medical care, but honestly, I couldn't tell you anything anyway. The doctors don't really know." Nurse Ayers shook her head.

"Has he been bedridden like that very long?" Otto asked.

"No. He was awake and moving around when I came yesterday." Nurse Ayers frowned as if an unpleasant truth had popped into her mind. "He's quite a bit worse today. Something unusual must have happened."

"Such as what?" Otto asked.

She shook her head. "I have no idea. Most of the time, he's pretty quiet. He watches television. He talks to his neighbor next door, but Mr. Brown is off visiting family this week. I can't imagine why Mr. Scavo is so much worse."

"We're working on an important case, Mrs. Ayers. We don't need a lot of his time, but we do need to talk with him for a few minutes. It's important," Otto said.

Ayers shook her head. "He's not going to be talking at all for at least a few hours. Not until that sedative wears off. You'll have to come back later, I'm afraid."

Gaspar carried the coffee cups to the sink and rinsed them out. "Does he have many visitors?"

"I know he doesn't have any family." She cocked her head and closed her eyes to think about it. "No visitors that I know of, now that you ask. He's never mentioned anyone, and I've never seen anyone here."

Gaspar gave Otto a quick glance before he said, "Well, we'll let you finish your work. We'll come back later after he wakes up."

Otto took the hint. She handed Ayers a card. "If you think of anyone else who might know more about Mr. Scavo, would you give me a call?"

Nurse Ayers didn't agree, but she didn't say no, either.

"Thank you," Gaspar said on his way to the door.

Otto followed him out. They returned to the rental, shivering until the heat warmed the SUV's interior. Gaspar pulled around Ayers's car and continued down the block and rolled onto the road.

"What did you find when you were searching for bugs?" Otto asked.

"Nothing. But I did leave a couple. We can hear what, if anything, is going on in there," he replied. He found the app on his phone that was connected to the bugs and their wireless recording transmitters and showed it to her.

She looked at the flat lines indicating that no one was talking about anything inside the duplex. "That'll save us a trip back, I guess. But we've learned nothing here."

"Except that whatever Scavo did yesterday that wiped him out, he couldn't have traveled to the Dakota and killed Simon Peck," Gaspar said.

"Right. He'd have died trying." She swiped a palm across her face. "Let's head back to JFK and catch the next flight to Palm Beach."

"Your wish is my command," he replied. "But can we stop for breakfast first?"

She smiled. Gaspar had his idiosyncrasies, but he was predictable.

CHAPTER THIRTY-FIVE

Friday, January 14
8:50 a.m.
Palm Beach

OTTO AND GASPAR SHOULD arrive today. Pauling was as ready as she could get.

She'd spent several hours last night learning everything about these two. She understood FBI agents and the department where they thrived. She'd lived in that world for a long time. She'd trained too many agents like them over the years. She knew how they worked, how they viewed the world.

What she needed to know could only be learned after they arrived.

They had unusual resumes, to be sure.

Otto was a star. The Director was grooming her for bigger things.

Gaspar was a charity case. His best days were behind him.

Pairing them felt like one of Cooper's typical Machiavellian moves. Which it probably was.

Yet, sending them on an unapproved hunt for Reacher, off the books and constantly below the radar, was far beyond typical. Even for Cooper. She hadn't believed it until the truth was confirmed by sources she trusted. Which took most of the night to accomplish.

Reacher was an off-the-books guy, too. But Pauling had expected to find some mention of him in government files somewhere.

"Government secrets" had to be one of the biggest oxymorons on any planet.

Bureaucrats could be divided into two classes. Paper producers and paper chasers. Everything, absolutely everything, was reported, recorded, and stashed—in triplicate—where somebody, somewhere, could find it. She should know. She'd spent two decades of her life on one end or the other of that continuum.

Still, she'd done a thorough search and found nothing mentioning Reacher at all. Not since he left the Army. Not so much as a whisper. Even his army pension records, which did exist, were behind a thick wall of classification that no one she'd asked could penetrate.

Not until she had exhausted every avenue had she accepted the only possible answer. His name had been systematically eliminated. From anywhere and everywhere. Quite a feat. She hadn't believed such a thing was even remotely possible.

But it had been done. What was it that Sherlock Holmes always said? When you eliminated the impossible, whatever remains must be the truth. Words she'd lived by for way too long to ignore them now.

And after all mentions of Reacher had been deleted, Otto and Gaspar were assigned to dig into his background to fill in the gaps in his resume since his discharge.

The pretext for their assignment was believable, on the surface. The Special Personnel Task Force existed. Otto and Gaspar had both worked cases there in the past.

But that was where plausibility ended.

No one could have a government file as clean as Reacher's was. No one born after 1900, anyway. Since 9/11, every sneeze and belch of every beating heart in the country was recorded somewhere by someone. Once recorded, stored forever.

Pauling didn't like it. Not at all.

Someone with enough juice to pull off an impossible feat like that was a man to be feared. Who was that man?

Only a few candidates existed. When she ran through the very short list in her head, she rejected them all.

Every government file mentioning Jack (none) Reacher could not have been created with disappearing ink. That was simply impossible.

She had no choice but to acknowledge the truth. One of the men on her short list had done this.

Which was as bewildering as it was shocking.

The only remaining question was *why*?

She guessed the time, and then looked at her watch. Her guess was ten minutes off. "Damn! How does Reacher *do* that?"

A second later, her doorbell rang.

She smiled. "Maybe now I can find out."

CHAPTER THIRTY-SIX

Friday, January 14
9:45 a.m.
Upstate New York

OTTO'S EXHAUSTION FINALLY OVERCAME her inability
to sleep in moving vehicles, and she'd managed an hour's nap
while Gaspar drove south. She awakened when the rental slowed
to exit the freeway.

"Good morning, Sunshine," Gaspar said with a grin.

She glanced at the snow-covered hills and a few low
buildings in the distance. "Where are we?"

"Breakfast. Where else?" He pointed ahead. "And not a
burger joint, as you requested."

"Great." She checked her watch first, and then the Boss's
phone. He hadn't called. Which was curious because he had to
know they didn't board the plane to Palm Beach. She dropped
the phone into her pocket.

They'd traveled more than one hundred miles before Gaspar
found the chain restaurant. A country themed place with a store

full of local crafts and tchotchkes on one side and a big porch with rocking chairs out front.

The parking lot was busy, which Otto figured was a good sign. Gaspar drove through the lot and around the building before he spied a car with its backup lights on.

"Anything showing on that app yet?" He asked as he waited for the car to pull out.

Otto checked his phone. "No. But it's still early. I doubt Scavo has slept off that sedative yet."

They went inside, used the restrooms, and joined the line at the hostess station. When they were finally seated inside, and the waiter had taken their orders, Otto asked, "Did you find anything else interesting while you were checking Scavo's place on your hands and knees with a magnifying glass?"

"No need to exaggerate. I didn't have a magnifying glass. Didn't need one with these peepers." He touched the corner of his eye with a forefinger, and she grinned in spite of herself.

The waiter brought coffee and left an insulated jug on the table when he rushed off.

"Found a few anomalies." Gaspar leaned forward, forearms on the table, to talk without being overheard. "The guy had no phone in the house."

Otto shrugged. "No land line phone is pretty common these days."

"I mean no phone of any kind. No land line. No cell phone. No walkie-talkie, even. Nothing." He paused a moment and lifted his coffee cup as if she wasn't firing on all cylinders and needed caffeine to wake up her brain. "Which I'd call pretty damned odd for a guy in his condition. He might need to call emergency services at any hour of the day or night. How's he going to do that?"

"Or maybe he had a cell phone with him. I keep mine with me all the time. So do you."

Gaspar narrowed his gaze. "You went into the bedroom. Did you see a phone of any kind in there?"

She closed her eyelids to visualize Scavo lying almost comatose on his bed. "No."

Gaspar nodded, but to his credit, didn't smirk. "Also, no computer, no tablet, nothing that would allow him to use the internet and reach the outside world."

Otto cocked her head. "That is odd these days, I guess."

"Damned odd." Gaspar raised one eyebrow. "Especially since he had a strong and fast Wi-Fi signal inside the duplex. I checked. Why have Wi-Fi available if you have nothing to access it with? What's the point of that?"

"Okay." He'd snagged her full attention. "What else?"

"The television and cable box were unplugged and disconnected from the wall. But the prongs on the connectors had marked up both outlets, like they'd been plugged in a few times by a guy with the shakes who couldn't find the insertion points. If plugging and unplugging was such a struggle, why were they unplugged today?"

"Maybe he's just paranoid about being watched or something," Otto said thoughtfully. "All of those devices are well-known monitoring opportunities. There's thousands of examples in the new TrueLeaks documents, for one thing, and that's been all over the news lately."

"Only way he'd be unaware is if he'd landed here from another planet this morning. Which we know he did not." Gaspar slumped back into his chair, looking at her as if he expected answers, which he must have realized she couldn't give. "Where is our food? Did they have to wait for the hens to lay the eggs or what?"

"The place is busy. You won't starve." She refilled her coffee and his. "Were you able to get one of your listening devices into the bedroom?"

"Close enough. We should be okay." He frowned. "Seemed like he doesn't get many visitors. Could take a while."

The waiter, a round tray hefted onto his shoulder, stopped at another table to drop off something and then brought their breakfast and a fresh pot of coffee. She'd ordered one egg and toast. Gaspar had ordered everything on the menu. Or at least, that's how the table looked after the waiter unloaded the tray.

"Anything else I can get you?" he asked.

Otto smiled. "You mean you've still got food in the kitchen?"

He frowned as if she'd spoken in tongues. "I'm sorry?"

She didn't explain. "Is there a shopping mall close by?"

His frown cleared immediately and he nodded. "Just about five miles further south right off the interstate. It's an outlet mall. Fifty stores. Opens at ten on Fridays."

He reached into his back pocket and pulled out a four-by-six-inch postcard and placed it on the table. He pointed to the small map at the bottom. "You can't miss it. Watch for the signs. Keep that with you. We've got plenty."

Otto nodded. "Thank you."

Gaspar had cleared one of the small plates before the guy scurried off. "We're going shopping?"

She nodded again. "And then we're going to find a hotel so I can get a shower. I'm sick of these clothes. I feel like I've wrestled a pig in a mud bath."

"Well, that's a little harsh. I wouldn't have put it quite that way. But now that you mention it…" He wrinkled his nose and sniffed loudly.

She rolled her eyes. "You don't smell all that great yourself, Cheech."

Gaspar laughed. "Let's say we spend a couple of hours and do all of that. Then what?"

"I'll let you know when I figure it out," she replied.

CHAPTER THIRTY-SEVEN

Friday, January 14
11:18 a.m.
Stanwix Village, New York

WHEN PARNELL PULLED UP to the curb in front of Scavo's duplex, it was well after eleven o'clock. He hurried to the door. He ran his fingers across the molding above the door and found a key right where Scavo said he'd hid the spare. He stomped the snow off his boots and stepped through to the oppressive humidity inside.

Scavo shuffled from his bedroom to the kitchen, wearing an oxygen cannula, and pulling a rolling cylinder. He nodded toward Parnell on his way to the sink, where he swallowed a handful of pills he'd dumped into his palm from a case on the counter. He opened the refrigerator for a bottle of water and shoved it into the pocket of his sweatpants. Then, he rummaged until he found a red plastic coffee tub, and set the machine to brew.

Parnell watched but said nothing.

The coffee finished. Scavo poured the hot liquid into two plastic mugs and carried them to the table. He pushed one toward Parnell and sat heavily in the same chair he'd occupied before. He drank about a third of the coffee and cleared his throat.

"Sorry to keep you waiting so long, General," Scavo rasped. "Some days are better than others for me. Today's a bad one."

"Tell me what I need to know, and I'll leave you in peace."

"Yes, I think we should." Scavo nodded. "Do you know what the Panama Papers are?"

"What?" Parnell growled. "I haven't been living under a rock, Scavo."

"Tell me what you know." Scavo closed his eyes to listen as if the visual noise was too loud.

"Confidential documents were stolen from a Panamanian law firm a couple of years back. Made a big splash, worldwide." Parnell recited the facts like a schoolboy being tested on his math tables. "Important people, some legitimate and some not, were exposed. Assets parked in shell companies throughout the Caribbean and Latin America."

"Placing assets in an offshore shell company is not illegal, although, for some politicians and celebrities, it became embarrassing." Scavo nodded, eyes still closed. "Conducting or concealing tax evasion, money laundering, and other illegal activities in shell companies *is* a big problem."

"And this is relevant to me how?" Parnell said, his patience exhausted.

Scavo stopped to drink the coffee, which seemed to soothe his throat. "When I persuaded the Colonel to tell me where he'd hidden the bulk of his money, he said only that I would never find it."

"Yes?"

He opened his eyes, and his voice was stronger when he continued. "But it was the way he said it. He was absolutely certain. No doubt at all in his mind. Well, it got me thinking, you know?"

Parnell asked, slowly. "Where could he hide that much money securely forever?"

"The answer had to be outside the country. Banking laws here are draconian." Scavo said. "The money wasn't all strictly legal when the Colonel received it. And he didn't want to lose any to taxes or penalties. And mainly, he didn't want anyone nosing around his business."

"Which led you to believe he'd created an off-shore shell company." Parnell would have come to the same conclusion. Sooner or later.

"When I went to the Dakota, I searched for anything that might have pointed me in the right direction. I found the vault. I knew how the Colonel's mind worked, so figuring out the combination lock wasn't difficult. The moment I saw all those bales of money. Knowing he'd been paid for that West African job." Scavo stopped. His face and ears were bright red. His eyes were furious. "Blood money. That's what it was. I paid for that money with five long years of my life in that hell hole."

The coughing began again. After a few minutes, he managed to get himself under control, but the episode had weakened him.

He closed his eyes briefly. Deep lines etched his pale, gaunt face. "I knew the Colonel wasn't coming back from London."

"How did you know?"

Scavo's flat brown eyes stared at Parnell. "I knew. Just leave it at that."

Parnell nodded slightly. The Colonel must be dead. He'd assumed as much.

"So I thought I had plenty of time to figure things out."

Scavo drank more coffee, which once again strengthened his voice. "I left the nine million in the safe, and I took everything I could find that might help me locate the rest. At that time, I only knew about his twenty million. I didn't know about your money. I found that later."

Parnell said nothing.

"I had an appointment to get my cough evaluated the next day. They found whatever this thing is that I became infected with at that wretched prison. They told me the prognosis was bad. Every word they spoke to me just made me more furious." Scavo drew a long breath. Another. A third. He calmed himself by the sixth. "They sent me to a hospital here for more tests. My health situation was deteriorating fast. And then I learned about the Panama Papers."

"You're saying there's a connection between my money and the law firm whose files were stolen?"

Scavo nodded. "The shell corporations exposed by that whistleblower were established with false identities. The Colonel set up two corporations. One for his assets, and one for yours. The money is stashed in the British Virgin Islands."

Parnell cocked his head. Scavo was smarter than any of the OSC fighters he'd met before, clearly. "How did you find the accounts, given the false identities?"

"That was the problem. If the Colonel had been available, of course, I would have simply beat the information out of him. Gladly." Scavo's smile suggested he'd have been happy to try.

"But he wasn't available. And he never would be," Parnell said.

Scavo nodded. "When the Panama Papers were published by media worldwide, the actual names of the law firm's clients were exposed."

"So you got lucky. You found the Colonel's name on the list." Parnell nodded. "That led you to the false identities and the shell corporations. You found both accounts and all of the money."

Scavo nodded. "It would have been easy to, shall we say, liberate the assets. Except for one thing."

"You weren't physically able to do it."

"The only thing I could do was wait. I knew you would come eventually." He grimaced. "If I lived long enough, I'd be here when you showed up."

Parnell considered everything he'd said so far for a moment. "How does Reacher fit into all of this?"

"That was the craziest thing." Scavo shook his head as if he was still bewildered. "I was living in some shack on the outside of this nowhere town because I could get the medical stuff I needed free at the local VA. I get a package delivered to my front door by a private messenger service. It's a box full of money. And a note telling me that I now own this place here." He waved an open palm around his palace." And a driver will pick me up in an hour to bring me home. The note says everything is compliments of the Colonel. The typed signature at the end was J. Reacher."

"But you didn't believe the Colonel took care of you?"

"Not a chance." Scavo laughed and coughed for a long time and spent a few moments to compose himself afterward. "So the driver brings me here. The place is furnished the way you see it now. Stocked with food. Clean clothes in the closet. And that's that."

Parnell cocked his head. "You think Reacher's involved?"

"I don't know what to think. I mean, I never met the guy. But later, when I heard that the nine million was missing from the Dakota, I thought Brewer took it. He had access to the apartment. But no way would he have helped me out. I doubt he has any idea who I am."

Scavo stopped to wet his vocal chords with more coffee and wheeze a few times. "On the other hand, Reacher had the combination to the vault. He'd worked for the Colonel. He was a soldier. He might have done it. Taken the money and helped me. I wouldn't have done it for him if our situations were reversed."

Parnell considered the points. He didn't respond.

Scavo drained his coffee. "Which one would you send the thank-you note to?"

Parnell shrugged. "Could go either way."

"I agree. Brewer had access. He could more easily have hidden the cash and use it more effectively. He's the logical bet."

Parnell nodded again. Reacher probably died a while ago. Brewer said Pauling took the money. She'd used Reacher's name when she helped Scavo. Had to be.

"What about Lauren Pauling?" Parnell asked.

Scavo shook his head. He frowned. "Who's Lauren Pauling?"

"You don't know her?"

"Should I?"

"Former FBI turned private investigator. A friend of Reacher's."

"Sorry. Never heard of her."

Parnell shrugged. "Have you contacted the banks?"

"It's better if you do it. They'll be less suspicious," Scavo said. "Your name is on one of the accounts. Mine isn't."

"Makes sense," Parnell said.

Scavo pushed himself upright and shuffled over to the refrigerator. He opened the freezer and pushed a few freezer bags aside. He pulled out a frozen pepperoni pizza.

He brought the box to the table and slid it toward Parnell. "My mother's still alive. And I have a sister. They're in Minnesota. They don't need a lot of money. If you give me your word that you'll take care of them, the rest is yours."

Parnell pulled the tape away from the box and looked inside. Documents. "What's this?"

"Everything you need to find what you're looking for." Scavo seemed extremely tired now. He closed his eyes again, and his chin dropped as if he was already asleep.

Parnell nodded. "What about you?"

"I won't be alive long enough to worry about it, General. Whatever is wrong with me is eating me alive. Surely, that's obvious." A grim smile slashed Scavo's gaunt features. "Now that you're ready to go, I don't expect I'll suffer much longer. Which is fine with me."

Parnell didn't reply.

Scavo made his way very slowly back to his bedroom. Parnell gave him time to settle into sleep while he reviewed the documents in the pizza box. He smiled. Scavo had been thorough.

Half an hour later, Parnell grabbed a heavy throw pillow from the cheap sofa. He followed Scavo back to his bedroom.

He held the pillow in place for a full five minutes until he was sure Scavo had stopped breathing forever.

Parnell removed the pillow to confirm.

Scavo's ghastly face looked no worse for the experience. His death would likely be attributed to natural causes. He'd been looking over the edge of his grave when Parnell found him yesterday. No one should be surprised that he'd fallen into the abyss.

Parnell dropped the pillow onto the couch. He picked up the

pizza box with his documents in it and glanced around the duplex one last time.

He shook his head. If anyone suspected Scavo was helped along to his place in hell, there was nothing Parnell could do about the forensics. His fingerprints were scattered throughout the place. He'd probably left DNA on more than one surface, too.

Briefly, he considered cleaning up, but that might set off alarm bells where no foul play would otherwise be considered.

He shrugged. Nothing more to do here.

He locked the door on his way out. His plan was almost complete. Only two steps left.

Find Pauling. Leave the country.

CHAPTER THIRTY-EIGHT

Friday, January 14
1:15 p.m.
Upstate New York

GASPAR WAS BEHIND THE wheel, driving toward the city again when his cell phone made an audible buzzing noise like a hive of angry wasps. "That's the bug I left in Scavo's apartment."

"You have a very odd sense of humor, Chico," Otto replied as she located his phone. "What am I looking for here?"

"The app is on the last page. Probably at the end of the icons. Open it and follow the prompts. You should find a recording of some sort has been downloaded."

"Okay. Found it. Is it saved on here so that all I need to do is play this?"

"The cell service is spotty between Stanwix Village and the city, but the app should have downloaded the whole thing and saved it when we passed through an area with good coverage." He pulled a cord from his pocket. "You can plug the phone into that outlet, and we can hear the whole thing through the stereo speakers, like a playlist or an audio book."

"Got it." Once she had the setup done, she said, "Ready?"

"Let 'er fly." When no sound emitted from the speakers, he said, "The system is voice activated, and there's some silence built into the beginning of the recording time so that nothing gets cut off."

Otto nodded. The next raspy voice they heard was Nick Scavo. The recording lasted quite a while. There were several long pauses.

Sorry to keep you waiting so long, General. Some days are better than others for me. Today's a bad one.

When the recording ended, Otto fished out the Boss's phone. When he picked up, she didn't give him time to say anything. "We need plane tickets to Palm Beach. We're an hour from JFK."

"I heard. Your flight departs in less than two hours. Can you make it? The next one doesn't leave until tomorrow morning."

"Tell them to hold the plane."

She heard nothing but long silence for a while until he finally said, "Ten minutes. No more."

"Ten minutes will be enough." She looked at Gaspar. He nodded and pushed the accelerator closer to the floor. "Do you know who Scavo is talking to? He calls him General."

"Send me the recording. I'll identify him as quickly as I can."

"Finlay will help, if you can't get it done immediately," she said.

"You must have a death wish," he replied coldly before he disconnected the call.

Gaspar grinned from ear to ear. "Suzy Wong, you're one brave cookie."

She shrugged. "He needed incentive."

She pushed the replay, and they listened to the entire recording again before they reached JFK.

Gaspar pulled as close as he could get to the departure level at JFK. They hopped out of the rental, grabbed their laptops, and dashed into the terminal.

CHAPTER THIRTY-NINE

Friday, January 14
1:55 p.m.
Stanwix Village, New York

PARNELL PUT THE RENTAL into gear and headed south
toward JFK. He stopped several times along the way to dispose
of the various items he'd accumulated, which increased his travel
time but couldn't be helped.

He dropped the gun and sound suppressor from a bridge into
the first big river. He smiled as he watched them splash into the
swift current. Both might be too heavy to travel far, but the
bottom of the river should cover them well enough. If they were
recovered someday, it would take a while to match them to the
Brewers' murders after he'd altered them.

The door-breaching tool rested further south at the bottom of
a deep lake well off the interstate.

He tossed the duct tape, twist ties, and used latex gloves into
four separate dumpsters at two rest areas, one on each side of the
road.

Everything else he'd bought for use at Brewer's place he'd thrown out the window into water-filled ditches when he was certain no one would see.

His evidence disposal techniques were not perfect, but under the circumstances, the best he could do.

He directed his energy to what remained to be done. Locate the right hotel room near enough to the airport. Make a few phone calls.

First, find Pauling. She had flown somewhere. Records existed. His sources could find those records. It shouldn't take long.

At JFK, he backed the rental into a space against a garage wall in the long-term parking lot. He chose a busy floor where cars might be left for a week or more by legitimate vacationers.

He removed Scavo's laptop and cell phone along with the few personal items he'd stashed inside, and locked the vehicle.

The sedan must have been registered in one of the states that didn't require a front plate, which saved him the trouble of removing it. On his way into the terminal, he tossed the sedan's keys into a wastebasket two floors below.

Inside the terminal, he studied the local hotel board. He found a low-end, no-frills roach motel located outside the typical monitoring radius of the airport. He memorized the address, walked outside, and grabbed a taxi.

An hour later, he'd rented a room, paying cash and using an assumed name.

He checked his watch as he considered who to task with the problem. He'd spent more time than he'd planned on the return from Scavo's place. It was seven-forty-five already.

He had limited information to supply. Pauling's name and departure city. Nothing more. Thousands of flights left JFK every day, and Parnell didn't know the date or time Pauling had departed. He didn't know her destination.

He had three sources he could tap. While calls requesting assistance were not unusual in Parnell's world, contacting the Pentagon was risky. Calls would be recorded. Questions would be asked. He factored all these variables into making the best choice. Safer to call Baghdad where the time was almost three o'clock in the morning and the right guy would be on duty.

Parnell located a new disposable cell phone in his bag, fired it up, and made the call.

After relaying his request and his number, the only thing left to do was wait for the data to come in. He showered quickly, toweled off, and stretched out on the bed.

Fifty-six minutes later, the phone bounced around on the bedside table, jarring Parnell awake. He cleared the sleep from his throat. "Yeah. What've we got?"

He wrote the information on the notepad next to the phone. "Uh, huh. Palm Beach? Uh, huh. Got it. Thanks. Yeah, doing great. Retirement is absolutely worth it. Thanks again. Yeah, I'll keep in touch. You too. You've got my number."

After the call, Parnell dialed the same airline Pauling had flown weeks ago. He booked the same non-stop flight to West Palm Beach, departing JFK at 8:15 a.m.

He made a few more calls.

He rechecked his watch. He had time to catch another couple of hours of shut-eye. He couldn't risk clogging the plumbing in this dump, so he took the cheap phone apart, placed the pieces on the bedside table.

He fell asleep feeling closer to his money than he had in years.

CHAPTER FORTY

Friday, January 14
4:28 p.m.
Palm Beach, Florida

ALMOST THREE HOURS AGO, Otto and Gaspar had
downloaded materials from the Boss before they boarded the
plane in New York. Their tickets were always for empty seats
not purchased by regular passengers in the first-class section of
the aircraft. If she'd booked and paid for her own ticket, she
wouldn't be sitting in 3A on a bet. The tail section was the safest
place for passengers to sit. Closer to an emergency exit in the
back was ideal.

Not that she'd request to move. Nothing would tank her
advancement potential faster than any public acknowledgment of
concerns about flying. Not to mention tipping off Gaspar to the
extent of hers. He'd mock her endlessly, which she refused to
encourage.

So she sat in 3A and spent almost three hours bouncing
through turbulence, drinking coffee, swallowing antacids, and

reviewing the files to distract herself from the inherent dangers of speeding through space sitting on enough jet fuel to destroy small cities.

Gaspar, of course, slept.

The files contained a curious mix of material. Sorted documents from the latest TrueLeaks mole were mostly about private contractors milking military coffers while U.S. armed forces were dying because of a shoestring budget.

The leaker's interests seemed to be related to shortages of manpower, equipment, and support for the troops. What he'd chosen to leak suggested he was an enlisted man or a low-level officer.

The Boss included the same conversations they'd received from Finlay. But no Reacher recordings dated within the past six weeks, meaning nothing after he blew up the house in Rocky Pointe, Maine.

When the flight landed at Palm Beach International Airport, Otto was no closer to knowing whether Reacher was dead or alive than she had been back in Detroit.

She said a quick prayer of gratitude for the safe landing. So many ways a flight could go wrong, and she was intimately familiar with every last one of them. Someday, her luck might run out. But not today.

She gathered her laptop and deplaned. On her way past 1A, she nudged Gaspar to wake him up and waited for him at the end of the jetway.

Through the big windows, waning sunshine bathed the pavement outside. Palm trees wafted in the breeze, and green foliage dotted the landscape. The effect of transporting from bleak, cold winter to verdant, warm summer in just a few hours jarred her senses as it always did.

She turned the Boss's cell phone on and checked for messages. Nothing. If he'd had enough time with the Scavo recording to identify the second voice, the one Scavo called "General," he hadn't bothered to share the name with them.

Gaspar ambled out of the jetway limping and lugging his laptop. "How about a quick pit stop and a donut or something before we get going?"

She nodded and walked with him. "Nothing new in the Boss's stuff, if you were wondering."

"I figured. If he'd found anything useful, he'd have called the moment you turned the phone on," he replied before they peeled off into the restrooms.

While she picked up cheap sunglasses at the sundries shop, he bought a dozen donuts and four large coffees to go. Gaspar gobbled two of the donuts before they collected the rental, where he slid behind the wheel without comment.

She'd stopped fighting that battle on their first day. He was right. He was number two, and number two drives the vehicle, even as number one drives the case.

"Have you ever been to Palm Beach before, Suzy Wong?" Gaspar asked while he was familiarizing himself with the dashboard of the Japanese sedan.

He preferred a Crown Vic to every vehicle on the road, and he complained about all the others. But Ford was no longer producing Crown Vics, so finding one on a rental lot never happened.

Otto nodded. "When I was working in accounting, we had clients down here. It's a different world from Miami or Detroit. Or New York, for that matter."

She passed the sunglasses she'd bought for him across the console and adjusted hers to fit her face. She held the shoulder harness away from her neck with her right hand and the donut in her left.

"No doubt about that. Thanks for the shades." He backed out of the parking space and slipped the aviators over his eyes before he rolled the sedan into the bright but fading sun. He grabbed another donut.

"Pauling's place is on Ocean Boulevard. I put the address into the GPS." She nibbled the fried dough. It settled like lead in her stomach, but she figured it would soak up some of the acid.

This was the first time in weeks when she hadn't felt engulfed in bone-chilling cold. The GPS led them north and then east. Gaspar drove with easy familiarity, and as the miles passed, Otto relaxed a bit.

He swallowed a big gulp of the flavored syrup he called coffee before he asked, "Did you learn anything new while I was sleeping?"

"Bottom line, still no hard evidence that Reacher's alive."

He grinned. "Guess I should bump my bet."

"You're a riot, you know that, Chico?" She scowled behind the sunglasses, which he couldn't see. But he must have felt the vibe.

"No hints about what Pauling did with the money?" His grin widened briefly before he popped half of a donut in his mouth.

"The nine million? What makes you think Pauling did anything with it?" She cocked her head. Sometimes his tangents were hard to follow. "Brewer didn't say Pauling moved the cash, only that she might know what happened to it."

"Seems obvious, doesn't it?" Gaspar swigged the coffee as he maneuvered around the heavy traffic. "Peck's dead, so he didn't take it. Brewer says he didn't take it, and we've found no evidence to the contrary. If the money had been there when the mysterious stranger arrived, who was probably Scavo's general, too, he would have had no reason to kill Peck. Who else could it be?"

"Your theories have more holes than a screen door." She paused while the GPS instructed him to turn east in another two miles.

"Maybe. But that doesn't mean I'm wrong." He shrugged. His all-purpose gesture for everything. "You think it was Reacher? Doesn't sound like him, does it? Reacher working with Pauling? No evidence to support that, either."

She viewed Gaspar as her best window into Reacher's head. His background was a lot like Reacher's. Same training. Both ex-Army. Both men. She tried to keep an open mind to his suggestions, even when they made no sense to her.

"Why would Pauling take the money?"

"Why not?" He shrugged again, slowing for the traffic light ahead. "The Colonel's gone. Disappeared. His family, too. Probably not coming back, the way it looks. Hell, the guy could be dead for all we know. And it wouldn't surprise me to learn that Reacher had something to do with all of that." The light changed. He turned right behind a long line of vehicles.

Otto didn't reply.

"No question. Pauling's involved. She knows what happened to the nine million, at the very least. And Peck's killer will figure that out pretty quickly, too. If he hasn't already," Gaspar said.

Otto felt the Boss's phone vibrating in her pocket. She dropped her nibbled donut into the empty bag. She maneuvered around the seatbelt to dig the phone out while holding the safety harness away from her neck to avoid decapitation.

"Yes?" Her tone was grouchy. She didn't care.

"You're on the ground, I take it," the Boss said.

278 | DIANE CAPRI

Otto said nothing. He watched them every second of every day, one way or another. He knew damn well precisely where they were.

"Pauling is expecting you."

Interesting. How did she find out? Brewer? "Any reason to believe she's hostile?"

"Any reason to believe she's not?" he countered.

Point taken. "So what's your suggestion?"

"Improvise." He disconnected before she could ask questions.

She sent a quick text. "What about Scavo?"

The reply was equally quick. "Nothing yet."

Gaspar glanced her way. "I take it he's as helpful as ever."

"He says Pauling knows we're coming. He suggests we improvise." She curled her lip and looked out the window.

Gaspar shrugged. "Sounds like a feasible plan."

They were traveling over a bridge. According to the GPS, the waterway beneath was called Lake Worth.

She wondered about the price of real estate on Palm Beach Island these days. And how Pauling could possibly afford to live here on her FBI pension and the income from her private investigator business. Not only to live here, but also in New York City, two of the most expensive places to own housing in the entire country.

Gaspar was right. The only answer that made sense. Pauling took the nine million. She was at the center of whatever was going on here. She had to have been involved before she met Reacher. Brewer was involved before Reacher, too.

But somehow, Reacher came on the scene, and something more happened. Probably something deadly, because violence was Reacher's way. Whatever that something was, it must have made Pauling a very wealthy woman.

"How far do you think she'll go to keep what she's already got?" Otto asked.

"As far as she can." Gaspar shrugged.

CHAPTER FORTY-ONE

Friday, January 14
5:32 p.m.
Palm Beach, Florida

PAULING GUESSED THE TIME and then looked at her watch. She'd missed again. But only by four minutes. She was getting better, but she'd been practicing the trick for months. and she only nailed the time about once in ten tries. Reacher was some kind of savant or something.

Otto and Gaspar were on the way. She'd confirmed their flight, and it had landed an hour ago. It was a short drive, and the President wasn't due back until tomorrow morning, so traffic was light. She expected them to pull up out front shortly.

She was ready.

She opened a bottle of crisp Chardonnay, poured a glass, and wandered out to the pool to wait.

Not ten minutes later, the front buzzer sounded. She set the wine glass on a table and went to answer the call. The buzzer sounded again just as she reached the intercom.

She tried not to smile. "Yes?"

"Lauren Pauling?" A female voice.

"That's right." She looked at the video screen. A man and a woman stood within range of the camera. She was attractive, Asian, tiny. He was older. Taller. Latin looking.

"FBI Special Agents Kim Otto and Carlos Gaspar. We'd like a few minutes of your time."

"Yes, Greg Brewer told me to expect you. Please come up." She pressed the lock release for the front entrance and watched the video until they stepped inside.

She waited for the knock and opened the door.

"I'm Lauren Pauling," she extended her hand. Both had solid handshakes, she noticed. "Please come in. We'll sit outside. Walk straight through to the pool. I've opened a bottle of wine. Can I get you something?"

"Sparkling water?" Otto asked.

Pauling smiled. "Of course. Just grab a bottle there in the fridge and a glass from the cabinet next to it."

"Do you have any coffee?" Gaspar asked.

"I have an espresso machine. You're welcome to make your own." She waved him to the open kitchen and left him to fend for himself.

She joined Otto on the patio. She retrieved her wine glass and settled into a gliding chair near the table. "I know you've been sitting for hours, so feel free to stand if you'd like."

Otto looked beyond Ocean Boulevard to the shoreline and the vast Atlantic on the other side. Stars sparkled in the dark sky past civilization's light pollution.

One of Pauling's favorite party yachts was out there, moving slowly across the near horizon. Windows alight and three hundred-plus passengers enjoying the mild January weather. *The*

Beachy Babe featured three decks for dining, dancing, and lounging during night cruises. Day cruises also included water toys like jet skis and scuba gear.

"It's magical, isn't it?" Pauling said. "Only a few hours from here by plane, right now, one can literally freeze to death. Seems impossible to me most days."

"I can see why," Otto replied. "Have you lived here long?"

"My husband bought the place for a song from a client. Poor guy was in a dire financial bind. That was long before we married." She paused. "After Hugh died, I didn't come here much for a while. Too many memories, you know?"

Gaspar joined them, his steaming espresso in hand.

Pauling raised her glass. "Death to our enemies."

Gaspar grinned. "I'll drink to that."

"I'm sure you didn't come here to look at the stars and drink coffee," she said, clearing her mind of sentiment. "So tell me how I can help you."

"We're looking for information on Jack Reacher from people who know him. Brewer probably told you that he's being considered for a classified project. We're tasked with completing his background check." Otto recited the facts, but she didn't seem to have her heart in it.

"Brewer mentioned all that to me, yes. But it seems like something more is going on here," Pauling replied easily. She slipped into the familiar techniques for handling witnesses that she'd honed to an art form during her years at the FBI.

Gaspar said, "Let's start there. You know Reacher. How did you meet him?"

"Not very complicated. Brewer hooked us up." Pauling sipped her wine as if she was discussing a social occasion. "Reacher was interested in an old homicide. The case was one

I'd worked at the FBI. Reacher asked Brewer because he thought the case was NYPD. But it was an FBI matter, so Brewer sent him to me."

Otto nodded. "And the old case had something to do with Colonel Edward Lane."

Pauling lowered her gaze briefly. "That's right. His wife was kidnapped and murdered. The case was never solved."

"Why was Reacher interested?" Gaspar asked.

These two were asking all the right questions. But she'd decided earlier what she'd leave in and what she'd leave out. "Because the second Mrs. Lane had gone missing. He thought the two cases might be related."

"Were they?" Otto asked. "The cases, I mean. I assume the two Mrs. Lanes were not related, right?"

"Correct on both counts." Pauling shook her head. "Except for the fact that the women were Edward Lane's first and second wives, the cases were not related at all."

"When was the last time you saw Reacher?" Gaspar asked.

"It's been a while." Pauling shrugged. "Much longer than I'd like, frankly."

Gaspar flashed a meaningful glance at Otto, and she frowned.

Pauling wondered what that was about. "Have either of you met Reacher?"

"Haven't had the pleasure," Gaspar said.

Otto changed the subject. "When's the last time you talked to Brewer?"

Pauling frowned. "Yesterday afternoon. Why?"

"Brewer might have mentioned some bad news if you'd spoken to him today." Otto cleared her throat. "Simon Peck was murdered sometime yesterday."

Pauling gasped. Her right hand flew to her mouth. "Why would anyone kill Simon?"

"Brewer caught the case. He called us over to Lane's apartment at the Dakota." Otto paused and glanced down for a moment. "The man who killed him used a knife first."

Pauling widened her eyes, and her nostrils flared. "Knife murders are crimes of passion, usually. Up close and personal. Was Simon killed by a lover?"

Gaspar shrugged. "We don't know. NYPD is handling the case. We haven't heard anything more from Brewer."

Pauling understood what they needed to know. She shook her head. "It wasn't me. I've been right here."

"We didn't think you killed Simon Peck, Lauren," Otto said quietly. "But you might be the reason he was killed."

"How could that be true?" Pauling gasped again. "I haven't seen Simon in weeks."

"Brewer's theory is that the killer came to steal the Colonel's money. When he found the money missing, he killed Simon." Gaspar cocked his head. "Brewer says you know where the money is."

"You know how this goes, Lauren. The killer used his knife to get information from Peck." Otto looked around the patio and the open pool deck. "I assume you're armed. How secure are you here?"

Pauling sat her wine glass down hard and clasped her hands. "You think this maniac is on his way here?"

"We're fairly certain of it," Gaspar said.

"Why?"

"I can think of about nine million reasons," Otto said.

Gaspar drained his espresso. "Now would be a good time to call Reacher."

Pauling was thinking the very same thing.

CHAPTER FORTY-TWO

Friday, January 14
6:45 p.m.
Palm Beach, Florida

DESPITE THE CIRCUMSTANCES, OTTO liked Lauren
Pauling as much as she'd expected to. She was the kind of
woman Otto had always admired. Strong. Self-reliant. Confident.
Competent at work and in life.

Pauling was older than Reacher's other women by at least
ten years. She was also ten times more beautiful. Tall, slender,
elegant. Her hair, frosted gold and blonde, fell to her shoulders in
big waves, as striking as her smoky voice.

It was easy to see why Reacher would have been smitten
with her. But what did Pauling see in him that Otto had
missed?

Engaging every ounce of her imagination, Otto couldn't
picture them together.

Nor could she imagine Reacher living here.

Pauling's home was as understated and elegant as the

woman herself. The spacious open floor plan was perfect for a single woman. Reacher's size would have overwhelmed everything in the place, from the furniture to the doorways.

Gaspar had returned to the kitchen for more espresso. While he was gone, Pauling said, "You're working for Cooper. Does *he* think this guy's coming after me?"

"He hasn't said, and we didn't ask," Otto replied. "But it's the obvious play, isn't it? The guy knows who you are, where you are, and believes you have his money. Why wouldn't he come after you?"

Pauling nodded. No hysteria. No overtly female reactions. Total acceptance of the situation the way it was. Otto admired that about her, too.

"How much time do I have?"

"Tonight or tomorrow, probably." Otto shook her head. She didn't know for sure. "Less than twenty-four hours, best guess."

Pauling nodded again.

Otto saw Gaspar was on his way back. "Is the money here?"

"What money?" Pauling replied.

"The nine million. Do you have it here?"

Pauling waved a hand toward her home. "Feel free to look."

Gaspar put his coffee down and went inside.

"Are you planning to take this guy down?" Pauling asked.

"Personally?" Otto shook her head. "That's not my assignment."

"I see," Pauling said.

Gaspar came back empty handed. He collected his espresso. "No bundles of cash inside, but you have a really beautiful vault. One of the nicest I've ever seen."

Pauling smiled. "My husband was an investment banker. He

had an appreciation for things like that. In an effort to avoid high-burglary rates and exorbitant insurance premiums, most of the better homes in Palm Beach have a locked safe. Ours is a bit more elaborate, perhaps. He used the room for his office."

"I'd like to see it."

Pauling nodded and Otto retraced Gaspar's path through the living area toward the bedrooms.

The sliding oak pocket door was open. The vault door was ajar. She slipped through into the room. Except for the vault door, nothing about the place was particularly impressive. No windows. No closet. An eight by ten space with slate floors and an unremarkable desk.

If nine million dollars had once been stored here, the cash was here no longer. The general wouldn't be pleased when he discovered as much.

Otto scanned the room one last time and walked back the way she'd come. Before she reached the patio, the Boss's cell phone vibrated. "This is Otto."

"I've put new intel on your secure server. Get to it as soon as you can," the Boss said without preamble when she took the call. "Share with Pauling. She's got solid credentials. Could be helpful because she knows some of the players."

"Okay."

"Here's the highlights. Scavo's dead." He paused. "Looks like natural causes, but probably murder by suffocation."

Otto didn't reply. She wasn't surprised. Scavo seemed to give the General permission to kill him near the end of their conversation. From what she knew about Scavo's condition, he probably wouldn't have objected.

"We've identified the General. Mackenzie Parnell. Two stars. Recently retired. They call him Nitro Mack because he's got a short fuse and once something sets him off, he takes out everyone and everything. No prisoners."

"That's just swell." Otto curled her lip.

"His name is all over the latest TrueLeaks documents." He paused for a breath. "Looks like Parnell funneled military contracts to the Colonel's OSC operation for at least ten years."

"This just gets better and better," Otto said.

"Parnell and his pal, Colonel Lane, are both listed as clients of the law firm that was exposed by the Panama Papers." The Boss seemed weary of normal human weaknesses all of a sudden. "Both own shell corporations under false identities registered in the British Virgin Islands, where the majority of such things are registered. Both corporations hold significant bank balances in Tortola."

"So we think Lane has bugged out to BVI and Parnell is on his way to join him?" Otto asked.

"That's one possibility. I can think of a few others."

"Such as?"

"Most likely, Lane is dead, and Parnell killed him for his share of the money they scammed."

Otto nodded, although he couldn't see her. "How much money are we talking about?"

"Looks like tens of millions. I don't have exact numbers yet."

"Where is Parnell now?"

"We're looking for him. Hard. Lots of resources deployed. With a little bit of luck, we'll find him before he leaves the country." He took a breath again as if all this talking was too much. Which it probably was. He was a taciturn man with few words to spare under normal circumstances.

"But?"

"He'll head Pauling's way as soon as he can get his plans in place." He stopped. "Expect him to arrive by tomorrow if we don't find him before."

"What about Brewer?"

He paused. "That's the other reason for my call."

Otto listened to the news and tried to take it all in. Brewer and his wife were dead. This time, no possibility of natural causes. Both were found executed by gunshot wounds to the head.

General Parnell was the prime suspect in all three murders, as well as the murder of Simon Peck.

"Listen up, Otto," the Boss said sternly, as if she'd been ignoring him until now. "Tell Gaspar this, too. The wide search parameters we've deployed mean this info is out there. Available."

"Good. The more people who know we're looking for Parnell, the more likely we are to find him before he kills again."

"Normally, yes. This is different." He paused, waiting. When she said nothing, he spelled it out for her. "Reacher will hear everything. He'll come. There'll be a bloodbath."

"What? You no longer believe Reacher is dead?" She mocked. "Shocking news. Just totally shocking."

"He'll protect Pauling. You don't have to worry about her. He's done it before." He said as if she hadn't challenged him. "Hard to say what he'll do to…bystanders. You and Gaspar stay out of the way. That's a direct order."

Otto's temper flared. "Yeah, so you can't find the guy. One guy. So when he gets here, we'll pass along your orders to *Nitro Mack*. That'll make all the difference. He'll simply turn himself in. For sure. That'll work."

Dead silence.

She disconnected, dropped the phone into her pocket. The sooner she metabolized the new intel, the better. Time was short.

CHAPTER FORTY-THREE

Friday, January 14
10:35 p.m.
Palm Beach, Florida

OTTO HAD DOWNLOADED THE new files and divided them three ways. She gave them a sanitized version of the highlights from the Boss.

For the next three hours, they each worked alone to wade through the files.

Otto had spread her laptop and notes on the kitchen table. Gaspar worked on the couch. Pauling took the small desk in the vault office.

Gaspar put his laptop aside and limped onto the patio to call home. He talked to his kids before they went to bed, and spent a few extra minutes with Maria, his wife. Otto knew because he'd done the same thing every night they'd worked together.

She felt a little stab of jealousy that she didn't have someone to call. Or even better, someone who cared enough about her to call first. Briefly, John Lawton, the hot treasury agent, flashed into her head. "Oh, good grief."

She noticed the tension in the sides of her neck. She'd been sitting on one calf, leg bent at the knee. The pins and needles sensation in her foot prompted her to walk around a bit.

When Gaspar came back, he said, "Any chance we could order a pizza? Do they even order pizza in ritzy places like this?"

Otto would have teased him about eating all the time, but the truth was that her stomach had stopped growling a while back, having given up the hope of dinner.

Pauling must have heard them because she walked into the kitchen with a phone in her hand and the pizza place on the other end of the line. "My favorite is pepperoni and cheese. New York style. What do you both like?"

While Pauling placed the order, Otto attempted to relieve the prickly pain in her foot on her way to the guest bathroom. She washed her hands and splashed water on her face. The new clothes she'd bought earlier at the New York outlet mall already looked like she'd been wearing them for a month. Nothing she could do about that for the moment.

Gaspar took his turn in the guest bathroom. Pauling had freshened up in the master. No sooner had they gathered in the main room again when the buzzer at the front door sounded.

For a second, Otto thought it could be Parnell, and touched her gun. Her reaction proved how jumpy she was.

One quick look at the security video feed showed only the pizza girl, laden with three big, flat pizza boxes and a twelve pack of beer, which let Otto relax a couple of levels on her internal threat meter.

Pauling grinned. "I know this place. I order from there frequently. It'll be okay. Come downstairs with me. I could use another pair of hands."

The exchange of cash for pizza and beer went smoothly. No explosive generals busted through the door wielding knives or guns. So far, so good.

They carried the pizza, paper plates, napkins, and beer outside to the patio table. Gaspar, of course, began gobbling like a hungry wolf immediately.

Pauling gaped at him, astonished.

"It's amazing, right?" Otto grinned. "And I can tell you for sure, he does absolutely nothing to burn off all those calories."

Pauling laughed. A genuine laugh. Which turned to uncontrolled laughter, complete with tears streaming from her eyes. The whole thing went on and on. Too long for the situation.

Otto cocked her head. Gaspar's eating habits were amusing, sure, but not that hilarious.

Was she hysterical? She'd learned that three of her friends were viciously murdered within the past forty-eight hours. She must have felt some responsibility. She seemed to be the centerpiece of Parnell's crime spree, after all.

Otto could understand if she'd gone a little off the rails. But they needed a reliably cool head and steady nerves from her. She'd been out of the bureau for a long time. Were her once remarkable skills too rusty now?

When Pauling finally got control of herself, she could barely breathe. Her eyes and nose were as red as if she'd been crying for days. She blew her nose on a napkin and sat back in the chair, exhausted.

Gaspar was the one who asked, "Are you okay? I mean, I'm glad to provide comic relief, but really, I'm just not that funny."

"Once I started, I simply couldn't stop." She patted Gaspar's arm. "I'm fine, Carlos. Thanks for asking. Kim, don't look so worried. I promise not to crack up when things are critical."

"Are you sure, Lauren?" Otto asked the question as gently as possible. "Because if you're not up to dealing with Parnell when he gets here, it's no problem. We're not alone in this. Cooper is marshaling backup."

Gaspar said, "With luck, they'll intercept him. We might never see the guy until he's arrested."

Otto didn't believe that for a moment, and she doubted Gaspar believed his own baloney. But the words sounded reassuring. Pauling seemed calmer.

"I'll be right back." Pauling pushed away from the table. Otto's gaze followed her until she disappeared down the corridor to her bedroom. "What do you think?"

"Your call, Suzy Wong. I'm number two, remember?" He'd already returned to eating the pizza. Which, in some crazy way, was also reassuring.

She shrugged. Nothing they could do anyway. They couldn't leave Pauling on her own, and they were better off together until Parnell was apprehended. They had one job. Stay alive and keep Pauling alive. Even if she was a thief.

CHAPTER FORTY-FOUR

Friday, January 14
11:55 p.m.
Palm Beach, Florida

WHILE PAULING WAS GONE, Otto asked, "Do you think she took the money?"

Gaspar swallowed the mouthful of pizza before he said, "Of course. Don't you?"

She played with her salad, moving the fork around the plate. She was hungry but preoccupied. "We've talked about this before. That's a lot of cash. It would have filled that vault at the Dakota, where we found Peck. And it would have filled the one here, too."

"She's had four months to figure that out. She's resourceful. She spent years dealing with money launderers and gangs and tax evaders." Gaspar had almost finished his large pizza by himself. "If she didn't take it, then who did?"

Pauling returned in time to hear the question. "If who didn't take what?"

She'd refreshed her makeup, which meant she looked less like a teenager who just got dumped. Her smile was wobbly, but she seemed better.

Gaspar raised both eyebrows, passing the question to Otto.

"We're talking about the missing money. From the Colonel's apartment in the Dakota. That's what seems to have started the general on this killing spree."

Pauling served a piece of pizza on her plate and a bit of salad, too. She twisted the top from one of the beer bottles and swigged.

Otto said, "So the question is, who took the money? The general believes you took it."

Pauling chewed for a while. "Why does he think that?"

"Probably because Brewer told him," Otto replied.

"I see." Pauling continued to eat her food. "How do you know Brewer said that?"

"Brewer told us that after the money was found, he'd turned the matter over to you. He said you handled it from there." Otto ate a few bites while she waited.

Eventually, Pauling said, "I see."

"Brewer's dead now, Lauren. His wife, too. Parnell killed them both. Don't you want Parnell to pay for that?" Otto asked.

"Of course, I do."

Gaspar said, "You know it's a crime to lie to federal agents in the course of an investigation, Pauling."

"I haven't lied to you, Gaspar."

"You haven't told us you didn't take the money, either."

Pauling cocked her head and swallowed her pizza. "Is there any chance that the money Lane had in that apartment wasn't dirty?"

Otto said, "Not likely."

"Maybe the money was put to better use than gathering dust at the Dakota. Maybe people who deserved it were helped. People Lane had maimed or left for dead, like Scavo." She swigged the beer and picked up another forkful of the salad. "Scavo needed a place to live and medical treatment he couldn't afford. He got that. If there were more like him, how can that be a bad thing?"

Otto nodded. "That's true. Did you help Scavo and people like him with the money, Lauren?"

Pauling shrugged. "Scavo said Reacher gave him the money. We all heard that."

"So you're saying Reacher took the money?" Otto asked.

"Scavo said Reacher is the one who helped him. Maybe Reacher had money from somewhere else?" Pauling ate more pizza, drank more beer.

Otto shook her head. "Reacher never seemed like the Robin Hood type to me."

Pauling replied, "I thought you'd never met him? How do you know?"

"She's got you there, Sunshine," Gaspar grinned. "Got any pizza you're not going to eat over there?"

Otto pushed the box toward him.

She might back Pauling into a corner. But did she need to? The three of them knew Pauling had taken the money from the Dakota, just like Gaspar said before Pauling walked in. No reason to make her admit it. Not at the moment, anyway. They had bigger issues to handle. She'd say nothing more on the matter for now.

"True, I haven't met Reacher. But the Boss says I may have my chance very soon." Both Pauling and Gaspar stared. "General Parnell is still in the wind. The Boss says he's on his way here. Law enforcement is looking for him all over the country. He says Reacher usually has his ear to the ground and is bound to hear about the manhunt. When he does, the Boss says Reacher will show up."

"Sounds reasonable." Gaspar grabbed another slice of pizza. Pauling seemed energized by the suggestion. Her eyes brightened and her face lost about ten years of worry. Her eyes fairly sparkled. She looked for all the world like a woman in love.

The truth gobsmacked Otto the moment she recognized it.

Pauling in love with Reacher?

The mere idea was like walking down a long corridor of distorted mirrors, where reflections were grotesque versions of reality.

How could a woman like Pauling possibly be in love with a man like Reacher?

Otto wouldn't have been more amazed if Pauling had pulled a mask from her face to reveal a lizard under the fake skin.

Gaspar, of course, saw the situation differently. "Let's hope the Boss is right."

She stood to pace the room. "Let's go over the important things we found in all the new files. Lauren, you start. Anything we all need to know?"

They each shared the salient points they'd uncovered, making sure all three were up to speed. By one thirty, they were ready for bed. Pauling insisted they stay overnight.

"I've only got one guest room. Gaspar, you get the couch." She smiled. "And tomorrow, we'll get you both some more suitable clothes."

"Suitable for what?" Gaspar said.

"There's a big annual fundraiser for the local cancer center on that yacht you saw earlier. I'm on the board, and I've volunteered to help. Starts at noon and ends after sunset. I can't miss it," Pauling said, looking from Gaspar to Otto and back. "Besides, we'll be better off away from here. If Parnell gets inside and doesn't find the money, he may give up."

Otto doubted Parnell would give up. He'd already killed four people. Nothing about him suggested he was likely to stop there.

"Lots of great stuff on Worth Avenue, Kim." Pauling smiled, woman-to-woman. "There's no better shopping in the country. You'll love it."

Gaspar groaned.

In the end, they agreed to stay simply because they had nowhere else to go.

Otto checked the Boss's phone one last time before she went to bed. No word on the manhunt for Parnell. Which couldn't possibly be a good sign.

CHAPTER FORTY-FIVE

Saturday, January 15
11:30 a.m.
Palm Beach

PARNELL DEPLANED IN PALM Beach where he collected another rental. A full-sized SUV this time, with enough cargo space to hold nine million dollars. He tossed his duffel into the back.

He'd added Scavo's laptop, cell phone and a box of documents, along with Brewer's cell phone, to his few personal possessions. He'd buy whatever he needed when he reached Tortola. He had the rest of his lifetime to accumulate things. For now, he traveled light.

Several times during the trip from JFK he'd considered whether he should forget about the nine million. He'd confirmed what Scavo told him. He had forty-six million waiting for him in a bank in the British Virgin Islands. He could collect Lane's twenty, too.

Sixty-six million dollars was more money than he'd ever

expected to have in his lifetime. More than enough to live very well for the next forty years, if he survived that long. Which he might. No reason to think he'd outlive that much money, though. Hell, he'd outlasted his karma many times over already.

He shook his head. The Pauling broad had already caused way too much hassle. Because of her, three more people than he'd planned were dead. Peck and Brewer and Brewer's wife. If Pauling had simply left the nine million in place at the Dakota, those three would still be alive right now. Why should she survive?

Nine million dollars was a lot of money to walk away from, too. And more important than the money was his pride. Walking away now would mean defeat. No general in any army would accept defeat on Pauling's terms. Certainly not General Nitro Mack Parnell.

He was close. Closer than he had ever been to everything he had sacrificed his entire life to accumulate. He was a young man still. Not quite sixty. That nine million was icing on his retirement cake, but it would go a long way toward the kind of life he intended to live now, after all the years of deprivation.

Not to mention the satisfaction of victory in his final campaign.

The decision was settled.

Eliminate Pauling.

Collect the nine million.

Leave the country.

Live happily ever after.

He grinned. Sure. Why not?

He drove away from the rental lot at Palm Beach International and detoured toward Travis Field, a private executive airstrip on the coast, closer to the Island of Palm Beach. No commercial aircraft landed here.

Travis Field was owned and operated by a collection of private corporations for the exclusive use of wealthy CEOs who valued privacy and convenience. These same CEOs avoided the cattle call and foolish theater that passed for security at the major airports.

All of which made the field perfect for Parnell's needs. The easiest, fastest way to move almost anything out of the country from here was by private jet from Travis Field. If law enforcement suspected illegal trafficking of any kind was conducted here, they were incentivized to ignore those suspicions.

Parnell assumed payola and kickbacks were involved, one way or another. But he didn't care. What he cared about was getting himself and his money twelve hundred miles across the Atlantic to the British Virgin Islands. Today.

He'd hired the right jet and a reliable pilot. A former Navy aviator who knew how to keep his mouth shut. He had a strong incentive to make the trip down at Parnell's expense because he transported illegal drugs on the way back, according to Parnell's source.

Parnell would pay cash. Half before takeoff. Half when they deplaned safely in Tortola. After that, he didn't care what the guy did on the return trip.

Private aircraft dotted Travis Field, but he saw only one Cirrus Vision Jet. The personal jet's distinctive appearance made it easy to spot. The single piggyback engine and V-tail were touted to reduce cabin noise.

The ballyhooed airframe parachute system seemed like an unnecessary precaution to Parnell, although he could see where the pilot might feel otherwise. Drug running was a dangerous occupation. Extra precautions were always a good plan.

Parnell had chosen the Vision Jet for two reasons. It could

fly farther, faster, and higher carrying more people and cargo. And it didn't require an entire flight operations department to fly and maintain it. Which meant he could keep the number of people who knew his destination to a bare minimum.

As an added bonus, the jet's fuel capacity was more than sufficient to cover the 988 nautical miles to Tortola nonstop. With luck, he'd be there tonight.

He drove the rental as close as possible to the jet and parked. A big man dressed in mechanics' garb lay on his back under the jet, working on the wheels. All Parnell could see was his fair hair and hands as big as turkeys. Not that he cared about the ground crew, anyway.

Before Parnell had a chance to ask, the pilot hurried down the flight stairs from the cockpit, right hand extended.

"General Parnell? I'm Bert Trout. People call me Fish." The slight, sinewy man's eyes crinkled at the corners. He nodded his head toward the cockpit. "She's a beauty, isn't she? Rides like a dream."

"Very nice, indeed." Parnell shook Trout's hand while admiring the jet, although performance was the only thing that mattered to him.

"I was just going over the preflight. Do you have time for a quick tour, sir? Show you some of the more sophisticated features?"

"I'm afraid not." Parnell shook his head. He dropped his duffel bag on the ground. "Stow that bag onboard for me. I'll have more luggage later."

"That's fine. You made it clear that you wanted to book the cargo space. Every inch we don't need for equipment is yours for the flight."

"I'm late for a couple of meetings. I'll be back as soon as I can."

"I think I mentioned that we'll need to take off by four-forty-five, at the absolute latest," Trout said.

Parnell's temperature went up a notch. He never allowed the hired help to dictate to him. "Why?"

"There's a party ship, takes a sunset cruise between five and six every night. Travels too close to our runway. We don't climb fast enough to pass over it on takeoff," Trout offered an apologetic smile. "By the time it's done and out of our way, we won't have enough visibility out there. We need to get up and out before, or we'll need to wait until tomorrow."

"Tomorrow is not an option. We leave today." General Parnell stated flatly. He turned to go and walked a few steps before he tossed the guy a bone, "I'll call you to let you know when I'm on my way back."

Trout said, "I can be ready to depart on thirty minutes notice."

"Make it fifteen, Fish," Parnell ordered.

"Yes, sir," the former Navy pilot called across the widening divide. "No problem at all."

Parnell had walked fifty feet toward the SUV when he heard Trout say to the big mechanic, "What an asshole. Toss his bag in the back when you're done, okay? I've got things to do before we take off."

Parnell fumed. Last month, he'd have tossed both men in the brig for such disrespect. Those days were over. The grease monkey wasn't Parnell's concern.

Four hours to deal with Pauling, collect his money, and get back here.

All he needed Trout to do was fly the jet. Whether the pilot made it back to Palm Beach alive afterward or not just became an open question.

CHAPTER FORTY-SIX

Saturday, January 15
1:45 p.m.
Palm Beach

PARNELL DROVE PAST PAULING'S Oceanview Boulevard address and parked on a side street a block away. Pauling's condo had a view of the Atlantic Ocean, which meant she was on the East side of the building.

He'd downloaded the real estate files and studied the layouts carefully. He'd wager that he knew more about Pauling's condo than she did at this point.

He approached from the northwest, where she wouldn't see him, even if she happened to be watching.

Which she wasn't.

In fact, she wasn't home at all.

Unfortunately.

He'd hoped to kill her while he was here. She deserved to die. She'd caused him a lot of inconveniences the past few days.

Maybe she'd come back before he finished moving the money.

Hey, a guy could dream.

Her condo was small. A big room for most of her living activities. Two small bedrooms. Two small baths. And the vault. Which was the only room he cared about.

Entering her building wasn't simple. She understood security measures, and she'd employed effective ones. But all security systems had one flaw he could easily exploit. The human factor.

He simply waited for one of her neighbors to enter or exit. On a beautiful Saturday like this, he didn't need to wait long.

Not more than twenty minutes later, two young women, dressed to the nines, constantly chattering on their way out to go shopping, didn't give him a second look. He stood aside, waiting for them to exit. When they did, he held the door for them, preventing it from closing again.

The privileged little tarts didn't even say thank you, he noticed.

He slipped inside Pauling's first line of defense.

The door locked and beeped to signal security cameras were operational. Which was fine. He'd be gone before anyone bothered to check the video.

He climbed the stairs to Pauling's unit. He pulled the latex gloves onto his hands and his tool kit from his pocket. At her front door, he slipped paper surgical booties over his shoes.

Pauling's locks were good.

Much better than average.

But not good enough.

He unlocked the door quickly.

Parnell grinned.

Inside Pauling's apartment, he spent no time admiring the view. He turned right and moved swiftly down the hallway. When he reached the open door to the vault, he was overwhelmed with a sickening sense of déjà vu.

He stared at the sparsely furnished little room as if he'd landed on Mars.

No money. Again.

Which was the first time in many days that Nitro Mack lost control.

He screamed like a crazy kamikaze. He pulled his new knife and used it to slash everything he could find. Upholstery, mattresses, carpets. Anything the knife would penetrate, he sliced to shreds.

While the knife destroyed, he swept the flat surfaces with his arm, knocking vases, jars, bottles, anything perched on any table or counter, to the floor where they shattered and splattered.

By the time he'd finished, the only things left were the cabinets on the walls. He opened the doors and swept dishes, glasses, and food to the ground.

If Pauling had been there, he'd have cut her to ribbons, too.

The whole tirade lasted a few minutes. Afterward, he was breathless, panting like a wild dog. His eyes scanned the destroyed apartment with something like disbelief.

Half of it, he didn't remember actually doing.

Which was always the way it was when he surfaced again after one of his episodes. While it lasted, he couldn't think. He didn't see or hear clearly. He simply destroyed whatever he could find.

He breathed heavily for several seconds. Where was she? What had she done with his money? He'd find her and choke it out of her, if he had to. He was beyond caring now. The bitch had to be dealt with.

He looked down at the slop covering the tile floors. Which was when he saw the flyer with Pauling's name on the top.

He picked it up. *The Beachy Babe*. A party yacht. A fundraiser. Today.

He stomped through the crap all over the floor to the patio slider and looked out across Ocean Boulevard to the Atlantic. There it was. He compared the yacht to the flyer. Definitely the same.

He watched the yacht and the people and the jet skis and the Zodiacs zipping to and fro for a while. His breathing slowed. His head cleared.

He knew where to find the bitch. All he needed was a Zodiac.

He might even have time to collect his money if she didn't waste his time.

Things were looking better.

CHAPTER FORTY-SEVEN

Saturday, January 15
4:05 p.m.
Palm Beach

THE FUNDRAISER ABOARD *THE Beachy Babe* had been in full swing for more than four hours. The perfect Palm Beach weather had no doubt encouraged the crowd.

Security staff for *The Beachy Babe's* owners roamed the decks stopping potential trouble before it got out of hand. They were big, bulky men dressed in the same casual clothing brands as the guests.

Pauling seemed to know several of them, and one had made a point of checking on her throughout the day. Or maybe he just wanted a date.

Otto had met four of the yacht's security team earlier in the day. She'd seen at least four more from a distance. She hoped there were more.

She'd noticed the satisfying bulges under their arms where their shoulder holsters rested, weapons within easy reach. They were using a wireless communications system similar to the one Otto, Gaspar, and Pauling employed. The system was voice activated, which was okay because it left their hands free. But for crowded conditions like these, voice activation wasn't ideal. A couple of times, her earpiece had intercepted the security staff chatter, which was a common problem with wireless systems. Another problem was weak or interrupted signals.

Unfortunately, this was the best they could do under the circumstances.

Maximum passenger capacity was 380, according to the posted signs Otto saw when they boarded, but all three spacious decks were teeming with partiers of all ages. She wouldn't be surprised to learn that the maximum capacity was viewed as a mere suggestion when a major fundraiser like this one chartered the yacht.

Tourist yachts could sink when overloaded, Otto knew. She kept her fingers crossed that *The Beachy Babe* would not go down today.

Across *The Beachy Babe's* stern was a large swim platform. From there, guests could dive into the Atlantic or jump onto the complimentary jet skis or dash around the vicinity in motorized Zodiac inflatable boats.

Otto's attention was drawn to the platform over and over again. She loved water sports. She'd been swimming her whole life. She'd learned to swim before she'd learned to walk. Too bad she couldn't participate this time.

The Beachy Babe's lowest deck was the largest. An art deco dining room complete with chandeliers and a full bar attracted an older, moneyed crowd. Casino style games had been running all day, with all proceeds going to the cancer center.

The middle deck was divided into three sections. The largest area was a club room with a DJ spinning pulse-pounding music and a dance floor packed tighter than a can of sardines.

The center section of deck two was an enclosed lounge with wraparound windows and a full bar.

In the third area, an open-air bow, young people slathered with oil and wearing the tiniest bikinis lounged as party-colored cocktails were replenished before their glasses emptied.

The noise on decks one and two was the most overwhelming because they were enclosed with wraparound windows that held the noise inside. OSHA couldn't possibly approve.

Deck three, the cabana deck, boasted a high canopy to shield passengers from too much sun. The open-air setup allowed the incessant noise to dissipate slightly.

The cabana deck was the only place where Otto could hear herself think or reply to Gaspar's conversations or catch occasional snippets of Pauling's voice through her earpiece.

Once they'd found a good observation point, where they could watch Pauling at her post near the bar, they'd perched. One of them stayed nearby at all times, while once an hour, the other took a brief lap around the second deck, scanning for threats.

Moving through the throngs was like swimming against the tide, which made threat assessment difficult, at best. But sitting all day in one position wasn't a good idea, either.

Either Otto or Gaspar stayed within sight and easy shooting distance of Pauling. And where the earpieces allowed them to hear occasional comments amid the noise, in case Pauling had the chance to shout for help, should the need arise.

It was Pauling that Parnell wanted. If he came, he'd come for her. Otto and Gaspar were prepared to deal with him on-board.

The Boss promised reinforcements when they returned to port at the end of the cruise.

Otto could see guests coming and going on the stairs to the lower decks from her perch. The cabana deck was the smallest of the super-yacht's three levels, which limited the number of people milling around at any one time. Another advantage.

There was one flaw in their stakeout location. Two crews from two local television stations had also established observation points on the cabana deck.

Both crews were flying commercial drones around *The Beachy Babe* and the frolicking guests enjoying water sports in the ocean.

The event was broadcasting live. Every guest, every couple, every swimmer or gambler or drinker, was captured on video. The video was shared instantly with the less fortunate who remained stuck on shore.

Every thirty minutes or so, Otto checked the Boss's phone for messages. The last time he'd contacted her was well before noon. "Nothing yet." Meaning Parnell had not been apprehended or located.

"Sunset is five forty-six, right?" Gaspar asked for the tenth time, kneading the folds between his eyebrows with his knuckles. "Less than two more hours of this, thank God. How do they stand it?"

Otto nodded. They'd covered the topic extensively already. What more could she say?

Pauling heard his lament through her earpiece. Her trilling laughter rang in Otto's ear. "Lighten up, Gaspar. Have some fun."

"I can get this level of chaos at home," was Gaspar's snarly reply.

Otto watched the drones flying overhead. They were not the kind she and her young cousins played with in the back yard on holidays.

These were huge spiders of carbon fiber and aluminum that made them lighter than their size might suggest, yet incredibly strong. They were held in the air by multiple propellers, and underneath they had high-quality steerable digital cameras.

Both operators were expert at maneuvering the surprisingly nimble drones remotely. The drones darted around *The Beachy Babe*'s decks, peeking into windows, zooming and retreating. Throughout the day, the huge drones rose to dizzying heights and showed breathtaking aerial views of *The Beachy Babe* in her full glory on televisions mounted everywhere.

Two screens were running in the corners of the cabana deck, displaying the broadcast as it happened, one tuned to each of the local stations. From her vantage point, Otto had a clear view of both.

If any disturbance broke out anywhere on the super-yacht, she'd see it quickly enough to hustle Pauling away from the trouble.

At least, in theory.

The Beachy Babe sailed north to south along the coast of Palm Beach and back again. The entire round trip took about two hours. They'd sailed the loop twice and already made the wide turn for the last leg of the trip.

The Beachy Babe's captain planned to offer passengers a spectacular sunset view to send everyone home happy about spending thousands of dollars to support a worthy cause.

On the swim platform, the water sports deck crew was rounding up the revelers as they returned. Collecting and stowing the water toys for the night.

318 | DIANE CAPRI

Finish the final leg and the day would be over.

Almost done.

Otto's tension eased a bit.

The cruise was coming to an end.

No sign of General Nitro Mack Parnell.

Pauling remained unmolested.

Gaspar was grumpy, but none the worse for wear.

All in all, this had been a better day than she'd feared.

Pauling had been right. *The Beachy Babe* was the perfect place to avoid the homicidal General Parnell.

The only troubling issue now was why the Boss hadn't found Parnell. They'd be disembarking soon. The manhunt should have been completed. Parnell should be in custody.

But he wasn't.

Where was he?

CHAPTER FORTY-EIGHT

Saturday, January 15
4:15 p.m.
Palm Beach

PARNELL RAN THE STOLEN Zodiac to the swim platform at the stern of *The Beachy Babe*. He'd spent way more time than he'd meant to simply find an inflatable boat. He'd been forced to deal with too many niggling issues to dwell on, but he was finally here.

Fish had warned him they couldn't take off after 4:45 p.m. He had fifteen minutes to do what he came for and get back to Travis Field.

The nine million was gone.

He'd accepted that.

But he still had time to make the bitch pay.

Which was exactly what he planned to do.

He left the Zodiac at the swim platform with a young kid from the deck crew.

"I'll be back in twenty," he told the kid.

He reached into his pocket and pulled out a Franklin. He palmed it over. "Keep my Zodiac right here, and I've got another one of those with your name on it. I can't be late. My boss will kill me."

The guy looked at the hundred-dollar bill and nodded. "You bet, mister."

Parnell barely heard him. He was already inside and running to climb the stairs to the first deck.

At the door to the makeshift casino, he stopped to scan the room. Wall-to-wall bodies.

He didn't see Pauling.

But he did see the closest big screen TV. The video feed happened to catch Pauling talking to two security guards twice her size.

"Gotcha," he said under his breath. She was on the cabana deck, two flights up.

He paused.

Something about one of the guys seemed familiar. Big. Maybe six-five. Maybe two-fifty. Huge hands. Had he seen the guy before?

Parnell shrugged it off. Probably dumber than a box of rocks. Most of those big gym rats were. Steroids fried the tiny brains they'd been born with.

He returned to the stairs and hopped up, two at a time, to the second level and then to the third. When he reached the cabana deck, he was barely short of breath.

At the top of the stairs, he saw her. Standing at the end of the bar, behind a small table. Now she was chatting with a nearly naked young couple wearing bikinis too small to cover a Chihuahua's privates.

He approached the bar and watched Pauling for an opening.

The bartender said, "What can I get you, sir?"

"Whiskey. Neat." Parnell barely noticed when the bartender placed his glass on the bar. He pulled a five from his pocket and stuffed it into the tip glass before moving away to make room for the next guest.

The naked couple was still monopolizing Pauling. How long could they stand there?

Parnell glanced at his watch. "Come on. Come on, already."

Five minutes passed. Parnell felt a trickle of sweat run down his temple. He wiped it off with his fingers.

The naked couple walked away.

Finally.

Parnell left the whiskey on the bar and made his move.

He approached Pauling as quickly as he dared. She didn't see him coming. He sidled around the table and stood next to her. He grabbed her arm. Tight.

She glanced up at him. She seemed to recognize him somehow.

Her eyes widened, and she gasped.

"Let's go," he said, close to her ear. "And act normally, or I'll kill you where your stand."

He jerked her sideways, and she stumbled into him before she steadied her footing.

"We're going down to the swim platform. Smile, say hi, but don't stop." Parnell spoke for her ears only.

They reached the top of the stairs before he saw a dumb ass security guy moving fast.

Parnell raised his right foot to descend.

Someone leaned in and shoved hard in the center of Parnell's back.

At the same time, Pauling jerked her arm from Parnell's grasp and stepped aside.

Parnell lost his footing.

He stumbled down, fighting gravity all the way until he succumbed at the middle of the flight. He tumbled ass-over-shoulders to the second deck.

"Stop! Stop him!" yelled a tiny Asian woman standing ten feet away from the bottom of the stairs where Parnell landed.

Parnell scrambled up and hurried around the corner toward the next flight of stairs.

The Asian woman came after him.

A tall, lanky guy hurried down from the third deck to follow.

Parnell ran hard. His head start and the crowds buffering his pursuers conspired to his advantage.

The distance between him and the Asian woman widened. When he hit the swim platform running, the kid was standing there next to the Zodiac, as promised.

Parnell ignored him as he shoved the Zodiac into the Atlantic and dived into the inflatable.

The motor started up immediately.

He opened the throttle and pointed the boat toward Travis Field. No time to go back for the SUV now. He couldn't take it to Tortola.

Parnell was breathing hard. He looked back at *The Beachy Babe*. The people milling around the yacht's stern grew smaller as the distance widened.

So far so good, but it wouldn't last. They'd come after him. He didn't have much time.

He pulled a disposable cell from his pocket and called Fish. "I'll be there in five, ten at the most. Coming in via Zodiac from the Atlantic. Fire it up. Let's go."

Trout's voice crackled on the line. "I've got your duffel on board, but what about the rest of your cargo?"

"Change of plans."

Parnell tossed the cell phone into the ocean.

CHAPTER FORTY-NINE

Saturday, January 15
4:25 p.m.
Palm Beach

OTTO WAS ON HER way up from the women's restroom on the second deck when she saw General Parnell grab Pauling's arm and jerk her aside.

"Over there! It's him!" she yelled to Gaspar over the deafening noise of the crowd. She probably blasted his eardrums when the voice activated communications system transmitted her alert. "He's grabbed Pauling!"

"On my way," Gaspar replied. She could barely see him in the crowd from her position below on the second deck.

She triangulated Parnell's course. He was headed toward the stairs. Only one way off the cabana deck. He had no choice unless he went overboard. She'd grab him when he reached the bottom of the first flight.

Gaspar followed her reasoning as if they were telepathically connected. He moved toward the top of the staircase as she moved toward the second deck's landing. Threading the crowd was worse than struggling through an airport security line on both decks. They made little progress.

Otto was smaller. She could fit through smaller spaces. She vectored to the right and was ten feet from the staircase half a second before Pauling lifted her foot to take the first step down from above.

A tight knot of passengers had gathered to watch across her path, blocking Otto from reaching the stairs. She tried to muscle them aside, but they were drunk and deafened by the noise or something. She couldn't get through.

Her view was blocked by passengers.

At the top of the stairs, Parnell's foot moved toward the first step.

His head swiveled, and his eyes were wild. Bewildered and carried by momentum, he stepped out on one foot, off balance.

At the same time, Pauling leaped backward, jerking her arm away from Parnell's grasp.

Someone shoved Parnell in the back. Hard.

Momentum should have carried them both all the way down, but Parnell tumbled alone.

Otto was stopped by a wall of people.

Gaspar rushed forward and slid down the stair rails to the bottom of the second deck and then to the bottom of the first.

By the time he reached the base of the stairs, Parnell was running toward the stern faster than Gaspar could ever hope to move.

"Stop! Stop him!" Otto yelled.

Parnell kept running.

In her earpiece, she heard Gaspar say, "I'm going after him. I'm taking a Zodiac."

"Gaspar, wait!" Otto said, still blocked against the second deck's side rail.

He replied, "Come after me."

That was all the time he had before he ran after Parnell toward the swim platform, as fast as his damaged leg would take him.

Otto found the Boss's phone.

The moment it rang, he picked up. "I saw. I'm on it. Be there soon."

He disconnected.

Otto stood there on the second deck, feeling helpless, watching Parnell zoom away in the Zodiac with Gaspar too far behind to catch up.

Otto glanced at the closest television screen. One of the reporters had his drone already on the Zodiac chase. The drone was high in the sky, way too high because Travis Airfield was in the Zodiac's direction.

She looked around for the drone operator. She saw him down below, on the swim platform. He must have followed Parnell and Gaspar, chasing his story.

Reporters could be reckless idiots. But she had to admire this one. The whole world could see Gaspar zooming after Parnell. Maybe the video would help.

She looked up to the cabana deck again. Pauling stood near the top of the stairs. In her earpiece, she heard Pauling's voice. "Now what?"

"I don't know." Otto shook her head. "Are you okay?"

"I'm fine."

"We know where Parnell is now. The Boss has teams on the

way to intercept." The drunks who had prevented her from moving had drifted over to watch the action on television. Otto could finally move. "I'm going after Gaspar. He's already out of range of our comm system. Call one of the security guys to stay with you. Parnell may not be working alone."

"But—" Pauling protested, but Otto was already halfway down to the swim platform.

CHAPTER FIFTY

PARNELL'S HEAD START PUT him several boat lengths in front of the second Zodiac. He swiveled his neck to look behind him.

The guy was gaining, closing the distance.

Parnell already had the throttle wide open. The Zodiac's motor had no more speed to give.

He hadn't seen the other driver before. Who was he? What was his skill set? Was he armed?

Could he shoot straight on the fly? Not many amateurs could.

He was too lean and lanky to be one of the security team. Was he just a stupid good Samaritan?

Parnell saw the shoreline at Travis Field straight ahead. He'd beach the Zodiac and run toward the jet.

He was too close now to give up.

He'd shoot the damn Samaritan if he got in the way.

Parnell slowed the Zodiac as he approached the coastline.

Up ahead, another jet took off from Travis Field. The jet built speed and began to lift before it ran off the runway and over the ocean, climbing all the way.

Parnell saw the perfect spot to beach the Zodiac and headed for it.

The damn Samaritan closed in behind him, following in Parnell's wake.

He found the shallow spot in the water line and drove the Zodiac hard toward the shore. He cut the throttle at the last minute and rushed toward land.

The Zodiac beached.

Parnell leaped out, crouching low in case the Samaritan was a better shot than most.

He climbed the short distance from the shoreline to solid ground. Then, he ran.

Behind him, he heard the second Zodiac cut its engine and beach.

Parnell looked over his shoulder. He couldn't believe it.

The Samaritan followed in hot pursuit. But he was limping, holding his right side with his left hand. He'd never catch Parnell in time.

Parnell grinned and increased his running speed. Fish was in the pilot's seat of the jet straight ahead, prepared to taxi toward the runway.

Above the roar of the Vision Jet's engine, he heard the unmistakable sound of gunfire and felt the zing of a bullet flying past his head. Eight inches lower and he'd have been down.

He glanced over his shoulder again.

What the hell?

The Samaritan had stopped limping and started shooting.

More bullets came Parnell's way.

He ran a zigzag until he could grab his weapon and shoot back.

The Samaritan doubled over and fell to the ground.

Parnell ran flat out toward the jet.

Fifty yards. Forty. He looked back again.

The Samaritan was still down.

Parnell sprinted the last ten yards to the flight stairs and rushed breathlessly up to the cockpit.

Fish had the engine spooled up and warm enough for takeoff.

Parnell pulled the stairs up and secured the door. "Go, go, go!"

As if flying amid gunfire was an ordinary routine, Fish simply said, "Ten-four."

The jet rolled toward the runway, picking up speed.

Parnell stumbled to the copilot's seat and buckled his harness.

He slipped the headset on and watched as Fish pushed the throttle to maximum for takeoff.

Parnell looked out the side window as the jet sped past the Samaritan, still not moving. He had hit the guy with a lucky shot. He shook his head and laughed.

Then he felt something warm and gooey on his left side.

What the hell?

He looked down to see blood pulsing from a side wound, plastering his shirt to his body.

Damn Samaritan had been a better shot than Parnell expected after all.

Good thing he killed him.

CHAPTER FIFTY-ONE

THE NEWS CREWS HAD sent the two heavy drones toward Travis Field as soon as the Zodiac chase began. The scene was broadcast on all the television screens on *The Beachy Babe* and presumably, everywhere else.

Otto reached the swim platform and looked around quickly for anything motorized that she could use to go after Gaspar.

If only she could talk to him. He was out of range of the comm system, and he couldn't answer his cell phone even if she called.

The crew had already stowed all jet skis and Zodiacs below deck. By the time she could retrieve one of them, she would be too late to help Gaspar.

The Beachy Babe was headed in the right direction, but the yacht would never reach Travis Field before Parnell got away.

Where the hell were the reinforcements? The Boss said they were on the way. From where? Alaska?

She was stuck. All she could do for now was watch the scene unfold on the television screens along with everyone else.

She saw Parnell beach the Zodiac and take off running toward a waiting Vision Jet, spooling up for takeoff.

She saw Gaspar follow and take a couple of bad shots that went wide, followed by one that looked like a solid hit.

Parnell shot back.

She saw Gaspar go down and Parnell make it to the plane.

She inhaled sharply. She knew what was coming next. The jet would take off, and Parnell would be gone forever.

She shouted to activate the mic on her earpiece. "Pauling! Gaspar's down! Get a medical team over to Travis Field!"

"I'm on it!" Pauling yelled in her ear.

The two drone operators were standing next to her, capturing every moment like a live sporting event. *The Beachy Babe* was still traveling toward Travis Field, almost directly in the Vision Jet's flight path.

The plane barreled down the runway, the engine straining to give the aircraft lift, running out of time to accomplish it.

Less than a moment's indecision.

She knew what she had to do.

Only one choice.

She had to bring that plane down. She couldn't let Parnell get away. If their roles were reversed, Gaspar would do the same.

The odds were against her. Despite the exaggerated reports in the media and all the squawking from the various government agencies, taking down any kind of jet with a commercial drone was entirely theoretical.

It had never happened.

Never.

Not once.

"Otto? Are you still there?" Pauling's voice in her ear.

Otto knew every possible disaster that could befall an aircraft. She'd made it her business to know. She knew the probabilities. The dangers. The rescue options. She assessed them instantly in every situation.

There were two narrow windows of opportunity to down the Vision Jet. One was on takeoff. The other, on landing.

Her only opportunity this time was on takeoff.

When the plane left the runway, it would barely be going fast enough to sustain flight. Very little maneuvering would be possible.

The pilot would be headed straight and climbing slowly to gain more speed, making the plane vulnerable to interception.

On top of which, the drone would be hard for the pilot to see.

His attention would be sharply focused on the tasks he needed to accomplish to get the bird in the air.

Which meant she had one chance.

And only one chance.

Right now.

Could she make it happen?

Could she be that lucky?

She could. She would. She had to be.

Simple as that.

"Otto? Otto!" Pauling kept yelling. "I'm almost there!"

Otto had no idea what she wanted.

Nor did she care.

The drone's operator stood two feet away on the swim platform.

In one fluid motion, she grabbed the remote from his hands before he knew what was happening, and pushed him backward. He landed on his ass, mad as hell.

"What do you think you're doing?" he yelled.

"FBI," she yelled back.

His eyes widened, and words failed him. Momentarily.

Which was the only moment she needed.

Pauling must have seen her take the remote. Her voice was breathless as if she was running. "Otto! What are you doing? Hold on!"

Otto's focus was on the job.

She maneuvered the big drone into the flight path of the departing Vision Jet.

From her vantage point on the swim platform it was hard to judge the distances, but the drone's onboard camera gave her a real-time view of the jet as it headed directly toward the airspace above *The Beachy Babe*.

The plane was far faster than the drone, so she had to hope the jet would simply run into it, sucking the drone into its single engine.

Jet engines couldn't handle debris. The engine's core should be thrown out of balance and would shear off fan blades as they rubbed against the casing. The engine would lose power, big time, maybe even start a fire, if her luck held.

From that altitude, the pilot would have no choice but to ditch into the ocean. If he landed well enough, Parnell and the pilot should both survive.

The jet would be buried in the ocean. Salt water would cover it completely in a matter of minutes, along with all the boats and bodies that rested in the mighty Atlantic's cold depths over the centuries. Spanish galleons, government navies, pleasure craft and commercial trawlers and sailing yachts carrying thousands of men were resting on the bottom of this ocean. More would follow.

Rescuers might never find the Vision Jet. But these two passengers could get out before the jet sank into oblivion, never to be seen again.

She'd haul Parnell's ass off to prison and leave him there to rot forever. And if he'd killed Gaspar, she'd do a lot worse than that.

Pauling's breathless voice yelled through the earpiece while she slogged through the crowds gathered around the televisions. Otto blocked the noise from her mind.

She held her focus.

The drone wavered in the wind.

The jet kept coming. Climbing slowly and steadily, which meant the pilot hadn't seen the drone, just as she'd predicted.

The jet closed the gap between the two in seconds.

The jet's engine sucked the drone up like a vacuum cleaner sucks dust.

The camera on the drone immediately cut out.

From the deck of *The Beachy Babe,* she couldn't see, but she heard the impact.

The engine's roar changed to an ear-piercing fingernails-on-a-blackboard squeal.

The engine coughed. It sounded like a bearing in desperate need of oil, which wasn't far from the truth.

The aircraft banked toward *The Beachy Babe*. Otto stepped forward, with her knees against the removable railing around the swim platform's edge, and held her breath.

The pilot leveled the aircraft for a water landing. He'd turned just enough to angle away from the yacht, preventing a full collision.

She allowed herself to exhale.

The squealing engine stopped.

There was a moment's overwhelming silence.

The jet sailed through the air on its way to a bumpy water landing.

"Otto! We're almost there!" Pauling's voice was closer now.
She opened her mouth to reply.
Before she could speak, without further warning, the Vision Jet exploded.
Otto snapped her eyes closed to the blinding flash.
A single massive pressure wave slammed into her. She slapped her hands over her ears. *The Beachy Babe* shook side to side, knocking screaming passengers to the decks.
She moved her feet in an attempt to remain stable. The yacht's metal railing jabbed her knees.
Her balance swam. As fast as she had snapped her eyes closed, she snapped them open.
But it was too late.
Her center of gravity had moved beyond the metal railing. She was leaning forward, moving fast.
She grabbed for the railing and missed. The bright metal sped past her hand. The side of the yacht flashed by.
Her arms outstretched and pinwheeling.
She hit the Atlantic.
Hard.
Force knocked the air from her lungs.
The cold Atlantic surrounded her and held her in a pressurized, claustrophobic embrace. She drifted down, down, floating. For some reason, it never occurred to her to fight her downward trajectory.
She felt a huge hand wrap around her bicep and hold on tight.
She stopped falling, and her body moved upward.
She blacked out.

CHAPTER FIFTY-TWO

Sunday, January 16
3:00 a.m.
Palm Beach

OTTO SLEPT FITFULLY. HER head throbbed. As they had been every night since the Rocky Pointe debacle, her dreams were nightmares about Reacher.

Dead or alive, he haunted her, whether she was awake or asleep.

She saw him running from the house on Rocky Pointe moments before it exploded. She saw him struggling to swim in the dark, cold ocean.

And then her nightmare turned to Gaspar. He was down. He'd been shot. He didn't move.

She heard her own whimpering. She lifted her eyelids slightly.

The room was unfamiliar. It smelled of antiseptic. The bed was high and the mattress narrow. Side railings held her captive.

She smelled something else. Something familiar. She turned her head to look.

Reacher sat in the straight chair in the corner, watching her. He looked young. Like the photo on her phone taken years ago. How could that be? He barely moved. His thick forearms rested on his thighs, a light dusting of fair hair barely visible in the dim light. His hands were clasped. Where was she? Not in her Detroit apartment. But where? Her head throbbed. She closed her eyes. Fitful sleep overcame her.

A while later, she awakened again. Her head felt better, but her brain was foggy still. Why was Reacher sitting in the chair in the corner? Was he actually there?

She lifted her eyelids a bit. No. It was John Lawton, the Treasury agent. The hottie. He flashed his megawatt smile. Had it been Lawton sitting there all along? No, that wasn't right.

She drifted off again, floating on some sort of drugs, she supposed. She was in a hospital, maybe. Which would account for the antiseptic smell and the high, narrow bed. She didn't know why. Or where. Or how.

She remembered the jet exploding in the air. Saw the explosion and the crash. Felt the percussive wave lift her from the swim deck and plunge her into the black, cold water.

She felt the Atlantic crushing her on all sides.

A big man hauled her up from the icy dark depths, and she fell into oblivion once more.

The pattern was repeated several times until once, maybe days later, she came fully awake. Her eyelids popped open.

Still nighttime. The room was dark. The hospital was quiet. Pauling sat in the chair in the corner. Her chin rested on her chest, which expanded and contracted slowly. She was sleeping.

Otto watched her for a while and tried to remember where she was and how she came to be here.

She pieced together memories of the drone and the exploding jet. Which didn't make any sense. The drone might have caused a fire, but not an explosion. Not like that explosion, anyway.

She worried around her fractured memory for a while. The Vision Jet was full of fuel, probably. But the explosion was more like the one that leveled the Rocky Pointe house. The explosion that Reacher built. Using C-4.

Yes. C-4 would cause an explosion as powerful as that.

Why was C-4 on that plane? How did it get there? Who put it there?

But wait.

C-4 doesn't simply explode. It requires a detonator, like a cell phone.

Which means the bomb on the plane didn't simply explode because of the drone. The bomb was triggered.

A bomb like that required advance planning.

Somehow, someone put the bomb on the plane before takeoff and detonated it once the Vision Jet was over the Atlantic, beyond *The Beachy Babe*, to minimize casualties.

She was too tired to decode any more snippets from her subconscious. She closed her eyes and drifted into oblivion once more.

CHAPTER FIFTY-THREE

Six days later
Friday, January 21
2:00 p.m.
Palm Beach, Florida

OTTO GAZED AT THE mesmerizing Atlantic sparkling in the sunlight. Pauling's patio provided the perfect view. No wonder she loved living here. Perhaps Otto should add a Palm Beach getaway to her bucket list.

She smiled. No way could she afford such luxury on a government salary.

Enjoy it while you can.

Which was another hour. She was booked back to real life this afternoon on a flight to Detroit from Palm Beach International. She didn't want to think about that just yet.

Pauling returned with two tall glasses of iced tea on a silver tray. The glasses and the tray were probably new. Parnell had destroyed everything breakable in Pauling's kitchen, but she'd done a remarkable job of putting her home in order again the past few days.

She slipped her sunglasses on, effectively masking her expressions from Otto's planned penetrating examination. This was Otto's last chance to figure Pauling out. She intended to make the most of the time she had left.

"My limo driver will be here to pick you up soon for your flight. He's very reliable," Pauling said as she settled into her seat.

"Good to know. Thanks."

Otto wasn't looking forward to getting on any kind of plane today. Or any day, for that matter.

The Vision Jet explosion invaded her dreams every night, and she suspected it always would.

Flying wasn't safe. It never had been. Never would be. Too many unexpected things could go wrong. And she was acutely aware of every single one of them.

"I'm sorry about Brewer and his wife, Lauren," Otto said quietly. "I know you were friends."

Pauling lifted a finger to the corner of her eye under the sunglasses. Her voice was thick when she quietly replied, "Me, too."

Otto waited while Pauling composed herself. It didn't take long. She'd seen a lot of misery in her life. Losing Brewer and Peck to General Parnell's particular brand of slaughter wouldn't totally derail her life, and Otto was glad of that.

But these losses were different for Pauling, too. Parnell went after Brewer and Peck because of the money. The nine million dollars. Pauling knew where that money was, and she must feel responsible for those deaths, at least on some level. Otto would have.

Still, Pauling was fine. She seemed to have had total

confidence that Otto would show up and work something out. Maybe that's why the Boss put Otto and Gaspar on Pauling's trail. Which made total sense, now that Otto understood the motivation.

"We know Parnell never found the cash because he kept looking for it right up until the end. He destroyed your home when he didn't find it here." Otto paused. "Where is the money now?"

Pauling barely moved a muscle, and her replies were as cagey as always. "I met the Colonel a few times, you know. He was a despicable human being. He hung his men out to dry. The ones he didn't outright kill, he left alone and broken."

Otto's memory flashed to the skeletal man she'd seen barely alive in that Upstate New York duplex. "Like Nick Scavo, you mean?"

"If the Colonel had nine million dollars in cash hidden in his apartment, you can bet that it was dirty money. He wouldn't have acquired it in any honest way." Pauling's mouth set into a hard, grim line. "The money didn't really belong to him at all."

"Brewer told us that he turned the matter over to you. Are you saying you didn't move that cash out of the Dakota? You don't know what happened to it?" Otto lowered her voice to a near whisper. "Peck and Brewer and Scavo all died for nothing?"

Pauling kept silent for a long time. Otto waited, applying what little patience she could muster to the task.

Finally, Pauling cleared her throat and said, "My guess is that the money gave some of the Colonel's casualties a helping hand. You could confirm with them, I suppose if you're so inclined."

The epiphany struck when she realized that Pauling's faith was not vested in Otto or Gaspar, or even the Boss. It was

Reacher that Pauling zealously believed in, for better or for worse. "And how was Reacher involved in all of that?"

Pauling's well-shaped eyebrows arched above the sunglasses. "What makes you think he was involved at all?"

"Because he was there. At the Dakota. Shortly before the Colonel and his family went missing. Nothing I know about Reacher suggests he's the kind of guy to lurk in the background." Otto paused. "Quite the opposite."

"It's not likely you have the full picture of the man since you get your information from Cooper." Pauling's equanimity returned, confirming Otto's instincts, and she changed the subject. "Have you talked to Gaspar since he went home?"

Otto shook her head slowly, which still made her head swim. "He's resting comfortably, Marie said when I checked in this morning. The bullet grazed his right thigh, which was his weaker leg, to begin with. Which was why he couldn't get up off the ground. She said he'll be fine, but he's on house arrest for a while."

Pauling grinned. "He'll hate that, won't he?"

"Maybe not." Otto sipped the freshly brewed tea. "He's a family man. Big time. He loves those kids and Marie like crazy. He'll be okay for a while."

"You'll miss him, though?" Pauling cocked her head, and Otto could feel her steady gaze behind the sunglasses.

"Yes, of course. We've been through a lot together."

"Hunting Reacher, you mean?"

Otto nodded before she remembered not to. She pressed a forefinger to the pain that throbbed briefly between her eyes whenever she moved her head at all. She circled back to the man for one last try. "Speaking of Reacher, was he here?"

Pauling turned her face toward the water.

Otto waited, but Pauling's reply was too long coming. "While I was sedated, in the hospital, I thought I saw him in my room."

"In your room?"

"Seated in the chair in the corner. I saw you a few times, too," Otto said. "You were there, weren't you?"

"I was. You were out of your head, though, for a couple of days. Heavy sedation like that can cause odd dreams that seem real. When my husband was dying, he experienced some of the strangest visions and swore they'd really happened." Pauling grimaced. "Of course, the pain meds were responsible."

"I remember the explosion. I was propelled off that swim platform. I'm a strong swimmer, but I would have died right there, no doubt about it." Otto chose her words carefully. "Someone came into the ocean after me. Right away. Pulled me out. Someone standing very close by. Someone paying attention to me instead of the blast. Not Gaspar, for sure, because he was at Travis Field, already down for the count. And you hadn't reached the platform yet. You were still running."

Pauling said nothing.

"It was Reacher. He was there, on the yacht, wasn't he?"

Still no reply.

"This is important to me, Lauren." Otto set her tea glass on the table and leaned forward. Seriously, earnestly, she said, "I *need* to know. Did Reacher save my life?"

"Reacher has saved a lot of lives, including mine," Pauling replied kindly. "Would it be so terrible if yours was on that list, too?"

Otto took her answer as a yes.

"What about the bomb? You know our best guess is C-4 in a laptop detonated by a cell phone. We never found Scavo's laptop. It was missing from his apartment. Which means Parnell probably took it with him on the plane." Otto narrowed her gaze. She put the question directly. "Reacher was the one who put the bomb on Parnell's plane, wasn't he?"

Pauling smiled. "Make up your mind. Is Reacher the hero or the villain here?"

Otto wished she knew the answer.

The pilot was a drug runner, but none of his rivals claimed credit for killing him. Although any of his enemies certainly could have rigged that laptop, that answer didn't feel right.

Maybe Reacher hadn't bombed the plane. Maybe he hadn't pulled her from the ocean. Hell, maybe Reacher had never been here at all. Pauling would say no more about Reacher's presence or the missing nine million dollars. Otto added the questions to a running mental list she planned to ask Reacher whenever she found him.

She glanced at her watch. The limo driver would be downstairs in ten minutes. She had one more thing she wanted to cover before she left.

"Do you know a girl named Jacqueline Roscoe?"

Pauling's breath caught, and her vibe definitely changed. "Should I?"

"She lives with her mother in a small town in Georgia. Her mom is the local police chief," Otto cocked her head. "Ring any bells?"

Pauling shrugged. Maybe she'd learned that all-purpose gesture from Gaspar.

"The thing is, kids these days have Social Security numbers and passports. And banking regulations apply to them, the same as anyone else. So when we set an alert on her tax ID, we came across something interesting." Otto watched Pauling, who barely moved. Otto would describe her behavior as wary when she reported to Gaspar. "Turns out, one of the big banks recently reported a significant sum of money deposited in trust for the girl. We dug into that a bit. The trustee named on the account, meaning the one who deposited the money, was listed as Jack (none) Reacher."

Pauling said nothing.

"See, I suspect that girl is Reacher's daughter. Which is why we've been watching her." Otto cocked her head. "And I wonder if that money came from that vault at the Dakota."

Pauling did not reply. The sunglasses masked her expressions too effectively.

"Which would mean that Reacher is the one who took the money, and the one who got your friends murdered, and the one who sent Parnell after you." Otto paused. She didn't believe any of it. Not a word. She figured Pauling didn't either. "What do you think? You know the guy. Am I on the right track?"

Pauling glanced at her watch. Her face broke into a big grin, and she fist-pumped the air as if she'd accomplished something special. "Your limo is here."

Otto let Pauling hustle her outside without further argument. There was no point to it. Pauling was smart and well trained and definitely knew how to avoid self-incrimination.

The sky was a perfect shade of pale blue. Thin high clouds and a mild breeze that felt warm. Otto knew this would be the last time she felt warm for a while. She turned her face toward the sun for a quick dose of vitamin D.

She had done all she could here. They parted with promises to keep in touch, but Otto knew that would never happen. Pauling was like the other women she'd met while hunting

350 | Diane Capri

Reacher. She wouldn't call Otto if her hair were on fire and Otto owned every fire hose in the country. Nor would she be any more forthcoming if Otto found a reason to contact her.

Otto shrugged and ducked into the back of the limo. She watched Pauling turn, shoulders slumped, head bowed, walking slowly back to her home before the limo pulled away from the curb, like a woman whose lover had left her once more.

The Boss would keep an ear to the ground, and Finlay would keep an eye on the Boss. Which, like all balances of power, was an uneasy equilibrium.

Otto figured it would be a good long time before Pauling saw Reacher again if she ever did. But the question that had plagued Otto for weeks had finally been answered to her satisfaction. Reacher hadn't died in that Rocky Pointe explosion last year. Perversely, she wasn't quite sure how she felt about the certainty that Reacher was still out there.

A few minutes later, the driver crossed the bridge and left Palm Beach behind. As the limo approached the airport, Otto's personal cell phone rang. She looked at the caller ID. John Lawton. The Treasury agent who'd been watching Brewer and now found himself with some extra time on his hands.

Well, well, well.

She smiled as she answered the call.

FROM LEE CHILD
THE REACHER REPORT:
March 2nd, 2012

The other big news is Diane Capri—a friend of mine—wrote a book revisiting the events of KILLING FLOOR in Margrave, Georgia. She imagines an FBI team tasked to trace Reacher's current-day whereabouts. They begin by interviewing people who knew him—starting out with Roscoe and Finlay. Check out this review: "Oh heck yes! I am in love with this book. I'm a huge Jack Reacher fan. If you don't know Jack (pun intended!) then get thee to the bookstore/wherever you buy your fix and pick up one of the many Jack Reacher books by Lee Child. Heck, pick up all of them. In particular, read Killing Floor. Then come back and read Don't Know Jack. This story picks up the other from the point of view of Kim and Gaspar, FBI agents assigned to build a file on Jack Reacher. The problem is, as anyone who knows Reacher can attest, he lives completely off the grid. No cell phone, no house, no car...he's not tied down. A pretty daunting task, then, wouldn't you say?

First lines: "Just the facts. And not many of them, either. Jack Reacher's file was too stale and too thin to be credible. No human could be as invisible as Reacher appeared to be, whether he was currently above the ground or under it. Either the file had been sanitized, or Reacher was the most off-the-grid paranoid Kim Otto had ever heard of." Right away, I'm sensing who Kim Otto is and I'm delighted that I know something she doesn't. You see, I DO know Jack. And I know he's not paranoid. Not really. I know why he lives as he does, and I know what kind of man he is. I loved having that over Kim and Gaspar. If you haven't read any Reacher novels, then this will feel like a good, solid story in its own right. If you have…oh if you have, then you, too, will feel like you have a one-up on the FBI. It's a fun feeling!

"Kim and Gaspar are sent to Margrave by a mysterious boss who reminds me of Charlie, in Charlie's Angels. You never see him…you hear him. He never gives them all the facts. So they are left with a big pile of nothing. They end up embroiled in a murder case that seems connected to Reacher somehow, but they can't see how. Suffice to say the efforts to find the murderer and Reacher, and not lose their own heads in the process, makes for an entertaining read.

"I love the way the author handled the entire story. The pacing is dead on (ok another pun intended), the story is full of twists and turns like a Reacher novel would be, but it's another viewpoint of a Reacher story. It's an outside-in approach to Reacher.

"You might be asking, do they find him? Do they finally meet the infamous Jack Reacher?

"Go…read…now…find out!"

Sounds great, right? Check out "Don't Know Jack," and let me know what you think.

So that's it for now…again, thanks for reading THE AFFAIR, and I hope you'll like A WANTED MAN just as much in September.

Lee Child

ABOUT THE AUTHOR

Diane Capri is an award-winning *New York Times, USA Today*, and worldwide bestselling author. She's a recovering lawyer and snowbird who divides her time between Florida and Michigan. An active member of Mystery Writers of America, Author's Guild, International Thriller Writers, Alliance of Independent Authors, and Sisters in Crime, she loves to hear from readers and is hard at work on her next novel.

Please connect with her online:

http://www.DianeCapri.com

Twitter: http://twitter.com/@DianeCapri

Facebook: http://www.facebook.com/Diane.Capri1

http://www.facebook.com/DianeCapriBooks

Made in the USA
Coppell, TX
24 May 2021